I0668853

AIRSHIP 27 PRODUCTIONS

Sun-Koh Heir to Atlantis
© 2018 Arthur C. Sippo MD, MPH
{This book is dedicated to my wife, Kathy, who is my editor, my partner, my friend, and my own Shani.}

Character Sun-Koh used with the permission of Edition Bärenklau
www.editionbaerenklau.de

Published by Airship 27 Productions
www.airship27.com
www.airship27hangar.com

Interior illustrations © 2018 Rob Davis
Cover illustration © 2018 Adam Shaw

Editor: Ron Fortier
Associate Editor: Rob Davis
Marketing and Promotions Manager: Michael Vance
Production and design by Rob Davis

All rights reserved under International and Pan-American Copyright Conventions. No part of this book may be reproduced in any manner without permission in writing from the copyright holder, except by a reviewer, who may quote brief passages in a review.

eBook Edition

by Arthur C. Sippo MD, MPH

TABLE OF CONTENTS

HERE COMES THE SUN (KOH)

BY ANDREW SALMON

few years back, talented writer Derrick Ferguson put together a list of Essential New Pulp reading so that newcomers to the pulp tradition and long time fans would have a jumping on point if they wanted to know what this whole New Pulp phenomenon was all about. The list, which has since been expanded and updated, contains what many believe to be the finest examples of New Pulp publications to date. I'm honored to have a release or two on the list myself, which is humbling to say the least. All of the authors and titles listed are worth your reading time.

Sun Koh Heir to Atlantis is on the list.

It deserves to be as you are about to find out if you are reading Dr. Sippo's classic for the first time.

It IS a classic.

As a New Pulp reader, fan and contributor myself, I've come across a handful of titles that I feel go a step beyond being merely a fine way to spend one's reading time. No, these books, for me, have that something extra that transcend the moment, break new ground and carve a little niche of eternity for themselves. I won't list my personal favorites—I'm sure every New Pulp fan has his or her list of their own. But I will say that Sippo's *Heir to Atlantis* has a place of honor on my list. I'm sure you'll add it to yours after you've turned the last page.

The debate has raged for almost a decade now concerning New Pulp's handling of the classic characters from the Golden Age. Some believe the writers of today should be focusing on creating new tales with classic characters that are indistinguishable from those from the 30s and 40s while other hold that these characters need to be re-invented from whole cloth for today's readers.

I fall somewhere in-between, believing the characters should be, for the most part, unchanged but that the "new" in New Pulp should not refer solely to the new writers pounding out purple prose. The New Pulp tales I enjoy most are ones that inject something the classic tales never gave

5

us. Historical perspectives, new interpretations of the racial stereotypes of yesteryear, more allegorical approaches—the possibilities for putting the *new* in New Pulp are endless.

And Dr. Sippo realized this when he sat down to bring a German pulp character from the Nazi Era forward for today's readers. The result was an edgy, inter-connected series of tales which form a comprehensive whole in *Heir to Atlantis*.

Make no mistake, Sippo's re-imagining of Sun Koh contains no sugar-coating and black and white has been blended into glorious shades of gray. It should be understood that Sun Koh is *not* a Nazi. He is a prince from ancient Atlantis but he does not mind working with Nazis at the outset as they present, for him, a way to further along *his* goals not theirs. Koh's involvement with the Nazis keeps the reader off-balance as there are moments when one doesn't know who to root for and tracing his character arc throughout the book provides subtle character development readers will appreciate. And you'll keep turning the pages as a result. Now isn't that the main goal of a great pulp story: to keep the reader turning the pages? Well, you're lucky Sippo is a doctor because your fingers will be shredded with paper cuts from flipping pages so quickly.

And there's so much more to the tales than the historical setting. Sippo blends in a cast of captivating characters from the German pulps, a role-playing game and his own fertile imagination. Exploring the similarities between Sun Koh and Doc Savage, Sippo gives us an interesting team of supporting characters: Alaska Jim, Minx, Sturmvogel, Rolf Karsten and Shani who all have much to add to the whole. Shani in particular. Here you'll find good guys doing bad things, bad guys doing good things and a world not so cut and dried as Classic Pulp would have us believe. Sippo weaves a rich tapestry you want to get caught up in.

In the pure pulp tradition, the stories are full of endless invention, breath-taking action and compelling dialogue. This one is definitely not for the kiddies. Trust me on that before you see Shani go into action in Episode 4.

If this is your first time sitting down with Sippo's Sun Koh, you are in for a treat. It represents the best of what New Pulp can be but, more than that, the characters and the tales will stick with you long after you've closed the book. You're in for a rollercoaster ride but, be warned, *Sun Koh Heir to Atlantis* does *not* come with seatbelts. Thankfully. Enjoy!

Andrew Salmon
September 13, 2018

How Art Thou Fallen From Heaven, Lucifer!

Isaiah 14:12 *How art thou fallen from heaven, O' Lucifer, son of the morning! How art thou cut down to the ground, which didst weaken the nations!*

May, 30, 1932—Borealis lights up night skies; disrupts wires. "There has been a large spot on the sun and we believe that this display is due to the sun spot."—Prof. Edward B. Frost of the Yerkes Observatory [Chicago Daily Tribune, May 30, 1932, p. 1].

Solar sun spot activity reached a critical high and the solar wind was buffeting the upper atmosphere. Electrical discharges caused the Northern lights to be visible as far down as the Midwest United States. The sky over London was alive with shimmering curtains of light. If anyone had been looking north east that night from Greenwich, they would have seen a bright flash in the direction of Norway and a shooting star heading south west over head over 100 miles high.

Each time the shooting star punctured the curtains of the aurora, a massive shower of sparks and ions sprayed out. Suddenly, the shooting star began breaking up into smaller pieces that burned and tumbled through the atmosphere overshooting England and disappearing over the Atlantic. One of the pieces slowed its forward momentum and began coming down over London. But it too began to spark and flash and soon it started breaking up as well, sending chunks southeasterly into the English Channel. One dark piece again changed direction and began falling into the city. A grayish white canopy opened and formed into a delta shape. Underneath it, a body dangled.

The delta shaped canopy rotated around above the city. It finally headed down again towards the ground and into the open area of Hyde Park. The figure dangling beneath it was pulling on the risers, guiding himself in. As he approached the ground, the nose of the delta pointed upward and slowed his forward speed until he stopped just a few inches above the ground. He landed on his feet and the inflated canopy over his head began to swell and float above him. Then it rapidly shrank and was absorbed into the pack on the figure's back. The figure collapsed onto his hands and knees.

He wore a bulky grey one-piece flight suit with many pockets and an integral back pack. It was made of a fabric which shimmered slightly in the reflected light of the Aurora. He had a helmet covering the top of his head and a mask with large mirrored eyepieces covered his face. A cowl covered his neck from the base of the helmet to the top of his torso. The mask retracted into the helmet, revealing a square-jawed masculine face, clean-shaven, with stony blue eyes the color of lapis lazuli. He took a deep breath and exhaled, removing his gloves.

The man rolled onto his back and looked up at the night sky. At first, all he could see was darkness and light, but soon his vision cleared and perceived color again. He studied the stars and found several that were familiar to him, but they were in different patterns than he remembered. The constellations had changed. He did a quick mental calculation and determined what the date was. He did it without thinking, almost as a reflex. The stars in this position indicated that he had succeeded in part of his quest. By his calculations, he was 10,853 years into the future from whence he had started.

Looking around him, he was suddenly aware that he was in a place called Hyde Park in the center of a city named London on the British Isles. He knew the date and time: 3:47AM in the morning, 31 May 1932 AD. He had a very strong sense of his position on the surface of the Earth right down to the minutes and seconds of his latitude and longitude. This puzzled him. How did he know all of this?

He then saw in his mind a map of London and somehow he knew that just east of him was a four-star hotel that catered to the wealthy foreign clientele that frequented this city. It had everything from a casino to a doctor and dentist on the premises 24 hours a day. And they were used to dignitaries who showed up unannounced without baggage or cash.

He steeled himself and set out for the hotel. From his left rear, he heard a man walking briskly towards him. He turned and saw it was a police constable on night patrol.

"What's all this then?" the constable asked.

The parachutist turned to face him. He understood the constable's words with no problem. He was even able to pinpoint which part of the old city in which the man had been raised. The constable was shocked at the size of the man. He was well over 6 ½ feet tall and with his suit must have weighed at over 3 hundredweight. He had not seemed that large from a distance because his proportions were so symmetrical and his movements so fluid, but up close, the man was a brute who exuded strength with every movement.

"Dreadfully sorry, constable" said the parachutist. "I ran into a bit of a problem with the aurora and had to ditch from my plane." The accent he chose for this response was high class Ox-Bridge with just enough insouciance to leave the impression of old money and a title. How did he know to do that?

The constable was startled and asked respectfully. "Are you hurt, sir? Do you need some assistance?"

The parachutist shook his head. "Thanks awfully, but I am all right. I just need to get some lodgings for the night. The Mayfair Metropole Hotel will do nicely. It is not far from here."

The policeman nodded and took out his notebook. "Please sir, I will need your name for my report."

The parachutist was taken aback. His name? What was his name? At that point, he realized that while some things were clear to him—preternaturally so—other details were fuzzy. His name was one of the latter.

With an extraordinary effort, he reached back into his memory and realized that he was covering almost 11,000 years of history. He finally was able to pull his name forward into the present.

"Ts|un K!oh" he replied. There was a dental click in the first name (|) and a post-alveolar click (!) in the second. The constable was baffled. "How do you spell that, sir?" Using his knowledge of modern English spelling (Where had he learned that?) the parachutist replied, "S-U-N K-O-H"

"Very well Mr..." the bobby paused. "Prince," said the parachutist. "Prince Sun Koh. Of the High House of Th!uleh‡ and heir to the Ocean throne." Again, he used more click consonants.

The bobby did not ask him to spell anything more. He figured this was some foreign mucky-muck and that it was best to keep clear of him. "Very good, sir. And you will be staying at the Metropole? Are you sure they will have room for you?"

Sun Koh thought for a moment and somehow he KNEW that they would. "Absolutely" Sun Koh replied. "If you will excuse me, it has been a tiring night and I need to get some rest. "

"Do you need any help getting there, sir?" asked the Bobby.

"No thank you, constable I will be fine. Ta!" The huge man walked off.

The constable shook his head, "Bleeding foreign gits. German prince, no doubt! They come to Oxford to learn our language and then act as if they own the place." He went back on patrol.

Sun Koh arrived at the Mayfair Metropole and the doorman escorted him inside. The receptionist was a tall asthenic man with a thin moustache and a fresh carnation in his lapel. "I am prince Sun Koh of the High House of Th!... Thule and I will require a suite."

The receptionist eyed the giant in the grey costume carefully. "Do you have a reservation, Sir?"

"No" replied Sun Koh.

"What about references?"

Sun Koh reached into a pocket of his flight suit and took out two flat bars of gold that were ~8x12x1.5 cm in dimensions along with a small sack of cut gems. He placed them on the counter and glared at the receptionist. The hard blue eyes became softer and took on the depths of the sea, swirling like whirlpools. "These are my references."

The man swallowed. He became queasy looking into those deep blue eyes. He felt compelled to obey this man. He did not ask him for a passport.

Sun Koh checked into a modest suite. He had placed the gold and gems in the care of the receptionist for appraisal in the morning. He knew that their value would be extraordinary and that they would more than pay for his lodgings.

He called down for room service and ordered a plate of cold chicken and salad. He also requested that the hotel tailor attend him for an immediate fitting. Afterwards, he lay nude in the clean sheets of the bed and slept for several hours. He dreamed that he was floating in a dark tunnel and at one end there was a bright white light while at the other was a low red glow like embers in a fire. He felt himself drawn in both directions bouncing back and forth. Suddenly the tunnel ruptured and a flood of images, sounds and thoughts assailed him. He awoke in a cold sweat. That had not been a dream but a recent memory. He had actually been in that tunnel and been worried back and forth like a bone being fought over by two dogs. They almost ripped him apart but in that last second, he was set free when the tunnel ruptured. That was when his mind had been filled with all the information he had been using since he landed. Why? How? He had no answer. It was one thing he did not know. He went back to sleep.

He awoke in the afternoon to find, as he had requested, some off-the-shelf clothing waiting in his sitting room. The fitted shirts and suits would not be ready until tomorrow. He dressed and ordered an evening meal of Beef Wellington with roasted potatoes and requested Yorkshire pudding with it. He knew what these foods were and what they tasted like, but he had never actually eaten anything like it.

He then took stock of his situation. Sun Koh had left his world 10,800 years ago because it was dying. The magnetic poles of the Earth had shifted and the crust had slipped slightly in preparation for a larger shift. Several cities of the empire had been left in ruins and the lack of a magnetic field had made the Earth vulnerable to the solar winds. In addition, a massive climate change had started melting glaciers all over the world. Already, the coastline of Atlantis had been retreating before the sea. Another crustal shift and it would sink altogether. Expeditions had already been creating underground habitats for many years as they realized the climate was changing and that the glaciers would inevitably retreat, but no one ever expected the poles to shift and wreak the havoc they did.

His father, King Fʘyunch!, knew that his kingdom was coming to an end. The Atlantean Civilization could not survive. So he decided to use the last great achievement of their technology to save his son and help him recover the lands of Atlantis when they surfaced again. His scientists had estimated that the next great Ice Age in which water would be locked in ice and the oceans would return to their lower level would be 11,000 years in the future. Until then, Atlantis would remain under water. The magnetic storms were already playing havoc with their technology and parts of the empire were disintegrating into barbarism. The slave races were overwhelming the Atlantean overlords by force of numbers. And there was the threat of the Basilisk race in the Lemurian realm resurging. Those things in Antarctica were stirring. The nightmares from the Dream Time were appearing around the world. With the fall of Atlantis, order was being replaced with chaos and the world would fall back into barbarism.

But there was hope that order could be restored. When the stars were right, the glaciers would return and all the horrors would retreat before it. When that time came the High House of Th!uleh‡ would return to claim its right to rule and restore order to the world.

His scientists had struggled to develop a method of sending vessels into the future along a warped trajectory in space-time such that the subjective time of flight would seem to be only a few weeks whereas the objective time elapsed would be—11,000 years. The trip would be made in paratime so that the ships would literally cease to exist and then reappear in the future without having occupied any normal space-time in between. Sadly there was no time to complete his original plan for a fleet. There was only one small vessel that could make the trip before the solar storms would make it impossible to do so.

So, Prince Sun Koh was sent to the future by himself in a ship that was heavily armed and sent into polar orbit. It carried sufficient documentation to establish his claims to Atlantis and enough precious metals and gems to fund him when he arrived there. And with the high-tech weaponry he had on board, he could defeat any enemy form his orbital vantage point. As the prince regent, he had received a tattoo on his back in the shape of the central continent of the Atlantic Ocean Kingdom. It established his rights to those lands. This was not an ordinary tattoo in which pigment is deposited below the basement membrane of the corneal epithelial layer so that it is not sloughed off with old skin. This was an active tattoo where the colored pigments were actually made by the basement membrane cells and renewed with each new layer of skin. This was a high tech tattoo that could only be duplicated with the most sophisticated biotechnology and could not be erased without flaying the man's skin. It could not be forged.

Meanwhile, treasure caches containing Atlantean technology, advanced materials, and rare metals and jewels were hidden around the world in mountain ranges so that the floods would not destroy them and the slave races would not find them. These valuable materials would aid Prince Koh in his mission. Hopefully, some of the underground colonies would survive and he could lead them to reclaim the world.

But something had gone wrong. The ship came out of paratime prematurely while he was doing a survey, and when it hit the full force of the solar wind, it started tumbling to Earth. The "weather" in paratime had been turbulent and it must have caused a feedback when the survey probe hit the solar wind pulling the ship out. As it ran the gauntlet of the Aurora Borealis, the ship broke apart. Sun Koh abandoned the main ship in an escape pod, but it too was damaged by the electromagnetic storm and he had bailed out at 10,000 feet. During this sequence of events, Sun Koh had been subjected to multiple electrical shocks from the solar storm and that nearly killed him. This, he reasoned was the cause of the violent pulling back-and-forth that he perceived in the tunnel.

Then he had a flash of insight. Somewhere between the worlds of the living and the dead was the collected knowledge of mankind. The Atlantean priests had spoken of it as the "Aether Record". In the Atlantean tongue

Ak!ash|ic||a. Then the word "Akashic" popped into his mind with its association with Theosophy and other occult disciplines in the modern world. Some ancient Atlantean adepts had claimed that they could tap into it, but most of them had gone mad especially when contemplating what horrors lay waiting in the Southern Oceans. It was said that not all portions of it were easily accessible and that those things most widely known among the populace were easiest to discern. Some parts were obscured by natural forces and others by active sorcery. Accessing it was not like reading a book or using a library. It was more like finding an ancient tomb and having to piece together what all the elements and artifacts meant. Sometimes it was easier than others. It was always easier to access general knowledge than specific information. Facts that had been written down seemed to endure more vividly in the Akasha than mere ideas, and the more copies there had been made, the easier they were to access. Even if no physical written record remained, the Aksashic imprint was still there.

Sun Koh cleared his mind. He realized that his knowledge of this present world was restricted to what he had accessed at the time of his re-emergence from paratime. He had no knowledge of world events since then. He could recall the long distant past with difficulty, and the recent past easily, but the present not at all. He had been well educated as a Prince, but now, he had the cumulative knowledge of the last 35,000 years of human history. The impressions from pre-humans, proto-humans, and non-humans going back even further were less well formed but with practice he thought he could sort them out.

He needed to try to access the Akasha regularly to keep himself updated. It had been rumored that the Aether Record gave one limited precognition. This would be a very useful skill. Sun began a series of yogic meditations to try and gain access to the current knowledge in the Akasha. By doing so, he unknowingly alerted a potential enemy as well as a future ally...

At Ealing Abbey on the outskirts of London, a monk stirred during his prayers. A feeling of dread came over him. He had come to London disguised as a Benedictine monk because of a premonition that his skills would be needed. He now was sure of it. He would monitor the papers closely and make contact with British security...

In Berlin, a dark man with reddish-brown eyes that glowed like hot coals awoke with a start from his meditation. He immediately made a phone call. A woman answered, "This must be you, Minx. Do you know what time it is?"

He smiled. His goatee made him look satanic. "Shani, my dear. It has happened again. I am certain that a new adept is here in Europe. I told you the Aurora was a sign! We must be prepared to find him. Tomorrow, we must poll our usual sources and keep our eyes on the foreign press."

"You mean today." The woman said sharply. Her German had an odd accent.

Ludwig Minx laughed. "Yes, I do. I have been in the spirit world and lost track of time. We will tell our Thule Society friends about this at a more decent hour." His voice became lower and more intimate. "Are you alone tonight my dear? Do you wish some company?"

She snorted and said "Good night, Minx."

He heard the click as she hung up and smiled. It had been worth a try. Then he went back to meditating…

The next day Sun Koh, properly dressed in a tuxedo, decided to dine in the hotel restaurant. He had a haircut, a manicure, and a pedicure and made several contacts that day. There was no gym at the hotel, but arrangements were made for him to work out at a nearby private club. Unlike some of the non-European guests at the Metropole, he was welcomed to use their facilities. He might be foreign, but he was obviously white and of Northern-European extraction. At his request, jewelers had presented him with accessories including rings, pocket watches, fobs, and tiepins. He requested certain custom-made items, which artisans were preparing for him. One they had found for him was a ruby tiepin with a gold counter-clockwise swastika in its center. This had been the symbol of the High House of Th!uleh‡. He wore that tonight.

The value of the small sack of jewels was extraordinary and, of necessity, an account had been opened for him at a local bank. He had several more trinkets in the pockets of his flight suit, which he kept hidden. It was a shame that most of the precious metals and gems had gone down with his ship. The suit was virtually impermeable and could defend itself against attempts to open it or carry it off. It was innocently stored along with his helmet in the upper shelf of his closet but it was dangerous for anyone other than him to handle it.

Sun Koh was a superb specimen. He was fully two meters tall weighing 22 stone with long legs, narrow hips, broad shoulders, and perfect posture. His skin was a bronzed color that looked as if he spent most of his time outdoors engaged in sports. His thick blond hair had a curling wave to it that gave him a boyish charm. And those piercing blue eyes were deeper and darker than anyone had ever seen before. They had depth and a patina that made them look as if they were constantly in motion. He kept his face smooth by actively suppressing growth of his beard through meditation. He moved gracefully with a rolling gait that kept his shoulders level. He was solidly built like a rugby lineman but looked more like a very tall field and track athlete. He looked like a German nobleman on holiday. Several females eyed him carefully as he walked past (and a few males as well). None of this was lost on him. Sun Koh had been raised at the Ocean Court and was keenly aware of how he looked and how he was perceived.

Entering the restaurant he ordered what he knew to be the chef's specialties, at least as of two days ago. He still had not been able to access the more recent Aether Record, but he had perused several London and Continental newspapers to keep himself up to date. His trip through the Aurora had not gone unnoticed, but they were calling it a meteor. He was intrigued by what was happening in Germany. The National Socialists were fighting a battle to establish ethnic purity and the privilege of the naturally superior races. They had taken the counter-clockwise swastika of the High House of Thule as their symbol. He searched his new memories and found that they anticipated the coming of a great race war and that they themselves felt connected to the ancient Atlantean civilization.

It became obvious to Sun Koh that the Nazis and their fellow Aryan Supremacists had to have accessed the Akashic record. There were too many coincidences. Racial purity had been part of the policy of Atlantean society. There had been nay-sayers and subversives who had spoken of the equality of all men but they had been brutally suppressed. There had even been religious prophets amongst the subjugated races who had warned that the racial supremacist policies would bring about the downfall of Atlantis. They had been suitably rebuffed, hunted down, and made an example to their fellows.

But then a nagging thought came into Sun Koh's mind. He knew the suppressed prophecies, and in retrospect, they had all come true. For some reason he had not seen this before. He had a disquieting feeling. Studies by many scholars in the early 20th Century were challenging the racist stereotypes that he, as an Atlantean noble, had assumed to be true. As he reviewed his recently augmented memory, he also saw many studies that reaffirmed the stereotypes, but he also recognized a number of flaws and biases in them. He looked around the dining room and saw several men

"Sun Koh was a superb specimen."

of non-European ancestry. They were well coiffed and intelligent. He felt somewhat uneasy around them, but he had selected this hotel because it catered to a wealthy foreign clientele with no questions asked.

He put his doubts out of his mind and enjoyed his dinner. Soon, he would establish himself and be able to afford proper accommodations with the right kind of people. The rack of lamb was medium rare and seasoned delicately. The mint sauce was a little too pungent for his tastes but he tried it anyway for the experience. They had some excellent wines in the cellar and he had a full-bodied Cabernet Sauvignon with the meal. Afterwards, he imitated several of the men and had a glass of Madeira with a mild Cuban Cigar. He had never smoked before and with his first puff, he registered alarm. The smoke was filled with carcinogenic chemicals and with strong physiological and psychoactive stimulants. As he accessed his memory, he found that a few researchers had suspected this but that there was no clear consensus about it. Most of those opposed to smoking at that time seemed to do so for religious reasons, which amused him. Are prophets always so prescient?

He snuffed out the cigar and took his Madeira with him to the Casino. He observed the patrons at the various games. There were Baccarat tables, Roulette, and dice games. He searched his memory and found that there were many systems for beating each of these games, but few of them were of any use. He found that the only mathematically sound systems worked with Baccarat. The other games actually required physically or mentally manipulating other players or the gaming pieces. He decided to try his hand at Baccarat first.

The concierge had arranged a line of credit for him of £100,000. He picked up his chips and sat down to play. The game was simple and the shoe of cards was small. After a few rounds, he had developed his own system that was ironclad. He also found that the cards liked him. His luck was excellent. With that on his side, he won over £25,000 in the next few hours. People took notice of him. Young women began to draw near him and make conversation. He recognized them as young ladies-of-the-evening, well dressed but not as well as the rich patrons. He was polite to them and bought them some drinks, but he concentrated on his game and most of them moved on to better prospects. The house changed dealers on him twice but he kept winning. He finally decided to move on to another game.

He took his tray of chips to the dice table and began to bet for and against other rollers. It was soon apparent that his luck was holding. He continued to win. He finally got control of the dice and rolled for himself. That is where he made real money. It was child's play to control the dice and make them come up however he wanted them to. He made hard points periodically, remembering to lose on enough occasions to make it look good. After several rounds of play, he was up over £60,000 and decided to pass the dice and move on.

He then went to the Roulette table and decided that this would be his big score. This was a European wheel with one '0' figure. He played conservatively at first betting on red vs., black, odd vs. even, and manqué vs. passé. His luck held good so he moved to the *douzaine* squares. He then became creative doing combinations of two and three adjacent numbers. Finally, he began to bet on single figures. All during this time, he had kept his eyes on the croupier and spoke short phrases to him. Subtly he was manipulating the man and learning how to control the ball through him. Again, they changed croupiers on him twice, but by then he had his technique down and he hit three numbers in a row. They changed the croupier a third time, and Sun Koh decided to punish the House. He placed £5,000 on '0.' It came up and he won £180,000. He let it ride. The pit boss grew nervous. He intervened and said that the House could not cover that large of a bet. Sun Koh looked up at him and said, "Very well". He could have made a scene but he decided to let it go. He scaled back his bet to £10,000 and let it ride on '0.' The croupier was nervous, but Sun Koh had him under control. His luck held and he won again. At that point, he called it quits, tipped the croupier, and headed to the cashier. He had won over £600,000 that night and nearly broke the bank.

On his way out, he felt a set of eyes following him intently. There was a hint of danger in them. He looked around and saw a tall handsome woman, coiffed like a patron, not a working girl. She was full-bodied with sensuous lips and a cascade of lustrous brown hair. Her strapless gown accented her décolletage and she pulsed her hips in a slow rhythm as he watched her. Her face was flawless, symmetrical, and beautiful in an understated way. Sun Koh knew immediately that she was trouble. Everything about her screamed that she was connected to British Internal Security scouting out potential foreign troublemakers. Looking at her even more closely, he realized that she was not just looking for anybody. She had been sent there to seek him out. They must have been tipped off by the police constable's report. He kept his face a blank slate but he smiled inwardly. He had wondered when they would get around to him. He had already made a connection to obtain a forged Bavarian Passport which would be ready in two days. He needed to stall for time before they decided to bring him in for questioning. He was not sure that if MI5 did so, they would ever let him go. So, he decided to distract them.

He walked up to the woman and introduced himself. "Good evening. I am Prince Sun Koh." She in turn gave him her hand and said, "Lady Felicity Knight". Sun Koh kissed her hand and escorted her to the bar for a drink. Closing time did not exist in this establishment. They chatted for a while. He told her that he had attended Oxford under his family name and that he was quite in love with London. This would buy several days as his sources tried to locate records of a German nobleman of his description but with a different name. She told him that her husband and she were separated and that she was living in London on her allowance waiting for her divorce to come through. He knew this was a lie. She placed her hand on his thigh. One thing led to another. Then they discreetly left for his room.

She was eager but not anxious. They undressed each other slowly and she marveled at the tattoo on his back. He told her truthfully that it was a map of his family estates.

They embraced in the sitting room and devoured each other's bodies until they were coupling wildly on the floor. Sun Koh was gentle at first but more forceful with time. Felicity had never experienced a man like this. He was tireless, attentive, and very knowledgeable. He knew her body better than she did. They made love all over the suite in different positions, finally ending up on the bed. She had a string of climaxes that wrung her out until she fell into an exhausted sleep. Just at that point, Sun Koh allowed himself to climax. It was a pent-up explosion that lasted for over two minutes. His body contracted multiple times. However, more importantly, his mind broke through and he once again accessed the Akashic Record. New information flooded into him and he knew of new dangers and new hopes. He had learned the secret of accessing the Akashic Record. One needed to bring oneself close to death to do so. Even the "little death" of orgasm was sufficient. With proper discipline, he should be able to duplicate this in a trance state.

He knew who was after him and why. In particular, he saw the image of a Basque priest from a hidden monastery lost in the Pyrenees who was somewhere nearby and who could now see him clearly. But he also saw the face of a Mephisphelean man in Berlin who had been searching for him and who now knew where he was. Sun Koh collapsed and fell into a deep sleep....

In Berlin, Minx awoke from sleep. He knew the adept was in London staying in a Mayfair hotel. Minx considered calling Shani but decided instead to call Jan Mayen. He went to a special radio and repeatedly sent out a brief coded message. He received a response a few minutes later providing him with a numeric key. He entered this on a keypad beside the transmitter and shortly heard Jan Mayen's voice clearly through the speaker. Other radios would only detect static. The scrambler worked quite well.

"Ludwig," said Mayen. "What is the problem?" He was speaking from his hidden retreat in the mountains of Austria.

"Jan, a new adept has arrived. I do not know where he comes from but he is strongly tuned to the Akashic record. I have never felt anyone with greater immersion in it. He arrived on May 30 and is now in London."

Mayen harrumphed. "There was a great disturbance in the stratosphere that night. A meteor came down from the North Pole and ditched out in the Atlantic. It passed right over England. Do you think he is from Aldebaran? Has he traveled here through space?"

"He seems quite human to me," said Minx. "I don't know where he came from. Maybe Shamabala or Agartha. But in any case the Occult Bureau at MI5 has been tipped off about him. We must get to him before they act. Can you take us there?"

"I will need to prepare the *Schimäre* for such a trip. I can be ready tomorrow evening."

"The sooner the better." Said Minx. "Shani and I will be waiting for you. I will get Schreck as well. He knows London better than any of us. Hopefully we will have this adept here for the next Thule Society meeting."

"I will begin making preparations. Listen for my signal at 1330 tomorrow and we will make the final preparations. *Auf Wiedersehen*."

"*Wiedersehen*" said Minx. He turned off the radio and went to the phone.

He dialed a number. There was no answer. He dialed another number. A sleepy woman answered.

"Gretchen. This is Minx. Put Rolf on the phone."

There were words exchanged and then a man in a curt voice said, "Minx, you fairy! What do you want?"

"Schreck! Get yourself packed in the morning. We are leaving for London tomorrow evening in *Schimäre*. The occult Bureau of MI5 has its sights on one of ours and we need to extract him. He is hold up in a luxury hotel in Mayfair without portfolio."

"Probably the Metropole" said Rolf Karsten. "It caters to foreigners and they ask few questions if you have money. He must be well heeled." Rolf was a private detective. He had worked in virtually every major city in Europe both for private clients and for the various police agencies. He was nicknamed "Schreck" which means "Terror." He had a reputation as the scourge of the underworld. He was an averaged sized man with brown eyes, dirty blond hair and a face that blended into any crowd. He could pass for Italian, Danish, English, even Hungarian. During the Great War he had run a spy network out of Soho in London. He had never been caught.

"That sounds right," said Minx. "We will sneak in to tomorrow night and fetch him. Be at my place at noon and we will proceed from there." Then he said with a smirk, "Give my love to Gretchen. You need to marry that girl someday."

Schreck made an obscene comment and hung up. Gretchen Schulman was his long-suffering secretary and occasional mistress. Schreck had two failed marriages behind him and Gretchen had one. They were in no hurry to commit themselves again. Theirs was a relationship of convenience. Gretchen was a buxom girl with slim hips, a saucy manner, and white blond hair. She was also the best records researcher in Berlin. There was no secret in an obscure file that she could not ferret out. She twisted men around her little finger and always got what she wanted.

Minx went back to bed. He had a long day ahead of him....

Fr. Aitor Txomin Axpe PJC was once again interrupted at prayer. He had a salacious vision of a man and woman copulating and recognized the man as the one he sought. He also recognized the woman. She had been taking notes in the Director's office at MI5's Occult Bureau during his visit. He frowned. So they knew where the man was and they had sent her to seduce him. Why did they play games with him? They acted like he was a gibbering idiot. The fools! They think this fellow is just another crackpot German cultist trying to infiltrate Britain's occult community. They do not realize how dangerous he is. Fr. Aitor had come a long way to warn them. He saw what the man had done to the British female agent. She was hopelessly compromised now by his sexual magnetism. But now Fr. Aitor knew where the adept was hiding. He would make his own plans to intercept him...

●●●

When Sun Koh awoke the next morning, Felicity was already gone. He had heard her get up and do a thorough, albeit brief, search of his suite before she left. She had found the flight suit and helmet, but they were too heavy for her to lift so she could not examine them too closely. The external fabric was flexible but had a smooth feel like silk. She could not get into any of the pockets. She padded bare-footed around the suite looking for anything of interest. She found nothing. She fetched her shoes and silently left the suite. Before she left she peered in at Sun Koh and he could feel her shiver. It had never been like that before. She felt herself getting aroused and suffered a moment of ambivalent horror, before she padded out the door. Sun Koh rolled over with satisfaction and went back to sleep.

Felicity put on her shoes in the elevator and ignored the knowing looks in the lobby from the staff. She went outside and a car parked down the street came forward and picked her up. She was brought to MI5 headquarters for debriefing. Felicity did not know at that time if she would ever see Sun Koh again. The thought gave her shudders of foreboding and longing all at once.

Sun Koh transferred his winnings from the night before to his British bank account and then transferred the total amount to a German bank which had an international branch in London. He kept the monies in pounds because inflation was destroying the Deutschmark but he wanted his funds protected from MI5 intrusion and he knew that a British bank could be all too easily compromised.

During his errands, he felt a sense of danger and he knew that the priest must be nearby. He had already picked up the British Security tails, but they were merely observers. The priest was another story. He was the one immediate threat to Sun Koh's life. At first, Sun Koh had trouble finding him. The priest apparently could ward himself against Akashic discovery. But Sun Koh had many talents and he soon was able to pick the man out of the crowd. Their eyes met. For the first time since his arrival, Sun Koh met a man whose soul he could not fathom through his eyes. In fact, as far as his Akashic memory was concerned, there was no one there. It was eerie. The priest wore a typical dog collar and black suit that fitted him poorly. It was good camouflage. He neither smiled nor blinked.

Sun Koh walked up to him and said, "I think we need to talk." The priest nodded and they walked together to Hyde Park and sat at an empty bench.

Fr. Aitor said in the ancient Atlantean tongue "We have been awaiting your coming Ts|un K!oh of the High House of Th!uleh‡. It has been a long time."

Sun Koh was stunned in the same tongue. "Who are you? How do you know my name?"

The priest replied, "I am Father A|it!or Txo!mi⊙n Ax!pe‡ warrior Monk of the Fortress Monastery of Saints Inigo and Xaber in the Pyrenees. Our order is known as the Paladins of Jesus Christ or PJC for short."

Sun Koh frowned. "St. Ignatius and St. Francis Xavier were Jesuits. There are no Jesuit monks. They are an active order, not a contemplative one." He searched his memory. "I have no knowledge of such a monastery."

Fr. Aitor smiled. "Oh, it is in the Aether records, my Prince. Everything must be. It is just hard to find. We were founded as a secret branch of the Jesuits and we are not contemplatives. We do warfare on behalf of the Church. Physical combat on occasion, but now it was mostly spiritual warfare. We ourselves dip into the Akashic Records. That is how I know you. It also helps that I am Basque, a descendant of the V|ashk! people who served the Ocean Throne millennia ago. You and I share a common heritage.

"I know who you are. You were conceived unnaturally by your father F⊙yunch! using all the best genetic material his geneticists could splice together. Your mother was a mere incubator. From childhood, you were trained to be the best at everything: science, sports, warfare, the arts, mental disciplines, and every other human endeavor. You were to be the greatest monarch in Atlantean history. Then the Great Chastisement occurred and it all started falling apart. However, your father elected to save you. He had invested too much in you. And so he sent you here to rule the world of the future."

The priest sighed, "Our order keeps the dark powers at bay. In earlier times we were men of action and we are still trained for that." Fr. Aitor shifted his balance and Sun Koh responded with a counter shift. It was imperceptible to the people around them but it was a Copernican change in the dynamics between them. Only a superior martial artist could have initiated this shift let alone sensed or responded to it.

"It is just like that," said the priest. "You have now come and upset the balance. It concerns us. We are trying to contain a great evil and your presence now threatens decades of planning."

"Is that why you tipped off MI5? To get rid of me? I am surprised that the Jesuits would cooperate with Protestant England."

"Not at all!" replied the priest. "Necessity makes strange bedfellows. Ever since the British offered to rescue Pope Pius VII from Napoleon, we have found constructive ways to help each other."

"Are you offering a truce? Or making a threat?"

Sun Koh retrieved that piece of historical trivia and gained a new insight into his enemies.

"But unfortunately, The Director at MI5's occult bureau decided to go after you himself. We would have preferred a constructive meeting like this one to see if we could avoid conflict."

"Are you offering a truce? Or making threats?"

Fr. Aitor smiled, but in an unfriendly way. "There can be no truce between us. What we both stand for is incompatible. But this is not the Middle Ages. Our order does not threaten people. It is our hope to dissuade you from certain courses of action which, in the long run, are not in your best interest."

"You mean you want me to repent and then you will help save my soul."

The priest's smile softened. "Yes. In the end, you will destroy your soul—both in this life and the next—if you do not rethink what you are doing. It was lucky for you that your ship broke up when it emerged from paratime. Impoverishment in the eyes of the world forces us to focus on enriching ourselves from within. I want to recruit you to our side. Ultimately, we will win."

"Will you?"

"Yes. Remember the prophets of your time. They were vindicated and they served the same Divine Master that I do."

Sun Koh paused. "Forgive me, but I still think that strength and proper breeding represent the future of Mankind, not coddling the weak and infirm. 'Survival of the fittest' as Darwin said."

The priest shook his head. "The whole of the people cannot be warriors or men of action. There is a division of labor in human societies and the diversity among people in genetics and temperament keeps society strong. If all men were warriors, then mankind would fight itself into extinction."

At that point bits of information from Sun Koh's enhanced memory surfaced to show that the priest was right. Sun Koh repressed this.

"I thank you for your proposal Father, but I have my own agendas and I intend to pursue them."

"MI5 is on to you, my Prince. They will move on you swiftly. I can get you out of this country and to safety."

"Thank you, but I can take care of myself. Good day, Father" Sun Koh stood up and walked away.

The priest shook his head. If MI5 moved on this man, there would be bloodshed. If only they had listened to his original plan! However, he saw that conflict was inevitable. Sun Koh would not cooperate with them and if he got to the Thule Society on the continent all Hell would break loose. He said a silent prayer and took a taxi back to Ealing Abbey. Maybe it would be better if MI5 took him out. But, Fr. Aitor had a premonition. Sun Koh was more formidable than anyone in this time knew. Well, he had planted the seeds. It was now up to providence.

•••

Jan Mayen arrived on the outskirts of Berlin at 1600 in his wonder craft, the *Schimäre or "Chimera"*. It was a pointed cylinder 30 meters long with retractable wings and two atomic powered engines underneath. It was capable of flying over 1100 k/hr and could achieve an altitude of 50 kilometers. But it was also a submarine and could dive to 500 meters depth and cruise at nearly 100 k/hr while submerged. Its atomic engines also made it capable of vertical take-offs and landings. The technology that created this vehicle was not unique to him. Mayen had inherited the technical notes of his grandfather who had been known as "Robur the Conqueror". Since then, Jan had hidden himself in the Austrian Alps appearing only periodically to obtain supplies and test his vehicle's capability. He had had a number of adventures, but needed to avoid government agents who wanted the secret of his vehicle. Luckily, no one knew his real identity and he was only known as the Captain.

The party he picked up included Ludwig Minx in full evening dress Rolf 'Schreck' Karsten, and a woman wearing a black chador, which covered her from head to toes. Only her eyes were visible behind a veil. This was Ashanti Garuda known also as Shani. Minx was disappointed at her concealing costume. After all, she was no Muslim! But, he held his peace.

On board the *Schimäre* were two other passengers. One was Alaska-Jim Hoover, a Canadian Trapper and outdoorsman. He stood slightly over six feet and wore buckskins and a coonskin cap. The other was Rudolph 'Sturmvögel' Rauhaar. He was a giant who stood 7 feet tall and wore black fatigues and combat boots with an Alpine service cap. He had been a special operations soldier in the Great War and—like many veterans—had returned to a Germany where there were no jobs and even less discipline. He had been a member of different paramilitary organizations and had gone to Canada and the United states to seek his fortune. Jim and Sturmvögel had shared more than one adventure with the Captain in North America and he had invited them to visit his secret headquarters in the Alps. When they had heard about the mission, they insisted on going.

The plan was to fly to England and then sneak up the Thames underwater to deposit Minx, Ashanti, and Schreck on shore. Schreck would do forward reconnaissance and affirm the target's location. Then Minx and Ashanti would make contact and retrieve him for extraction to Germany.

Schreck was put ashore at a deserted dock around 1730 London time. He was dressed in a better suit than he usually wore and had been properly coiffed by Gretchen to be a passable as an upper-class Brit. He would rendezvous with Minx and Ashanti in the lobby of the Ritz at 1900.

Schreck scouted out the Metropole and spotted the Internal Security people almost immediately. There were at least four of them inside the hotel and three more outside. There was also a small lorry parked up the street with a driver who was reading the paper and watching the Metropole. He went into the bar and struck up a conversation with the bartender. His English was quite good and no one suspected him of being anything but a normal patron. He made inquiries and discovered the interesting story about what happened last night in the casino. Some German prince named Sun Koh had come close to breaking the bank and then retired to his room with a voluptuous patroness who did not leave until the early hours of the morning. The bartender smirked. She had been walking oddly when she left. The maid who cleaned his suite gossiped about the disarray and the smell of sex that pervaded every room.

Schreck kept his appointment with Minx and Shani. He told them what he had discovered.

"Sun Koh!" said Minx. "Can it be?" He looked at Shani.

"The legendary prince regent of Atlantis!" She said. "That must have been his ship that broke up over the Ocean a few days back." Both men could feel the haughtiness through the thick veils that covered her. "I am glad I came prepared."

"I am surprised that you did not sense him yourself, my dear." said Minx slyly.

"Who says I did not? I have been on alert since you called me that first night. I sensed that certain preparations would be in order. Now I understand why." She looked at Minx through the veil. "You forget that I am a devotee of Kali, the Mother of Death. I am not a spy, a soldier, or a liberator. I do not rescue people. It is my job to subdue and/or eliminate. I have been preparing for that mission for several days. He will submit to us and we will take him."

"Well, we better move quickly," said Schreck. "British security is planning to snatch him tonight. They may send that Knight woman back as bait."

"We will not give them the chance," said Minx. With a flourish he produced a bright yellow rose in his right hand from nowhere and with a gesture, made it disappear. "Just like that, we will take him from under their noses."

Schreck went back and waited in the lobby of the Metropole. Sun Koh came down to dinner at 2035. Schreck called the Ritz and informed Minx and Shani who took a cab to the Metropole. When Shani came out of the cab, she had undergone a transformation. She had removed the chador and emerged in a red and gold high-necked sari that was slit high up the sides by her legs. She had a womanly figure but carried herself like an athlete. She wore golden sandals and her toenails and fingernails were painted blood red. Each of the great toenails and thumbnails had a golden counter-clockwise swastika imbedded in the polish. She also wore finger and toe rings of red, white .and yellow gold. On her palms were tattooed small black swastikas. She had a golden ring piercing her right nostril and a diamond stud embedded in the left side of her nose. On her forehead between her eyes was a red tikala mark of the same shade as the nail polish. It had an embedded golden Swastika just like those on her nails. Her eyes were violet and full of light. Her hair was jet black and full, cut short around her shoulders. On her right upper arm was entwined a golden snake bracelet. Every eye turned when she entered the dining room. Sun Koh was no exception.

He was stunned. She was the most beautiful woman he had ever seen. Her skin was a café-au-lait color: dark yet light and smooth. She looked like one of the highborn women of the southern climes of Atlantis. His augmented memory informed him that she was a true Aryan obvious from an undiluted bloodline going back 10,000 years.

She and Minx sat down and ordered drinks. She eyed Sun Koh from across the room in an inviting way. His danger sense started tingling, but not as it had with Felicity Knight. This was a sweet danger. One where the pay off was worth the risk.

Sun Koh signaled the waiter to send a bottle of champagne to the newcomers table with his compliments. Minx stood up and came to Sun Koh's table. He clicked his heels and said. "I am Professor Baphomet, a magician and prestidigitator from Berlin. My assistant, Miss Ashanti Garuda, and I would be honored if you would dine with us."

Sun Koh accepted. When he sat with them, Shani looked deeply into his eyes and said in the Atlantean tongue. "Prince Ts|un K!oh. Do not be alarmed. We are from the Thule Society in Germany. Do you know of us?"

"Indeed." Sun Koh replied in the same tongue. He searched his memory. "I am surprised you have been bold enough to show yourself here, Shani. That is your nickname? The British Secret Service wants you for terrorist acts committed in India. You must know there are agents all around us tonight. They are bound to recognize you."

She smiled and sipped her champagne.

He turned to Minx and spoke in German. "You, my friend, are a well known stage performer who recently retired to devote himself full time to the work of the Thule Society." Minx nodded.

"Your highness," Minx said in Sanskrit, "We are here to rescue you from the British swine and take you to where you have friends. Do you trust us to help you? "

Sun Koh nodded, "I know who you both are and I am glad you came. I was hoping that I would be able to travel to Germany on a Bavarian passport in two days, but MI5 is moving fast. We must go tonight. Do you have a plan? How do you propose we get out of here?"

Minx shrugged his shoulders and held his hands palms up. "The simplest way is by distraction and misdirection. A specialty of mine. Let us have dinner while we discuss the plan."

They ate dinner switching between English, German, Atlantean, and Sanskrit to confuse any eavesdroppers.

"I didn't know there were that many agents in the hotel until I came down to dinner," said Sun Koh. "It is likely that they will try to steal my flight suit while I am down here. Ha. They will be in for a big surprise if they try. It can defend itself. We will have to recover the suit before we leave."

"No problem. It will fit into our plans but we must be quick," said Ashanti.

At the end of the meal, Minx said, "All right, here we go." As the waiter came to clear the table, Minx stood up and said "No need my good man." He pulled the tablecloth out from under the dishes and, with a flourish, spun it over the table he then pulled the cloth away and the dishes, utensils, and glasses were gone.

"Where did they go, you ask? Why they are right here." With another flourish of the tablecloth, the dishes reappeared. It was simple trick. An expanding false table top that fit on top of the dishes that could fool the eye for just a few seconds.

Then Minx turned to the next table and took an empty champagne bottle that was upside down in its bucket and started pouring champagne from it into his cupped hand. The wine disappeared. He made a tossing gesture and the bottle itself vanished.

He turned to the next table where the waiter had just brought the ingredients for cherries jubilee. Minx took the matches and one by one set he tips of the fingers of his left hand on fire. Then he began to juggle the small fires overhead. Suddenly, one of the flames fell into the Jubilee pan and there was a loud explosion followed by flames and smoke. Multiple other explosions occurred around the room. Heavy smoke started to billow out of the pan and it appeared that Minx's left arm was on fire. Women screamed, and people started stampeding towards the exits. Out in the street there was pandemonium. Explosions, flames, and smoke filled the sidewalks. Smoke poured out of the hotel lobby. The noise was deafening. In the confusion, the MI5 agents on the ground floor lost Sun Koh and his companions, assuming they had gone out into the street with the other patrons.

They had actually exited into the kitchen and started climbing the utility stairs to the roof. Sun Koh stopped at the floor where his suite was to fetch his suit and helmet. Minx continued up to the roof, but Shani followed Sun Koh. Sun entered his suite and was confronted by three men and Felicity Knight. She was leading them to the bedroom where the flight suit was hidden. Sun had locked the bedroom door before he had left. The door was heavy enough that breaking it down was not an option so the British agents were trying to pick the lock. They had a heavy-duty utility trolley to carry the suit to the elevator.

"What are you doing in my room?" said Sun Koh. That is when the first Security agent drew his gun and fired. Sun Koh sidestepped the shot and spun, kicking the gun from his hand and striking the man's chin with the heel of his hand. The man went down. Another man came forward with a sap while the lock picker dropped his tools and reached for his gun. Sun stepped between them leaped into the air and kicked them both in the chest. He grabbed the neck of the one nearest the bedroom door and squeezed a pressure point. The man's eyes rolled back and he went down. The man with the sap recovered and ran towards him. Sun grabbed his arm and flipped him overhead. He struck the wall above the door and fell senseless to the ground.

Then from behind him, Felicity called "Hands up, Sun. I have you covered." She held a small pistol. Sun Koh looked at her with his merciless blue eyes. He took out his key, opened the bedroom door, and retrieved his suit. Felicity called out, "Stop! I mean it." Koh went up to her and slapped her face. She dropped the gun and started blubbering. He walked past her. Sun Koh despised weakness.

Meanwhile out in the hall Shani was confronted by two armed agents who came towards her from opposite directions.

"That's far enough mem'sahib. Savvy?" He stood a dozen feet away from her on her right.

"You're a right fine little bird, ain't cha" said his companion on her left. Suddenly, the eyes on Shani's snake bracelet opened and glinted green. The snake hissed and spread its hood. It spit venom into the eyes of the first agent. Shani was wearing a live Cobra as jewelry!

The second agent heard his friend scream and opened fire. Shani ran forward and up the wall, somersaulting overhead. The shot missed her and hit the first agent. She landed deftly and attacked the shooter. It was an incredible display. She used her hands, feet, knees, elbows, and even her head. The man was pummeled into insensibility.

Then Sun Koh came out into the hall carrying his suit and helmet. The first agent had recovered and he was about to shoot Sun. Shani leaped in front of him and took three shots center of mass on her chest. Sun reacted quickly, leaping over her and charging the man, but by then the agent was unconscious. Sun turned to Shani. She was back on her feet and there was no blood. The bullets had not penetrated her sari. She smiled at him. "Woven spider web. Softer than silk, but stronger than steel. Come on."

They ran up the last few flights to the roof. Sturmvögel and Alaska-Jim were throwing fireworks and smoke bombs into the street. The *Schimäre* was floating directly over the hotel. Minx motioned to them from the hatch and they all piled in.

"Okay, Captain. Take her away!"

The atomic engines roared and the ship climbed into the sky faster and faster. It soon disappeared from sight.

EPILOGUE

Fr. Aitor Axpe watched the entire spectacle from the street. Sun Koh had gotten help and from the wrong people. Destiny—no—providence had chosen a different course for the world.

"We will meet again, Sun Koh" he murmured. He shook his head and walked into the night.

THE END

THOU PREPAREST A TABLE BEFORE ME

Psalm 23:5 Thou preparest a table before me in the presence of mine enemies: thou anointest my head with oil; my cup runneth over.

It was a dark night over Europe in the first days of June 1932. Clouds obscured the stars and the remnants of the Aurora Borealis that had filtered down from the Arctic. A bizarre aircraft with retractable wings and two engines slung below the fuselage was flying at 800 k/hr towards the Austrian Alps. This was the *Schimäre*, the mysterious multifunction vehicle of The Captain and his crew of dedicated followers. They had just completed a rescue mission from the very heart of London.

Sun Koh, the Prince Regent of the House of Thule and Heir of Atlantis, had abandoned his damaged time vessel over England and the Thule Society had mounted a mission to extract him. He had traveled from almost 11,000 years in the past to prepare mankind for the new Ice Age and the reemergence of his ancestral realm from the Atlantic Ocean as more and more of the world's water was frozen into polar glaciers. But his ship came out of paratime prematurely during a solar storm and had been broken apart by waves of electrical discharges. During this disaster, Sun Koh had experienced a connection with the Akashic Record and the cumulative knowledge of the Earth had been infused into his mind. This had permitted him to comprehend his surroundings and plan an escape from England, but British Security moved faster than expected because a mysterious Basque priest representing the Vatican had tipped them off. Sun Koh had just barely escaped the trap set by MI5 with the help of Thule Society agents from Germany. Now within the hour, they would be safely in The Captain's hideout in the Austrian Alps, The Aerie.

Flying the unusual aircraft was The Captain whose secret identity was Jan Mayer, the brilliant inventor and his co-pilot Gunther Raus whose code name was Tyrann. Sitting with Sun in the passenger's compartment were an eclectic group of people. There were chairs and tables attached to the floor and some soft bench style seats along the walls. Sitting at one table was Alaska Jim-Hoover a Canadian trapper and outdoorsman dressed in Buckskins and a coonskin cap. Next to him in black fatigues and an alpine service cap was his friend and ally Rudolf "Sturmvögel" Rauhaar, a former special service soldier from the Great War who stood over seven feet tall. Across from them was Rolf "Scheck" Karsten, the private detective. At the next table was Ludwig Minx, also known as Dr. Baphomet, the stage magician and mystic. Lying on one of the benches was Ashanti Garuda, the Daughter of Kali whose nickname was Shani. She was dressed in a red and gold sari. There were three bullet holes at the center of her chest but no bleeding. The bullets had been stopped by the fabric of the sari, which was made of woven spider's web, and the force had been attenuated by the specially treated cotton padding she wore as an undergarment. Her dress protected against small arms fire and even knife blows. The three shots she had taken to the chest had bruised her and she was meditating to speed her healing. A pair of gold sandals were on the floor next to her. On her fingernails and toenails was blood red nail polish with gold inlay counter-clockwise swastikas on her thumbs and great toenails. On her forehead was a tikala or caste mark of the same blood red color with a golden swastika inlayed in it. She had coiffed herself this way to draw the attention of Sun Koh whose ancestral house symbol was the swastika. On her right upper arm was a small live Golden Cobra that looked like a long snake bracelet.

Sitting at her head and looking at her with admiration was Sun Koh, Prince Regent of Atlantis. He was a bronze giant over two meters tall with wavy blonde hair and deep blue lapis lazuli eyes. He was well muscled but, because of his perfect proportions, he looked more like a track athlete than a weightlifter. He was watching Shani's breathing and was satisfied that she had not suffered any significant ill effects when she had shielded him from the British agent's gun fire.

"Magnificent, isn't she" said Minx in German. "She is a consummate predator and assassin, formally trained in the fighting and mystical arts of India as well as those of Tantra and the Kama Sutra. Those two British agents were lucky. She could have killed them both."

Sun Koh looked at him. "They will both be in the hospital for a while. That man she pummeled was barely breathing."

"They deserved it." said Shani who lay still with closed eyes. "Imperialist bastards." She was wanted by the British for acts of terrorism in India and had sworn eternal enmity against England.

Sun Koh, asked her gently. "How are you feeling?"

She took a deep breath. "Still a little sore. I have suppressed the pain. By morning, I'll be fine."

Sun saw the concern and desire in Minx's eyes. He knew the magician was attracted to the Indian woman, but he could see that she did not reciprocate. As far as she was concerned, they were colleagues. Nothing more.

Sun Koh also felt a strong attraction to Shani. She had deliberately made herself up to look like one of the highborn women from his time. She made him long for his own world. But most of all Sun Koh appreciated her courage and tenacity. She did not fold under pressure and openly revealed her identity in England even though she could have been arrested. And she knew the old Atlantean language. At least a passable version of it. Minx did as well.

The Magician and the Daughter of Kali had both trained with the same Agartha master a decade ago. He had taught them the Atlantean tongue as a secure way of communicating even in a crowd. Now they were working full time for the Thule Society in Berlin.

Sun Koh addressed Minx. "So you are members of the new Thule Society? The original was founded by Rudolf Von Sebottendorff in 1918 and headquartered in Munich. After the Nazis infiltrated it, he left in protest and the Society was disbanded in 1925."

"Yes." said Minx. "Many of the original members were more interested in racism and right-wing politics than the occult and have risen to high positions in the Nazi Party. When Von Sebottendorff left Munich in 1920, he founded a secret conclave of Aryan adepts in Berlin of which we are members. Now, we are the only ones who understand the true significance of Thule! These National Socialists flirt with our ideas and pay lip service to them, but their leader, Hitler, is far too obsessed with anti-Semitism and not enough with recovering Germany's occult roots. He is decidedly not one of us."

"But the Nazis and Hitler are the future of Germany!" chimed Sturmvögel. "We need order and discipline to recover out greatness."

Minx clucked, "What we need, Sturm, is sound leadership based on eternal principles and ancient wisdom! We see sitting before us the man who should rule and who in fact has been chosen by fate to rule the world."

Sun Koh smiled wryly, "Well, if so, fate should have left my ship intact!"

Minx gestured "That is only a minor inconvenience. You are prince of the blood and a Man of Destiny. You have been equipped with all you will need."

Sturmvögel spoke up, "So how does it feel to know everything, Herr Koh?"

Sun Koh replied "It is not what you think. The Akashic record contains the summation of all human knowledge but not all of it is easily accessible. General knowledge and that which has been written down or printed many times is easiest to trace and access. Particular details in the lives of individuals are not as easy. Try picking out the face of friend in the crowd at a sports event and you will understand what I mean."

Schreck chimed in "Well isn't there an index?"

"There are several actually," sighed Koh. "Not all of them are modern and many are in foreign languages—mostly dead languages. Few are alphabetical. Some are phonetic. The vast majority are topical with some quirky or biased ways of categorizing the contents. And none of them are even close to being complete."

"But now you can solve many of the great mysteries of history. You can tell us what the original author of a book really meant," said the private detective.

Sun Koh shook his head. "If it is a mystery, it means that very few people—if any —knew the truth and that is the hardest type of information to access. Especially if someone was trying to hide it. You can't completely block access in the Akashic record, but you can camouflage it.

"And a book has only one author but thousands or millions of readers. It is hard to hear that one lone voice. I have discovered that many authors "go with the flow" when they write and do not fully understand what their work really means. In that case, the story may be archetypal and better interpreted by analysts other than the author.

"The most frustrating thing is in the various academic disciplines. The experts themselves do not always agree and it is their opinions that I am privy to, not the underlying truth of nature itself. I need to decide what opinion if any is the most credible and in some cases none of them are!'

Alaska-Jim was chewing tobacco and spitting into a cup. "I can't figure out how you fit all that stuff into your head. All that book learning would give me a headache."

"It could. But I was a practitioner of a mental discipline from Atlantis that utilized parallel processing across various quantum states to solve complex equations. Part of the discipline was the capability to compress huge amounts of information into simply formulated but infinitely complex algorithms. If I had not been able to do that, the full force of the Akashic load would have either driven me mad or killed me."

Alaska-Jim spat into his cup. He, Schreck, and Sturm looked at each other in bewilderment. "Any of you sidewinders understand what he just said?"

Minx laughed. "The carnal mind of the West is not ready for such truths. Only Shani and I can really understand this through our yogic training."

Sturm stirred angrily, "Mystical nonsense! What is real can be seen and touched. I have no need of this non-Aryan dreck."

"But it is Aryan and it is not nonsense," said Shani. She sat up. "It is part of the heritage that you have lost."

Jim cackled. "I've been telling him. The Indians and Eskimos have strong medicine practices that you can't just dismiss. I've seen things…"

The Captain came back into the passenger's cabin. "I have been listening to this incredible story. Tell me, Herr Koh. Will you rebuild your ship?"

Sun Koh shook his head. "I am afraid not. I had dozens of atomic warheads and many other weapons on board. They were irreplaceable. And the technology was too advanced. We could not duplicate it for many decades."

The Captain gestured around him. 'Well, this ship is rather exotic for its time, and I was able to build it anyway."

"Advanced as it is, its design is quite simple," said Sun. "It could be improved with better materials and more advanced technology. Besides, you have not equipped her with dozens of atomic missiles such as I had. The cost to duplicate my craft would have been in the vicinity of 500 million US Dollars at the current rate of exchange. And the technologies needed to accomplish this are beyond the capabilities of your small Alpine workshop. You would need whole new industries to provide what I would need. So there are many reasons why I cannot rebuild my ship. Aside from the quality assurance issues, and your backward technology, the cost alone would be prohibitive.

"I am like an aircraft designer marooned on a desert island. Theoretically, I could design and build a plane to fly me to safety. In reality, if I can not climb that coconut palm to get food or find a source of fresh water, I will be dead in a few days."

Sun Koh looked around the opulent cabin. "I have meant to speak with you about something. The engines you use are atomic powered aren't they? You use a relatively cold form of nuclear fusion to convert hydrogen into helium, yes?"

The Captain nodded. "It was a process taught to my grandfather by a Sikh genius who roamed the oceans sixty years ago in a submarine. Grandfather was a colonist on his secret island base. When the Sikh was lost at sea, grandfather assumed leadership of the colony and built a heavier-than-air flying ship called the Albatross. He used the alias Robur and flew around the world in it several times. Later he developed a vehicle that could move swiftly on land, sea, and air. He died when the first proto-type—*The Terror*—was struck by lightning."

"This basic design—especially the engines—is based on Atlantean technology" replied Sun Koh. "That Sikh must have had a source from one of our caches. Possibly the one in the Himalayas."

Alaska-Jim chimed in, "What all is in these caches?"

Sun answered, "Gold, jewels, other precious metals, exotic materials of industrial or tactical importance, technical designs, and even libraries of information."

Shani spoke up, "The Agarthic master who instructed Minx and me was a descendent of Genghis Kahn. He had access to many exotic materials including certain purified isotopes of heavy elements such as Uranium. He disappeared a few years ago and no one has been able to contact the Agartha since then. He used to speak of a hidden place in the Himalayas."

"Yes," said Sun Koh. "There is quite a lot in that region which remains mysterious even to me. Someone has placed wards on it to dissuade anyone from finding out about it. It is safe to assume that the cache there has been compromised."

"Were there other caches?" asked The Captain.

"Yes. Several," Sun replied. "There were none in Antarctica because of the things that live there. And the land of Lemuria—which included what today is known as Australia—was itself occupied or haunted by other races—human and otherwise. The North American Rockies were controlled by the subterranean empire that still exists below them today. But the other continents were under our hegemony. That is where the caches were placed.

"They were placed on the highest mountains with markers that could only be seen from above so that primitive people could not find them until they developed the ability to fly. Some were found anyway and are lost. The major one in the Andes was discovered just three years ago and looted. Its contents are wreaking havoc in the United States right now. The one in the Himalayas has been also been breached. There was another in Africa, but it was found by an errant British Lord at the turn of the Century. "

"Do you know where the others are?" asked Sturm.

"Vaguely. Most of them are minor compared to these four. I know where they were supposed to be but the landscape has changed dramatically in 11,000 years and no one since then has known their exact locations."

Minx became thoughtful. "My prince, you said that the caches were preserved on mountains. What about the Alps?"

Sun Koh smiled. "I wondered when you would put that together. Yes indeed, there was a large one planned for there and as far as I can tell, no one has yet stumbled onto it. I think our first order of business should be to find it."

•••

They arrived at the Aerie and under the cover of darkness, the *Schimäre*, hovered into its secret hangar high in the mountains. The hidden base was contained in an old mine from the last century. Jan had extended the tunnels and connected them to his mountain villa, which was at the ground entrance. The *Schimäre* only came and went at night or when the visibility was low enough to prevent detection.

The base's ground crew began a post-flight inspection while the passengers and crew went to sleeping quarters. The next morning, Schreck was taken into town and put on the train to Berlin. He had a few active investigations in progress and he needed to get back to them. Minx and Shani stayed behind to help debrief Sun Koh.

Sun Koh was up at 0600 local time. He knew the time exactly. He also knew his exact location on the surface of the earth within a meter. It was another of his augmented powers since tapping the Akashic Record. His room was simple but comfortable. The only things he had brought with him were the tuxedo he had worn to dinner and his flight suit and helmet. He went into the corridor and found his way unerringly to the dining hall. He had a rather exact layout of the facilities in his augmented memory. Many of the base personnel were already at breakfast as was Sturmvögel.

"Guten tag, Herr Koh" Said Sturm. "Did you sleep well?" The tall blond soldier-of-fortune was eating a hearty breakfast of prepared meats and rolls with a pile of scrambled eggs and a large mug of black coffee. His face was handsome if angular and he had a ten cm *renommierschmiss* dueling scar on his left cheek. His hair was crew cut short and spiky. He was wearing his trademark black fatigues.

"Indeed. It is good to be out of that degenerate England and among friends. You are up early."

"Jim and I are going to do some climbing today. I bragged to him about the beauty of my homeland when we were in Canada. The weather has cleared, and the visibility is excellent. Now he can see it for himself."

Alaska-Jim came and sat with them. He was dressed in Amerindian style furs and leather with a cold weather cap. "Good Morning," he said. "Are you thinking about coming with us on the climb? The scenery is magnificent, and I love the cold crisp air." He helped himself to bread and sausages. Jim had the weathered look of a man who worked outdoors and who could handle himself in any survival situation. Sun Koh saw that he carried two .45 caliber revolvers on his belt, several knives, a hatchet, and an unusual double-ended metal tomahawk. He should have been hot in those furs but he looked comfortable.

Sun Koh replied, "Not today, thank you. I need to talk to The Captain about finding the Alpine Cache. The sooner I find it, the sooner I can take my place in this society."

"Pah, society!" said Jim. "I prefer the great outdoors. Society just makes men soft."

"When the next Ice Age comes," said Sun, "the soft and the weak will not survive, but civilization must. We will need the hidden materials and technology to get us through, especially when Atlantis rises again."

After eating, Sturm and Jim headed off to climb mountain peaks and Sun Koh sought out The Captain, Jan Mayer. He was in his office/laboratory tinkering with some gadget. Sun recognized it as a mechanical valve that could be used in a chemical synthesis process to control the flow of product into a reaction vessel. It was quite complex. This was one of many devices that Jan Mayer had designed and patented. His manufacturing plants turned his designs into valuable products. This paid for all of his secret work on *Schimäre* and other projects.

"*Guten Morgen, Herr Koh*. What do you think?" He pointed to the valve.

Sun mused, "It would work better if this flange was twisted another ten degrees. The feedback struts are too thin and I would recommend using a different grade of steel due to the temperature of the reaction. Otherwise it will foul too easily."

Jan Mayen was surprised and delighted. The suggestions were excellent. They discussed the matter and Jan made some notes.

"Now Jan, there is something you can do for me."

"Of course!"

"I need to find the Alpine Cache. Do you have any aerial reconnaissance photos?"

"Ah," said The Captain. He took out sets of photographic maps. "I took these myself from the *Schimäre*."

They examined the maps. "Nothing." said Koh. "I see no signs of the aerial symbols they were supposed to use."

Jan asked, "Can't you …'access' its location?"

"No," Koh replied. "I have tried, but all I know is what they planned to do. I am sure that they did plant the cache, but it was intended to be hidden and I can't locate any specific information on it. Maybe they did not have a chance to mark it before the crustal shift. Everything for the next 2,000 years after that is very fuzzy."

Then a light dawned in Sun's blue eyes. "The African cache was completed late too. And it was different from the others. Maybe that is the key…"

•••

Sturmvögel and Alaska Jim drove along a rugged trail high into the mountains. They reached a rest area that was quite high and parked. Overhead loomed a large peak with an 850 meter sheer face over the roadway.

Sturm said, "Here it is. We climb up to that ledge and make our way around to the other side and you get a magnificent view of the whole range."

Alaska-Jim looked at the cliff face. "Pretty sheer. At this temperature, we could have running water and rock slides, too. "

Sturm sniffed, "Come on, old man. We have scaled worse cliffs in the Yukon before."

As they approached the face, Jim stopped and looked intently at the escarpment. "Do you see it, Sturm?"

Sturmvögel nodded. "Yes. Yes, I do."

They scaled the cliff face using pitons and guide lines. Sturmvögel led the way with Alaska-Jim on belay. Jim would follow on once Strum was stabilized up above. They made rapid progress demonstrating their expertise—and some of their arrogance. They both wore crampons over their boots and light climbing gear. Sturmvögel's powerful hands and fingers allowed him to get firm holds even without pitons and he scaled quickly.

Strum had reached the ledge at the top of the face and anchored a large piton with a ring through which he wound the belay rope. "Okay, Jim. Start climbing up to me!" he called.

Suddenly from the shadows on the ledge, a shot rang out and struck the piton dislodging it. Sturm lost his balance for a second but then regained it and held the full weight of Jim's body on the rope. Then an ice axe hit the rope and cut it. Strum fell backwards on to the ledge and heard Jim scream.

"I bring greetings from Colonel Gruber."

"Hold still, Sturmvögel" said a voice to his right. He turned and saw a man with an automatic pistol emerge from behind a rock. "Hello, Rudolf" the man said. "I bring greetings from Colonel Gruber." From behind him, Sturmvögel heard footsteps coming around the ledge. There were three men behind him similarly armed.

"We have been waiting for you, Sturm. The Unit has unfinished business with you."

Strum spat at him and cursed. "Cowardly dogs! Sneaking up on a man like that. Ambushing unarmed people was always your specialty. You have killed my friend! He did nothing to you."

"He was your friend and that was enough. Besides, we need no witnesses. It was a climbing accident. The rope parted and you both fell. Don't make this any harder than it has to be, Rudolf.

"You are never unarmed. Take out your pistol slowly using two fingers and throw it over the edge." Sturm reached into his jacket to his shoulder holster and pulled out his Mauser.

Suddenly from behind the three men there was a loud war-hoop. The man in front of Sturm looked up and aimed his gun behind his three companions. There was a "whoosh" sound and a spinning object wheeled through the air and hit him in the face, splitting his skull. The three men were distracted and looked behind them. In that instant there was a double report and two of the men went down with .45 slugs in their chests. The third man fired wildly but could not see who had fired the deadly shots. Sturmvögel rolled to his feet and struck the man behind his right ear. The man collapsed to the ground.

Alaska-Jim popped up just over the ledge. His pistols were in his hands and he was supported on the face by his crampons. Sturm moved quickly to secure the site and verified that the three men were dead. He retrieved the strange object that had crushed the first man's skull. It was a tomahawk with a shaped metal blade backed by a spike at each end and an asymmetry between the sides of the blades. When thrown, it developed aerodynamic lift and could whirl through the air like a flying disk over long distances. He knew that it also could return like a boomerang. It was Alaska-Jim's trademark weapon. The original had used stone heads but Jan Mayen had made this high-tech version for him.

"They were sloppy," said Jim. "They came up here yesterday and waited all night for us. They forgot that we were wilderness trackers. Their feeble attempt at covering their tracks stuck out like a sore thumb."

"Now you know why I had to leave Germany," said Sturm. "They actually thought that cutting that line would make you fall. They never saw how Red Indians climb mountains." Sturm shook his head.

"If you do it right, you don't need ropes and every man climbs for himself," said Jim. He kicked the prongs on his boots into the rock wall. "These crampons are amazing! They made it easy to shimmy sideways along that rock face and come up behind these bushwhackers."

"You learn something new every day. Now let's learn a little more from our friend here."

Sturm frisked and disarmed the unconscious man. Then he roused him and interrogated him. Intensely…

Several hours later, he and Alaska-Jim returned to the rest area. The four bodies had been stuffed into crevices on the mountainside. They would never be found. The two men drove back to Jan Mayen's villa without speaking.

Jan Mayen was clearly annoyed. "So these men were sent to kill you? How did they know you were here or that you would be on that mountain today?"

Sturmvögel did not flinch or make excuses. He sat upright in his chair as if at attention. "I had written my mother that I would be here with you in Austria at this time and that I was planning to visit her in Nuremburg next week. As for climbing that mountain… well, there is this barmaid at the Inn in town. I told her about it."

They were sitting around the table in the conference room of the villa with Sun Koh, Tyrann, Alaska-Jim, Minx and Shani.

"And what other things have you told her?" barked Jan. "Have you comprised the secret of my Aerie?"

"No! Never, Jan! I would never do that."

Minx got up and stood in front of Sturm. He held Sturm's left hand as it lay upon the table. His dark eyes began to glow with hints of dark red light. Sturmvögel's face went blank and his eyes glazed over. After a few moments, Minx backed off.

"He is telling the truth," he said as he turned to go to his seat.

Sturm shook his head to clear it and said loudly, "What the Hell was that?"

"Just more of that 'mystical nonsense,'" said Minx. "Be happy. It just saved your hide."

Sun Koh's danger sense was alerted. He spoke up, "Tell us about this Colonel Gruber."

Sturm looked to the ground and then faced Sun Koh. "He used

to be Captain Constantine Gruber, my company commander in the Sturmabteilung—the SA. There was a Communist newsman who was a constant nuisance to us. Gruber assigned my squad to rough him up. Our mission leader was Gruber's brother, Hans. Well, we cornered the man outside his house one night and tossed him around. A little *Zusammenstöße*. His wife came out screaming and tried to interfere. Hans started beating her and stripping off her clothes. He was going to..."

For the first time, Sturmvögel showed signs of embarrassment. "I am a soldier, not a degenerate or a criminal. The man was fair game. He was our mission. Abusing women is beneath contempt."

He composed himself. "I stopped Hans. Physically. We argued briefly, and he tried to pull rank, but we had already been there too long and needed to leave. When we returned to headquarters, he started in with me. He pulled a knife. We fought, and I killed him with my bare hands.

"Constantine was furious and tried to court-martial me. But the colonel overruled him and said it was a fair fight. He ordered Gruber to leave me alone. But even he was disappointed with me. The whole unit changed towards me. I knew that Gruber wanted me dead and that it was just a matter of time. So, I left Germany and went to America. That was five years ago.

"We learned from our interrogation that the colonel died of a heart attack last year. There was a struggle for power and Gruber won. He is the new commander of my old unit, and he has gotten quite chummy with Ernst Röhm. Those bastards on the cliff were from an old Alpine unit. They were supposed to work me over and finish me, making it look like a climbing accident."

"Weren't you taking a chance letting them get the drop on you?" asked Minx.

"Luckily, Jim and I were wearing Jan's marvelous long underwear. It not only insulates from the cold but protects from injury. Anything from falling rocks to pistol bullets. And there were only four of them. It almost wasn't fair."

Sun Koh responded, "But now Jan has been linked with you and this endangers all of us. The last thing that we need is to be at odds with the brownshirts."

Shani could not contain herself. "I think you are a brave a noble soldier, Sturm. What you did was right. You protected that woman's honor."

"I wish I could be so sure," said Sturm. "It turns out the man's wife was a Jew."

Sun Koh did not change expression, but he was shocked by this comment. There were Jews throughout Germany. Many of them were either secular or had converted to Christianity. In any case, as a whole, they were more German than Jewish. A large number of them were well educated and in the professions. Their contributions to European civilization were disproportionately greater than that of other ethnic groups. If only these fools would listen to the man Einstein and not dismiss Relativity as "Jewish Physics"!

But it was from them that the prophets of this civilization had come. They were the same kind of prophets who foretold the downfall of Atlantis and may have hastened it. Sun did not know what to make of this. As he reviewed the history of the last few hundred years he saw the simple religious pride of some Christians mutate into an irrational paranoia taken up by secular men. Subjugate these Jews, by all means. All lesser humans were meant to serve the true Aryan Master Race. But this fear and hatred was depriving the Masters of useful slaves.

"Enough!" Sun Koh slammed his palms onto the table with a loud report, making it quiver. He stood up and faced Sturm.

"You have endangered your benefactor and the rest of us with your carelessness. I can feel it. For all of our sakes we will have to deal with the SA and neutralize Gruber."

Sun Koh moved away from the table and called Sturmvögel to stand in front of him.

"You are a soldier and a man of honor. In the coming years I will have need of men such as you. I will forgive your error and promise to save your life. But, you must pledge to me undying loyalty as your liege. I offer to make you my Man-at-Arms and personal bodyguard. I have many things to do for the good of the Aryan Race and the world itself. Join with me and, I swear, we will deal with Gruber so that you may walk openly in Germany as a hero, feared by your enemies, protected by your allies, and respected by the people. Will you join me?"

Sturmvögel knelt on his left knee and said. "I swear to pledge my honor to you, Prince Koh and my fealty. I will fight beside you for the right, the Reich, and the Aryan people. Let us return order to Germany, but most of all let us restore the honor and dignity befitting the Master Race!"

Sun Koh pounded his fists on Sturm's shoulders and said, "Arise Sturmvögel, Man-at-Arms and First Knight of New Atlantis!"

Alaska-Jim Hoover came forward. "I come from good German stock, myself. I will stand with you and Sturmvögel, my blood brother. Your enemies are my enemies. Your friends are my friends. Your families are my families. We need a new world order and I want to be a part of it."

Sun Koh clapped Jim on the shoulder and shook his hand.

"Comrades," said Sun. "Our first great task is to uncover the last great cache left by my father, King FⓄyunch! Jan and I have poured over the maps and we have discovered something fascinating. The Alpine range rings the country known as Switzerland. This tiny nation has remained independent of outside rule for hundreds of years. It had never been fully conquered by any empire in all of history. There are old stories about armies that tried to invade but were beaten back by the very land itself: rockslides, avalanches, and alterations in the landscape. Sometimes it seemed that the Earth opened up and swallowed these invading armies whole.

"Many of the mountain people have come down to live in the valleys and Cantons. However, we examined aerial photographs and found that there is one area in the most rugged part of the Alps where a significant human population remains. This area has large farms and agricultural facilities far in excess of the needs of their population, yet they export only lumber, milk, and some cattle. There primary exports are hard woods and firs from heavy forests, which seem to grow back rather quickly. Much more quickly than we could explain.

"I think we must take the hint from the African cache. It was located in a remote area and protected by a servitor race. It was only recently that this race had degenerated to the point that an outsider could steal the treasure.

"I think that my father did the same thing here. It had been too late for an elaborate mountain cache, so he hid the treasure underground and left servitors to guard it."

Jan Mayen was puzzled. "How could they hide such a thing in the heart of Europe over all these centuries? There has been no hint of a hidden underground treasure or guardians."

"Sure there were. Even before the Romans there were legends," said Sun. "But everyone had dismissed it as superstition."

Minx's eyes lit up. "The fabled Zwergkönigreich! But no one has ever found it."

Koh nodded, "Information about it is very well warded. All I see in the Akashic records are legends and exaggerated folktales. But I think we have found the entrance to Zwergkönigreich here." He pointed to a photograph of a deeply forested valley in Northern Switzerland. "We will need more information. Jan, we need some aerial photography with special filters. I know you have them. Can we do that today?"

Jan scratched his chin. "Yes. I can use the cloud generators to hide *Schimäre's* launching." He looked sternly at Sturm. "We must be careful now."

"But it is most important that I find the cache before the Thule Society meeting next week," said Koh. "Then I can deal from a position of strength!"

•••

Two days later at dawn, *Schimäre* flew over the deeply forested area in the Northern Swiss Alps. Three figures jumped out of the plane and parachutes opened. One of the parachutes was triangular. The figures landed in an open meadow on the edge of the forest. One was Sun Koh wearing his flight suit and helmet. The next was Sturmvögel in his Black fatigues and a Metal Infantry helmet. The third was Alaska-Jim in Buckskins and a paratrooper's headgear.

They quickly deflated their chutes. Koh's was resorbed into his suit. Sturm and Jim rolled theirs up and stashed them. Sturm was wearing a combat vest with a bayonet, Combat Knife, and "potato masher grenades". He wore a Luger pistol in a shoulder holster. He also had an automatic rifle designed by Jan Mayen that used the 7.92 mm Mauser cartridge. It looked very much like the American BAR but with a larger ram's horn magazine. He also carried several packages of plastic explosives. Jim carried his usual set of wilderness weapons, some grenades, a sawed-off double-barreled shotgun and a late-model Winchester Repeating Rifle designed to use the .45-70 US Government cartridge.

Sun Koh had declined any of the weapons that Jan offered, but he was far from unarmed. His flight suit doubled as body armor and in his right hand he held a gray plastic handle with an odd metal comb on the end that was bent forwards at a 30° angle.

He spoke up, "Okay, the recon photos show that all the forests in this area have been harvested regularly except this one. This has all original growth and has remained undisturbed for centuries. There are several paths that lead into this forest from the agricultural areas. The IR photos showed the ground temperature in there to be 5°C warmer than in the surrounding valleys and there is a deep heat source at the forest's center. There are also what look like human and animal shapes wandering around in the thick woods. We will follow this pathway into the forest center."

The men strung out and entered the forest with Sturm in the lead followed by Sun Koh and Alaska-Jim. As they went in deeper, Koh confirmed that these woods did not have the same flora as the other forests in that area. The trees were thick with aromatic wood and that grew like olive trees: sending out shoots from the main trunks that spread and created miniature circular groups of trees. Such trees were virtually immortal. There were many ferns, vines, and bushes but few grasses. As they penetrated deeper into the woods, all three of them became aware that they were being watched. They communicated by whispers using the Ojibwa Indian Language. Sun Koh called a halt. His danger sense was tingling.

"There is something just over that rise," he said. Sturm could not see anything. "Let me take the point," Koh said. He moved ahead of Sturm and carefully mounted the rise. Suddenly, there was a grayish blur and something leaped up at Koh from the ground. He sidestepped and brought up the handle in his right hand. For an instant, a bright bluish light was projected from the handle into a shape like a halberd blade. There was a buzzing sound and the distinct tang of ozone. Sun lashed out and there was a brief scream like that of a child which was cut off abruptly. Something flopped on the ground for a few seconds then lay still. The bushes rustled around them. Sturm and Alaska-Jim fired randomly into the brush. There were a few more screams that faded and seemed to retreat.

Sturmvögel and Jim came up to see what Sun Koh had found. The creature had been 2.5 meters long and was covered with white, black, grey, and pink scales. In the middle portion, it was as thick as a man's leg. The black scales formed vertical stripes on its sides alternating with stripes made from pink and white scales. On its back the scales were arranged in short horizontal gray and black bars on a background of random scale colors. The creature had a set of forelimbs that were 50 cm long and ended in a 'hand' with four clawed digits. The most medial digit was opposable. The head had large liquid black eyes and a bulging cranium. The jaw was short but pointed and was filled with rows of undifferentiated reptilian teeth. There were small vestigial hind limbs almost ¾ of the way down from the head. Sun had cut its head off just above the forelimbs the cut was straight with some singeing.

Sturm whistled. "Mein Gott! It's a tatzelwurm! I have heard of such things living in these mountains, but I thought they were fables. It looks like some kind of snake with arms."

Jim looked at it. "It ain't no snake. It looks more like a stretched-out Gila monster with a big head."

Sun Koh nodded. "You are right, Jim. This is an ancient slithering lizard from the early Triassic. It is a living fossil. A forerunner of some of the Basilisk races that arose during the Mesozoic and which lived in my time in Lemuria. This species has the intelligence of a chimpanzee and, like it, is quite aggressive. Their bite is poisonous. The Lemurians used to use them as animal watchmen. Look over there." On the ground was a simple hand axe made by lashing a shaped stone onto a stick. "They can make and use simple tools, but they are not strong enough to fight a man hand to hand. They depend on their bite as their primary weapon." Sun Koh held up the handle with the metal comb. "My holographic plasma blade came in handy. It can be shaped into any of several pre-programmed forms for different tasks. It can even form a shield."

Sun looked up and sniffed the air. He sensed more danger. "We have a reception committee coming at us from all sides." There was a low grunting roar and a great black hairy creature with a long snout and sharp teeth reared up on its hind legs. It was almost ten feet tall! On its neck was a spiked collar attached to a chain. The bear slammed forward on all fours and on its back was a saddle with a rider. He was dressed in a steel helmet shaped like a bullet. He had a steel breastplate and interlocking steel plates covering his arms and legs. His shoulders were broad, but his legs and body were stubby and short. The rider would have been only four feet tall without his helmet. He had a pointed beard and his features were wide and blunted. He squinted in the daylight and his pupils were mere pinpoints. His nasty looking crossbow was loaded with a huge steel-tipped bolt. Other bears began to appear with their riders. Some of the riders held large barreled harquebuses that used some closed firing mechanism instead of a flintlock. Sun could see rifling in the barrel and huge spare cartridges on the saddles with glassy tips and brass casings. They were 40 mm diamond tipped armor piercing shells. Even Sun's flight suit could not stop them point-blank. Slithering among the mounted monsters were tatzelwurms armed with spears and clubs.

Sun Koh said. "You are seeing creatures from a world long gone. European cave bears were far larger than their modern relatives in America. These have been bred for war. Lower your weapons but do not let go of them."

One of the bears lumbered forward. His rider's helmet was larger and had a crest on it. He began speaking in a grunting language that was unlike any human tongue. Sun Koh searched his vast memory and found that he had to access the non-human part of his database to understand him. Sun responded in similar grunts and nasal chuffs. The rider was astounded. They spoke back and forth. Then the rider turned and conferred with other riders.

"What did he say, Prince Koh?" asked Sturm.

"He was pronouncing a formal death sentence on us for trespassing in accordance with their treaties with the surface dwellers. I rebuked him and identified myself as the Prince Regent of Atlantis. I demanded safe passage for us to parley with his chiefs. He was shocked because he thought that no human knew his language. They normally communicate with the surface people using an early Germanic dialect."

Strum shook his head. "They really are dwarves aren't they? And they live under the mountains."

"Actually, Sturm, they are descendants of the Neanderthals who once occupied Europe. Our ancestors came here 30,000 years ago and almost drove them to extinction. The Neanderthals were not our ancestors no matter what your scientists may believe but a completely separate species. They were cave dwellers before we humans arrived, and we drove them deeper into the Earth. In my time, there were over a million of these people living in this area. They were great miners and provided our empire with metals, minerals, and jewels in exchange for food, lumber, and other goods. It looks like my father chose them to protect the Alpine cache. This explains why the surface people export treated dairy products here like cheese. Adult dwarves cannot digest milk."

"What are they trading now for food?"

"Minerals, gold, fertilizer and very likely protection. There has never been a successful conquest of Switzerland. I suspect an almost feudal relationship between the dwarves and the surface people here." Sun shook his head. "That will have to change. The servitor races must know their place and shall not enslave their betters."

Sun Koh became impatient and called out to the senior dwarf. They exchanged words rapidly and fiercely. This dwarf's name was unpronounceable, but a close approximation would be Purtilretemkin. He wanted the three men to drop their weapons, but Sun Koh refused. He knew that guests were allowed to take their weapons with them. Only prisoners were disarmed. Finally, after consultation, the dwarves agreed to escort the three men to the council of chiefs. There was no one ruler in Neanderthal civilizations.

They proceeded on foot to the center of the forest and came upon a depression in the ground that looked like a sinkhole. Discrete battlements of

"Sun Koh responded in similar grunts..."

thorn bushes and earthworks surrounded it. Sun Koh learned that these battle bears were carefully bred from the stock that lived in this one forest. The bears were primarily vegetarian and ate off the land.

Several paths wound down along the walls into the bottom where a single large building was built against the wall. This was the egress into Zwergkönigreich, the kingdom of the Dwarves. Inside the building were boxes and bags full of foodstuff: grain, vegetables, prepared meats. There were even some live cattle. The interior of the building was illuminated by multifaceted crystals embedded in the ceilings that glowed with a whitish-yellow light. Even so, the lighting was dim by human standards. Set into the wall were three large elevators.

Strum looked around and saw sealed barrels attached to the walls and floors. Wires ran to them. He turned to Sun. "They have explosives mounted all over. In case of an invasion they could destroy this whole place and seal off any outside access."

Sun nodded. "I am sure there are other entrances."

The elevator was as large as a salon. The three humans were escorted by dozens of the four-foot warriors. Sun Koh noted that their pupils were now normal sized in the dim light. The door was closed, and the senior dwarf stepped to the wall, pressed a button, and spoke into a hole. There was a hum and the elevator began to descend. Light came from the faceted crystal in the ceiling.

"We are descending using electromagnetism. There are no winch cables. It is all controlled from below. They have rudimentary electrical technology probably powered by geothermal energy."

As they descended, the air pressure increased as did the ambient temperature. They went down over 1500 meters before they reached the bottom. The three men were led out into a large foyer. A strange wheeled vehicle like a small truck with an open top awaited them. They sat in the back of it. With a hum, they drove out of the foyer. In front and behind were other vehicles loaded with armed dwarves. There was a mild tang of sulfur in the air.

They went through a large cavern filled with supplies from the surface and then passed into a system of tunnels. They drove for almost thirty minutes. Sturm was sweating. The air was thick. The temperature must have been 30° C and the humidity was high. Jim was wearing his usual buckskins but did not appear at all uncomfortable. Meanwhile, Sun Koh's flight suit maintained a comfortable temperature for him.

They finally left the tunnels and parked the vehicle. They got out and proceeded on foot thorough more tunnels until they passed through a checkpoint and entered a series of finished corridors. There was not much decoration on the walls of the corridor. What little ornamentation seen was minimalist using basic colors and almost abstract. The most prominent decorations were horns, skulls, and bones of various animals. There were no pictures. Crystals emitting whitish-yellow light illuminated everything.

Finally, they were escorted into a large room filled with dwarves. They saw the first females there. Both sexes wore simple leather and cloth buskins. The females were slightly shorter than the males and had less facial hair. They were stocky by human standards. Many of them had thin mustaches, but no beards. Their faces were broad featured and not at all attractive by human standards. The average male was 125 cm tall and weighed about 90 kilos while the average female was 120 cm tall and weighed about 70 kilos. All the females had Wagnerian chests.

Sturm winced. "Ach! They all look like my aunt Myrtle."

The room had a raised dais with a table behind which several older dwarves of both sexes were seated. Several hundred dwarves sat in rows of seats facing them. There was a space between these two groups which was filled with armed guards and it was here where the three humans were brought. They were offered chairs at a table facing the dais and sat down. On the table were stone goblets and a pitcher full of water. Sun Koh removed his helmet. He drank some water and encouraged Jim and Sturm to drink up. The room was sweltering.

A seated female dwarf in the center of the dais began speaking. Sun Koh replied and then others from the dais addressed him. The discussion went on for several minutes. Meanwhile the dwarves conferred with other dwarves all over the room and some even went outside the room to speak to others.

When he had the chance, Sun Koh turned to his compatriots. "This is fascinating. There are around 100,000 of these people. They have been here since the end of the last Ice Age. They have no ruler but instead rule by consensus. Families are matrilineal but the males associate themselves into lifelong working groups."

"So the wives wear the pants in the family?" asked Jim.

"No" said Sun. "There are no wives or husbands. These are not humans. The females go into estrus only once every year or two. Unlike human women, they are not receptive to sexual intercourse outside of that. There is no pair bonding and males have little to do with raising children until a boy joins his father's working group around age twelve. When they are old enough, the young men can form their own working groups. Until then, they are not allowed to mate. Even then, the men live in their matrilineal family compound for their whole lives. Mating is strictly for reproduction and it is controlled by the women elders who choose who mates with whom. It is unusual for the same male and female to mate consecutively."

Sturmvögel scowled. "Do the men and women never associate in between, my Prince?"

Sun Koh smiled wryly. "The males and females associate freely until the females go into estrus. Then they are sequestered. But this is a subsistence economy with little leisure time. Males and females do different kinds of work. Males do mining, heavy manufacturing, construction, hunting, surgery, butchering cattle, and all the policing and fighting. Lots of fighting. That is how one earns the right to mate. One earns credit for economic achievements as well, but physical health and prowess in battle are the primary factors. Females do most of the light manufacturing, housekeeping, food preparation, medical care, and child-rearing. Both sexes participate in education and scientific study, though generally in different areas.

"They grow many kinds of fungi which provide food and clothing but still need to import animals and plants from the surface. There are large shallow pools of water with bacterial mats that scrub the carbon dioxide from the air and generate oxygen using the energy from sulfides. Until recently, they lighted their caves with natural gas lamps but they have since discovered electricity. They hope soon to be able to grow surface plants by lamplight and even raise their own cattle. The ventilation was usually accomplished by a clever system of thermal vents, but this limited the depths to which they could go. Now they have simple electrical fans and the air quality is much better.

"There is also very little art here. Virtually no literature except for oral legends and family histories. They use runic writings but in a most primitive way and only for practical reasons. I doubt whether they could even comprehend more than simple mathematics. And music is virtually nonexistent. They might enjoy listening to human music, but they lack the ability to truly appreciate it or make it themselves."

"No sex, no music, no arts? Sounds very dull. Do they at least have beer?" Sturm asked.

"Several kinds. And hard liquors. Their livers are much more resilient than ours. They do ferment other things like mushrooms and fruit, but the result is quite musty and not palatable to humans from what I can recall.

They also have mind-altering drugs, many derived from fungi that grow freely down here. Most of that is for what we would call 'religious' uses. But I would stay away from most of that stuff. The distilled liquors and some of the beers are okay but most of the other things can be toxic to humans."

Jim spoke up, "What have you learned about the cache?"

Sun shook his head, "They are being very cagey about that. They are happy to tell me about their lives and were fascinated to hear the story of my arrival, but the cache is a secret from their distant past that they are guarding jealously. It is so taboo to go near it that they will need a very wide consensus among their people before they would consider even discussing it with us. It seems that there were many pretenders who have come here before searching for the cache. That is why they negotiated the death penalty for interlopers in their most recent treaties with surface humans."

One of the dwarves on the dais called out to Sun Koh. "He is asking me if I have any proof that I am the Regent of Atlantis," he said.

Sun stood up and peeled down the top of his flight suit. He then tuned his back to the dais. On it was tattooed a map of the ancient Atlantean land mass. Several dwarves approached him and examined his back. This started a whole new round of consultations. Sun put his suit back on.

Several minutes later, he was addressed by a female. Sun looked grim but nodded to her. He spoke to several other dwarves and then turned to his men.

"They cannot get a clear consensus. This is a very primitive culture and their attitude is less concerned with abstract notions of ownership than with the concrete idea of possession and the status quo. They want to settle this in their traditional way with a trial by ordeal."

Sturmvögel snorted. "That is ridiculous!"

But Alaska-Jim interjected, "No Sturm. It makes sense. The Indians used to do that kind of thing. A public spectacle like that will convince everyone. And frankly, it is the only way we will get out of here alive."

Sturm nodded with resignation. "What do they want you to do?"

"Nothing much," said, Sun Koh. "Just wrestle their champion warrior off the back of his war bear."

•••

The ordeal took place in a large oval cavern lined with tiered stone benches like an amphitheatre. It could seat around 12,000 people and the seats were full. There were several large faceted light crystals in the ceiling, but the ambient light level was like early twilight. The field in the arena was firmly packed clay. At one side of the oval was a large viewing box where the people from the dais now sat. They had a three-foot-tall hour glass.

Sun Koh came out of a tunnel on to the field. He had removed his flight suit and was wearing a leather cuirass and breechcloth provided by the dwarves along with simple high-topped leather moccasins and a leather helmet. He held an 8 foot steel pole that was wrapped with leather. It had a conical spear point on one end and a three-pronged trident on the other. The tips of the trident were sharp with trailing curved hooks behind them for grasping. In his other hand was a large net made of braided mushroom fiber.

Sturmvögel and Alaska-Jim sat on the sidelines opposite to the dais box. They had retained their weapons but kept them slung over their shoulders. Armed warriors surrounded them in the bleachers. There were also harquebus snipers on the top tiers all around the arena. Jim seemed unperturbed and was enjoying the spectacle. Strum had surreptitiously slipped a primer into one of the plastic explosive bars. If anything went wrong, he would not allow these *zwerg* to take them alive.

From the other side of the arena a gate opened, and a dwarf came out similarly dressed as Sun Koh. He was quite large for a dwarf: Just over five feet tall and almost as broad as he was tall.

Sturm whistled. "*Ach du lieber!* A giant dwarf? He must weigh 140 kilos. He is bigger than Sun Koh.!"

Jim nodded thoughtfully. "This is going to be some match."

One of the males on the dais spoke into a box and his voice was amplified over the entire arena. He spoke in the usual grunting chuffing manner of the dwarfs and then pointed to Sun Koh and presented him as "Songkohffenskin". There were polite howls and grunts and slapping of hands on the benches. The Dwarves did not clap. Sun Koh's danger sense tingled.

Then he presented the giant dwarf as "Dariduforbogskin". The crowd went wild with hoops, howls and screams. The males started beating their chests and the females made a horrible yodeling noise.

And then he called out the name "Haugsporiss". Out of another gate came a roar and a huge collared bear ambled on to the field and came to the dwarf's side. There were chains on his collar but no saddle. He reared up on his hind legs and was over twelve feet tall! He weighed 1500 kilos and the ground shook when he walked. His roar sent the crowd into more paroxysms of cheering. Dariduforbogskin leaped effortlessly on to the bear's back and hugged the creature's midsection with his legs.

Strum said, "Prince Koh told us that he would have around twenty minutes to unmount his opponent and replace him on the bear's back. Once he does that, the match is over. If he does that!"

Jim answered, "It is not that simple. This is an ordeal and it must be accomplished with honor. If Sun Koh commits what these people considered to be a foul, he will lose. The bear is like a totem to these people. He cannot injure it in any way or he forfeits."

With a shout, the male dwarf turned over the hourglass and the battle was on. The mounted bear charged Sun Koh. Sun leaped into the air in a cart wheel spin to one side. He flicked the edge of the net into Dariduforbogskin's face as he did so. The bear charged past him.

Sun landed on his feet and raised both arms as if in triumph. The crowd roared.

The Atlantean knew that he his primary job was to win over the crowd and hence the consensus of the people. He would have to show-off some to do it, but he also needed to get that dwarf off the bear to win.

The bear circled around and came at him again, running faster than a race horse. This time Sun faked running to the right but somersaulted back to his left at the last second. He then stuck out the trident and hooked Dariduforbogskin's cuirass with the trident's hooks. He yanked hard but found that the dwarf and bear were working as one body. Sun was wrenched off his feet and flung about as the bear and rider tried to break his grip on the trident. Sun was being shaken through the air as the bear ran and bucked.

Finally, the bear reared up and Sun flung his net onto the bear's left front paw. As the bear fell forward onto all fours, his paw yanked Sun Koh over his back. This allowed Sun to unhook the trident and get free. As Sun passed over Dariduforbogskin's head the dwarf shot out a strong right arm and hit him in the gut.

Sun rolled free pulling the net off the bear's claws and, once again, preened at the crowd. They cheered. Dariduforbogskin turned Haugsporiss. This time he had the bear rear up on it hind legs to attack Sun. This meant that the dwarf could not see Sun Koh. He was letting the bear do the fighting. The bear lumbered forwards sweeping giant clawed paws though the air. Sun Koh backpedaled but Haugsporiss was fast and knew how to trap and kill his prey. Sun realized the thing would fall on top of him in a moment and crush him.

In that fleeting second, Sun Koh did a rapid bit of lateral thinking. He knew he could not dismount Dariduforbogskin merely by snagging him with the trident. He and the bear were too well integrated. And he couldn't hurt the bear. The only way to dislodge the dwarf champion was by using the bear itself to dislodge him.

Sun Koh recalled one of the Trickster legends of these people. In that story the Trickster spirit appeared as a simple fox being chased by a bear-mounted hunter. The fox tangled the hunter in some thorn bushes and the bear himself pulled his rider off as the bear turned to chase the zigzagging fox. This gave Sun an idea.

As the bear charged him, Sun flung the edges of the net in front of him as a distraction. The bear slowed his forward momentum confused by the flinging net. Sun Koh flashed the net around, expanding and contracting it over his head. Finally he spun the net up right in front of the bear. The creature roared and started to fall forward. But while Haugsporiss was watching the net, Sun had dived between his legs and came up behind him. He then shoved the trident up into Dariduforbogskin's cuirass again and dug the point into the ground as a fulcrum. As the bear fell forward, Sun used the leverage of the trident with his own strength and the momentum of the bear to pull the massive dwarf off his mount. Dariduforbogskin was thrown a dozen feet. Taking the opportunity, Sun Koh grabbed the bear's fur and pulled. He somersaulted over the bear's rump and landed on his back gripping tightly with his legs. He grabbed the chain reins and twisted the bear around to face his previous rider. He then made the bear rear up and roar.

Dariduforbogskin knelt in the dust and made submission. Sun Koh had won!

•••

The dwarves held a great banquet in honor of Sun Koh's victory. They had killed a fatted calf and several other cattle and roasted them on open spits. There was every manner of prepared vegetables, sausages, and libations. Sturmvögel sampled several strange brews that night, but found only one that reminded him of that heady beer they served at the Hofbrauhaus back home. He was careful though not to drink too much. After all, he was bodyguard to his Prince.

Sun Koh meanwhile toasted the prowess of Dariduforbogskin and Haugsporiss and praised the dwarves of *Zwergkönigreich* for their faithfulness to their traditions and to the honor of the warrior.

After dinner, one of the older females from the dais came to Sun Koh and solemnly anointed his head with oil declaring "Songkohffenskin" to be an honorary citizen of *Zwergkönigreich* and the rightful heir to the cache that had been entrusted to the dwarves by the King of Atlantis. Sun Koh knew that as the Prince Regent and Heir of Atlantis, he should find this ritual to be an insult. He was their rightful sovereign, but he also knew that these people had lived without sovereigns for so long that they had forgotten their place in the world. In their minds, they were honoring him. But he also knew that he had their trust and that they would honor his rights to the cache as their ancestors had promised. Looking into his vast store of knowledge, he realized that this was right for these people and that, as a man of honor, he should not interfere with them. At least for now.

The three humans were then led by the dwarves to a heavily guarded cavern. The cavern was dark, but with a command, the light crystals were activated and its contents revealed.

Sun Koh was stunned. He had expected that there would be between 200 and 300 metric tones of gold in the cache. What he saw was twice that much. And this was only one of three such caverns. It seems that when this place was built 11,000 years ago, the Dwarves had struck a large vein of gold and mined it out. This had been added to the cache. Other smaller veins had been found subsequently, but the dwarves kept those for themselves.

He was led to other caverns in the cache, which contained rare minerals and many gems. Sun Koh collected several pouches of gems. He gave one pouch to Dariduforbogskin. He then tossed one each to Sturmvögel and Alaska-Jim. "This is for coming through Hell with me."

In a sealed cavern were a collection of exotic materials and purified isotopes that were the key to the development of advanced technologies. Sun indicated that he wanted it kept sealed for the time being.

A further cavern was filled with literally thousands of stone tablets, which contained technical information on advanced technologies. In one corner of the cavern was a collection of hyper-diamond crystals within which was contained the sum total of the knowledge and literature of Atlantis. Sun knew that the stone tablets contained enough information to build a reader for the crystals. That would come later.

Sun Koh was tired as were his companions. They needed to sleep. Tomorrow would be a busy day.

•••

The next morning just before dawn, *Schimäre* hovered over the deep forest which Sun Koh and his men had entered the day before. It had been holding vigil there all night. Tyrann was at the controls while the Captain slept. In the back, Minx and Shani were also sleeping. Then he heard a voice on the radio.

"This is the *Erbe* calling to Rescue One. Can you hear me? We have found refreshment. Stability is established. We need to bring home some bacon." Tyrann responded and woke the Captain. He exchanged signs and countersigns with Sun Koh confirming that everything was all right. Sun Koh instructed him to land just outside the forest where the main path came out. By the time they landed, Minx and Ashanti Garuda were also awake.

They opened the cargo doors as Sun had instructed. In the distance, they heard a humming sound as strange vehicles came down the path. In the lead vehicle was Sun Koh dressed in his flight suit and helmet with his visor open. Sturm and Jim were with him. On the floor of the vehicle was a pile of gold ingots, each weighing about 20 kilos, and a large wooden chest. There were two vehicles behind them with even larger piles of gold ingots. There were several dwarves accompanying the vehicles. They started unloading the bars. The astonished Captain had Tyrann show the dwarves how and where to load the ingots into *Schimäre* to maintain weight and balance. Meanwhile Sun Koh gave him a brief rundown on what had happened. The last thing to be loaded was the chest. There were a total of 260 ingots. It was well within *Schimäre's* lifting capabilities.

Sun and his two companions bid farewell to the dwarves as they drove back into the woods. Then everyone boarded the aircraft and it hovered just above the ground. For safety's sake, the Captain decided on a horizontal take off across the floor of the valley.

When they were finally in the air, Sun Koh called The Captain to the passenger compartment. He addressed all those assembled there.

"Each of you will receive 10 bars of gold for your help in rescuing me from England. This includes Schreck and Tyrann. Jan, for your help, your hospitality, and the use of your machines this is for you."

Sun tossed him a pouch filled with diamonds. "Now we can talk about upgrading this crate of yours." The Captain clicked his heels and thanked him.

Next Sun turned to Minx. "Without you I would likely have been trapped by MI5. My house and I owe you a great debt. I have something special for you." He handed the magician a gold ring with a large opal stone set in it. The stone was a dark blue-green with a streak of deep red and many iridescent colored highlights. It seemed to shimmer with an inner light from the moment that Minx touched it. The colors swam across it and never seemed the same from one moment to the next.

"I know, Herr Minx, that in your discipline, a master is not at his full potential until he has been given such a stone by a grateful ruler. It will be a focus for your power. May you use it wisely."

Minx went down on his left knee before Prince Sun Koh and kissed his right hand. "Indeed, I am fortunate that I have a master who understands what this means. I am your servant, My Prince, from this day forward."

Turning to Shani, Sun looked into her dark eyes. In spite of herself, she quivered. Those stony blue eyes!

"And for you, dear Shani. You used your body to shield me from harm. This is my gift to you." He gave her a polished rounded gem with a flat back that was the color of blood. She stared at it. Strange electrical twinges went through her hand. It was a perfect ruby of incredible depth with a cat's eye refraction line down its long axis that followed you around the room. It actually seemed to look back at her and blink. She had never seen anything like it. It was perfectly shaped to be worn as a tikala.

On instinct, she wiped the red dot off her forehead and placed the ruby in its place. It stuck firmly as if by magnetism. She felt a heightening of her perceptions and a tingling in her limbs.

"This Tiger's Eye Ruby is very rare, Shani. It was worn by the priestesses of Atlantis to open the Third-Eye. You see how it hugs your flesh. It was made to be worn like that. It enhances the senses and increases physical strength and stamina. May it give you long life."

She bowed to him and said, "My Prince, you do more than honor me." Their eyes met and they both felt a deep longing. Minx watched them with mixed emotions. He wished that Shani would look at him that way.

Sun Koh addressed them all. "We have now found the cache and have become united together as more than friends. But we still have much to do. Colonel Gruber must be dealt with. We need to meet with the Thule Society next week. I must assume my place before the people of this world. And we must plan for the next ice age and the return of Atlantis from the depths of the sea. Come! Let us plan our future and that of the world."

And *Schimäre* continued its flight to the Aerie.

THE END

SIT THOU AT MY RIGHT HAND

Psalm 110:1 The LORD said unto my Lord, "Sit thou at my right hand, until I make thine enemies thy footstool."

It was 1630 in the evening on Saturday, June 4, 1932 when Rolf Karsten entered the bar at the hotel in the small Austrian alpine town. When the barmaid came over, he ordered a Pilsner and some *Weiner schnitzel*. The place was virtually empty. He chatted up the barmaid as he ate. Her name was Beattie. She was a handsome girl in her twenties with a full figure. In ten years, she would lose her figure and become a rounded hausfrau like her foremothers. By then she would have married a local man and had several children. For now, she flirted with the customers and turned the occasional trick for the climbers and skiers who came through town.

When he was finished eating, Rolf moved to the bar and struck up a conversation with the *barmixer*. The regular evening dinner crowd started to come in. Rolf blended in with them. No one noticed him leave.

A short time later Rolf "Schreck" Karsten, the private detective, was in the conference room at Jan Mayen's villa discussing what he had learned. In that room were the inventor Jan Mayen, his lieutenant Tyrann, Sturmvögel the seven foot soldier/adventurer, their buckskin clad friend Alaska-Jim Hoover, the former stage magician Ludwig Minx, and his beautiful associate Ashanti Garuda, the Daughter of Kali. Also sitting at the table was a bronze giant of a man with blond hair and blue lapis lazuli eyes: Sun Koh, the Prince Regent and heir of Atlantis. They were listening intently.

"The girl did not betray you, Sturm. She is an aging barmaid and you are a source of adventure to her: her way of experiencing something other than this dismal little *bergstadt*. She brags about you and must have let slip your climbing plans to the barman. He is the one who informed on you."

"Well then we need to teach him a lesson," said Sturm.

Schreck sighed. "*Nein.* He is well known in this town and a great source of information. You want to know who is sleeping with whom? Ask him. He will know. Trust me; he is one of those marginal people who are a perfect intelligence source. He has ambiguous loyalties and can be persuaded to divulge information for a price. A perfect spy. You don't want to eliminate such people. You need to cultivate them. We can make use of such a man in the future. Besides, he only sold information. The man you really want is Herr Manheim. He is the one who fingered you to the SA."

Jan Mayen spoke up, "The local lawyer? He has a reputation for shady dealings. He moved here after a scandal in Salzburg that ruined his marriage. He is also a prominent member of the Nazi Party."

Schreck nodded. "Manheim alerted Col. Gruber to Sturmvögel's presence and passed on the word about the planned climb. You have been here before, eh, Sturm?"

Sturm nodded. "Three times. I visited my mother in Nuremburg the last time"

"*Ja.* Someone must have seen you there and they heard that you came through Austria. A discrete call for your whereabouts went through party channels. You are hard to miss. If there is anyone who is a danger to us, it is Manheim."

Tyrann addressed the detective, "You were a spy in England, Herr Karsten. Does that mean that your loyalties are ambiguous too?"

Schreck smiled. "I was a spymaster! It was my job to find spies and exploit them."

Sun Koh spoke up. "Someone must pay for that assault on Sturmvögel and Jim, but we must do so in a way that will not bring a reprisal. Then we can concentrate on establishing an identity for me in this time period and depositing our treasures from *Zwergkönigreich.*"

Schreck pursed his lips. "Such things have to be handled delicately. I have a plan. The SA is under pressure from the government to disband and they are resisting. They are precipitating quite a lot of violence against their opponents and using it as a cover for purging their own ranks. We can use this to our advantage. It is a good thing you took those weapons, wallets, and passports from the assassins, Sturm. We will make good use of them. They had already checked out of their hotel and their bags were in the car. We will leave them there. Jan, do you have a syringe to draw blood from me?"

Jan nodded, somewhat puzzled.

That night, Herr Manheim was at home reading a legal brief. He heard a car drive up and stop outside and then there was a noise elsewhere in the house. The housekeeper was long gone. He took his service revolver out of his desk and went to investigate. As he opened the office door, it was slammed back against him! A dark figure dressed in black from head to toe floated into the room and shut the light. Manheim could not see the figure's face, but it had a single glowing red eye on its forehead with a bright slit for a pupil. He lifted his gun, but it was kicked out of his hand. It was as if the red eye could see in the dark. The figure assaulted Manheim and beat him unmercifully. He tried to fight back but the figure was too fast and strong. He was thrown around the room. The lawyer was bleeding from several places when the figure finally closed with him and pulled out a pistol. It shot him through the heart and then dropped the pistol on the floor.

The figure then picked up the lawyer's gun, placed it in his hand, and fired it once out the open window into the woods. Then the figure took out a vial of human blood and sprinkled some on the lawyer's body and hands. The figure retreated out of the house sprinkling blood as it went. It entered a waiting car, which drove off.

A few minutes later, Ashanti got out of the car and vanished into the night. She was dressed in climbing gear and wore a tiger's eye ruby in the middle of her forehead.

The car drove on to Salzburg. It was left parked outside the train station. There was blood inside the car and on the key, along with a trail of blood on the sidewalk heading in the general direction of the station entrance. Schreck pocketed the vial, which contained his blood and caught the late-night train to Germany. He would leave a little blood on the train to make the illusion complete. His blood type matched that of two of the assassins according to the ID they had carried. When he crossed the border, he would use one of their passports. If his plan went well, Gruber's people would assume that there had been a trap for the men they had sent to kill Sturmvögel and that one of them had survived long enough to execute Manheim as a traitor before attempting a return to Germany. It would appear that he had been wounded himself by Manheim's gun and never made it home.

There were many skirmishes between the SA, the Communists, and the Socialists. This would just be another one. Schreck did not worry about being seen. He had one of those faces that were just not memorable. He had also worn gloves and left no fingerprints. He planned to make his way back to Berlin and his Gretchen. He had several cases still pending that needed to be resolved.

•••

A freight package had arrived for Sun Koh from England on Friday. It contained the balance of the fitted clothing that he had ordered in London and a small package with the forged Bavarian passport he had purchased there. Schreck still had some connections in the London underworld from the spy ring he had run there during the Great War. They had shipped the materials to Jan Mayen in Austria right under the noses of MI5. This would permit Sun Koh to travel freely into Germany.

That Sunday morning, Sun Koh was dressed in a hunting shirt with buttoned pockets and epaulets, jodhpurs, and riding boots. He and Jan Mayen were discussing modifications to *Schimäre*.

"We can create hull plates which we can vary in color and pattern electronically. There are certain scintillation patterns that at a distance will make *Schimäre* virtually invisible to the human eye. And engine noise can be cancelled with a built in anti-noise generator. These are possible with your current technology. In the future we can use even more sophisticated camouflage techniques, but this should do for now."

Jan marveled. "This would allow us to operate with impunity in the daytime. I looked over those equations you showed me yesterday for projecting interference patterns that mimic 3-dimensional objects. Theoretically that could be used for disguising a ship as well."

Sun Koh smiled. "Don't try to run before you can walk, Jan. To make that work you need to learn how to project beams of coherent light of immense power. That will take some time."

Jan shook his head. "Time! That is all we have been hearing for centuries: '*Give us time.*' And as time goes on, human misery gets worse. Those in power suppress advances that would uplift the masses because they know that eventually there will be a leveling of social standing and their privileges will be gone. Did you know that the steam engine was first developed by Heron of Alexandria in the 1st Century AD?"

Sun Koh nodded, "Yes. And the Romans suppressed its use because it would have eliminated the need for slave labor."

"Exactly! They wanted to perpetuate slavery and so they suppressed a technology that could have started the Industrial Revolution in the time of Christ!

"That was why that crazy Sikh founded the Colony almost 90 years ago. He claimed that he had the backing of the Nine Unknown Men of Hindu legend who revealed to him certain hidden knowledge of physics. We colonists carried on after he disappeared. Now we have the most advanced laboratories and manufacturing facilities in the world hidden on a Pacific island. We are holding back our technological advances to keep the corrupt modern political regimes from exploiting them for war and conquest. Once we are strong enough, we will simply supplant them."

Sun Koh was aware of the Colony. He knew that the people at Jan's secret Alpine base were colonists and members of a Technocrat conspiracy, which wanted to replace all known governments with multinational technological conglomerates in competition with each other. This competition would spur them on to greater technological advancements to the benefit of mankind. But first, old notions of politics and privilege needed to be discarded and replaced with scientific efficiency.

The Technocrats were also eugenicists who wanted to apply science to the improvement of man himself. This was the most controversial part of their program. It called for the suppression of bad genes and the active advancement of good ones. But who was to say what genes were good or bad? The Technocrats believed that the Aryan Race was generally superior and that all other races needed to be suppressed by sterilization.

Sun Koh knew quite a bit more about human genetics than anyone else because he had access to the old Atlantean data that had helped to create him as a genetic superman. But what he knew about modern human genetics was limited and most of it seemed to be based on chauvinism and prejudice other than good science. He did believe that the genetically superior should be placed in positions of power and that technology was the way forward for mankind, but one could not reduce politics to technological competition. And using sterilization instead of the natural process of "survival of the fittest" reduced a complex interaction between organism and environment into a simplistic enforcement of superficial prejudices based on very limited knowledge.

As with so many other things, Sun Koh kept his opinions on this to himself. These were his allies and he needed to work with them until he was in a position to set their agendas.

Sun Koh changed the subject deftly. "Have you made contact with your private banker in Zurich? Did he receive the gold?"

"There is no problem. The passbooks will be issued tomorrow for everyone including you. I used the Four Seasons Hotel in München as your address and I vouched for you personally. The Colony has been doing business with this firm for over eighty years."

"*Sehr Gut*," said Sun. "Tomorrow I need to check in at the Four Seasons and verify the status of my Deutsche Bank deposit in London. Now, I have some design ideas for personal weaponry and tools. Nothing too far advanced."

Jan was excited. Weapons design was a hobby of his. "My fabrication shop here can make anything you like. You must show me what you had in mind." They began to draw up schematics.

In a palatial drawing room in the mountains outside of München, two men were conferring feverishly. "After all these years, he has really returned. I did not think it was possible. You assured me that he would be dead!"

"We were sure he was. There is no way he could have survived."

"Well he did! Even though his plane exploded. Now, he has disappeared and it is certain that he will surface soon. He must be stopped!"

"I know. We have people searching for him. When he shows up, we deal with him before he can reveal his true identity."

•••

The trip to München was uneventful. Jan Mayen flew them in his private plane. The plan was for Prince Sun Koh to establish his lodgings at the Four Seasons Hotel and then to make contact with the Agartha underground in Bavaria. Even though the Thule Society now met in Berlin, Bavaria—and in particular München—was still the center of Agartha occultism. Sun Koh had known that and that was why he had chosen a München address when he landed in London. He had more natural allies there than anywhere else in Germany. The Berlin circle was composed of adepts that were active in the Weimar Government. Sun Koh would have to meet them and gain their support if he was to have any influence in Germany.

The entourage included Sun Koh, Jan Mayen, Minx, Shani, Strurmvögel, and Alaska-Jim. For this trip, Sun Koh had imposed on Jim to wear a simple suit and not his usual buckskins. It made him look awkward, like a shepherd on his first trip to the big city. Sturmvögel was harder to disguise because he was so tall. He wore a fake beard and a wig and was dressed as a chauffer. He kept his eyes downcast and did not speak. In wealthy circles, no one took notice of the servants.

The Four Seasons was on the *Maximilianstraße* in the center of the city. It had over 300 rooms on four floors with the top floor broken into suites of various sizes.

In the lobby, Sun Koh spotted several observers who watched him as he checked in. He identified an MI5 spy, one from the Bavarian Secret Police, and a House Detective. There also were two SA bullies trying to blend in.

Then there was another man whose identity Sun Koh could not determine. He was not a private detective, but he was not a policeman either. He was too well dressed to be another agitator. The fellow was gone a moment later. Sun Koh's danger sense was alerted. This fellow posed a real threat.

Prince Sun Koh was given a large suite with accommodations for all of his guests and his servant. After everyone settled in, Minx made a phone call and spoke in what sounded like gibberish. It was actually the Atlantean tongue, which was used by Agartha adepts to keep their communications private.

Sturm looked at the décor in the suite and frowned. It looked decadent and effeminate to him. Playing the chauffeur, he got to sleep in the servant's room which was clean but plain. He much preferred it to the gaudy gilded wallpaper and brocade furniture in the main sitting room.

Shani languished barefooted on a love seat wrapped in a pastel sari. She was reading a book printed in Hindi script. On the soles of her feet and the palms of her hands were tattooed small black swastikas. As a devotee of Kali, she had twelve such marks on her body: palms, soles, inside the arms, inside the thighs, on the dimples of her buttocks and on the sides of her breasts. She had a ruby stud on the left side of her nose and what looked like a snake bracelet entwined on her right upper arm. The snake was no bracelet. It was a real Golden Spitting Cobra named Shakti. As usual, she wore the tiger's eye ruby as a tikala mark.

Jim sat by a reading lamp chewing tobacco and spitting into a coffee cup. He wished that Tyrann had come. One needed at least four people to play poker. Jan and Sturm would play, but Shani did not and no one trusted Minx. They had seen him do card tricks on the *Schimäre* that first night. It did not seem fitting to ask Sun Koh to play. Besides they all knew he had phenomenal luck at cards.

Sun Koh was in the master bedroom doing his daily routine of meditation and exercise. So far he had not been able to dip back into the Akashic record since his tryst with the MI5 woman. He had tried several meditation techniques, but they had not worked. He decided to run through his mentalism routines and isometric exercises. Minx knocked and entered the room.

"The meeting is set for midnight, my Prince. Xaux will see us at the *Germanenorden* Lodge. There will be others with him. We will need his backing at the Society meeting this Friday. He asks that just the two of us attend."

Sun Koh nodded, "Very good. With their backing, we will influence the Society to take a stronger stand against the current government. The inefficiency and corruption of the Reichstag is intolerable. Germany needs strong leadership if we are to accomplish our goals."

The phone on the bed stand started ringing. Sun Koh had a premonition of danger. He answered the phone himself.

"I am amazed," said a whispered voice on the phone. "You had the nerve to come here. We thought we had finished you, but you survived."

"Who is this?" demanded Sun Koh.

"Oh come now!" said the voice. "You know so much and you don't know who I am? Stop playing games. We want the treasure. Now. All of it. It would have been so easy had you just been dead. Two more years and it would have been over."

Sun Koh was genuinely puzzled. "What are you talking about? Were you responsible for my aircraft…"

"The crash? Of course. You thought we have forgotten about you? Prince Raimund, you disappoint me. You will not get a way with this. You have twenty-four hours to turn the bankbooks over before we take you down. I will call again this time tomorrow." There was click and the conversation ended.

Minx's keen hearing had made him privy to the call. He looked at Sun Koh. "This man claims to have caused the destruction of your ship, my prince. He wants the gold we recovered. The nerve of him!" Minx eyes blazed like glowing coals. His voice became deep and resonant, almost sepulchral. The stone opal ring on his finger began to glow and its colors swirled.

Sun Koh put up his hands, "Minx, relax. There was something wrong with that call. He called me Raimund. There is no Prince Raimund in Europe. But somehow that name is familiar." Sun Koh skimmed his Akashic data. "There were rumors almost twenty years ago but they were hushed up."

Minx cleared his throat. "I think we need some specialized help in tracking down this Prince Raimund."

Sun Koh said, "Call Schreck. We need to turn his Gretchen loose on the archives in Berlin."

•••

The Lodge met in an old Masonic Temple. Minx and Sun Koh were ushered into the central chamber. They walked between the pillars of

Jachin and Boaz into the room, which was shrouded in shadow. Benches lined the walls and several men in hooded cloaks sat in them. In the center of the room was a marble altar with a large leather-bound volume of the Upanishads on it. On the far wall was a two-level dais with three thrones, the center one larger and on a higher level than the other two. In that sat a large old man with leonine hair that was blond but going to grey. This was Xaux, the Agartha representative in Germany. There was a man on either side of him. The one on the left was the well-dressed man from the Four Seasons lobby.

Minx and Sun Koh went to the center of the room and stood behind the altar. Xaux saw the opal ring on Minx's finger and smiled with approval. Minx introduced Sun Koh and described the destruction of his ship, his landing in London, and his rescue. He didn't discuss the excursion into Switzerland or the finding of the Alpine cache. During the introduction, Sun Koh took off his shirt and showed the tattoo map of Atlantis on his back.

Xaux spoke up. "Greetings, Prince Sun Koh. I am delighted that you have been brought safely to Bavaria. Exciting things are happening in this country. The Agartha have waited a long time to break the hold of the Jews and their Christian stooges on the descendants of the Master Race. This Friday, the Berlin Thule Society will meet and there will be a very special guest. He comes to us asking for our support for his party. They are still a minority, but they have the will to rule and to crush their opposition. He is not one of us, but he will be useful to us.

"Prince Sun Koh, at the Thule Society meeting, we will negotiate an alliance with Adolph Hitler and his National Socialist Party which will return order to Germany and eventually place you on the throne of a united Aryan Empire!"

Xaux and Sun Koh discussed the up-coming meeting and planned their strategy. The man on Xaux's right was introduced as Baron Rudolf von Sebottendorff the original founder of the Thule Society who fled from Bavaria years when the Socialist Government sought his arrest. Sun Koh could not help but notice the discomfiture of the young man to Xaux's left. That man was introduced as Count Francis Rákóczi of Transylvania. Sun Koh was surprised. He recognized the name and realized who this man really was.

The Count spoke up several times during the discussion. It became clear to Sun Koh that he was not as enthralled about an alliance with Hitler as Xaux was. He also kept referring to the "true Germanic nobility".

Sun Koh realized that Rákóczi was a monarchist and that he thought the true solution to the political chaos in Germany was a return to the traditional monarchy that the British and French swine had destroyed by their "war to make the world safe for democracy."

Sun Koh made assurances that the true nobility would be restored once he re-established the Ocean Court and that the anarchist myth of "human equality" would be relegated to the ash heap of history. The Count appeared to be satisfied with this assurance, but Sun Koh detected a mental reservation in him and his danger sense still tingled. This Rákóczi would bear close scrutiny.

His business with Xaux was completed and Sun Koh departed for the Four Seasons. He left Minx behind with the Lodge. The recent gift of the opal ring from his sovereign, Prince Sun Koh, required special mystical rites and an initiation into higher mysteries.

The taxi dropped Sun Koh off at the Hotel. The Prince's danger sense was immediately stimulated. There were several men on the sidewalk waiting for him. They rushed him from all sides. A different man grabbed each of his arms and legs. This method of take-down was used in prisons and mental hospitals to restrain violent berserkers. Then a man came up behind him and slipped a wire garrote around his neck pulling it tight. They were trying to topple Sun Koh to the ground. Meanwhile three men were approaching him from the front. Two had brick bats and one was a huge pugilist with cauliflower ears and wearing brass knuckles. Sun Koh knew that if he was taken to the ground he would lose all leverage and could not defend himself. The five men continued to pull on him as the other assailants ran forward.

In the suite four floors above, Shani was in a lotus posture meditating and wearing the tiger's eye ruby tikala. She was waiting for Sun Koh and Minx to return. She could feel Sun Koh's presence outside the hotel through the tikala gem. When the assault began, she was instantly aware of it. She ran out into the sitting room where Jan, Sturm, and Jim were playing a three-handed variation of Euchre called '500' which Jim and Sturm had learned in America. She told them that Sun Koh had been ambushed and needed help. The three men were armed with pistols. They piled out of the suite into the stairwell. Shani hoped and prayed to Kali that they would get to Sun Koh in time!

This street ambush would become a part of the legend of Sun Koh. It was retold by German propagandists who made the assailants everything from Communists to Zionist fanatics. In fact, the men were criminals and

SA thugs who had been paid to rough up and abduct Sun Koh. The number of assailants varied from twelve to fifteen men in the retellings. The actual story is not as dramatic, but amazing nevertheless.

Sun Koh knew that if he lost his footing it was all over. Like Atlas, he needed to keep his feet in contact with the Earth to fight back. He concentrated and began funneling his *prana*—his inner power—into his legs and feet. One of the exercises that he had been taught was to resist being toppled over by controlling his center of gravity. It came in handy now. He tightened his neck muscles into a solid column that protected his throat and larynx.

Sun Koh twisted his arms and grabbed hold of the men restraining them. His right hand grabbed his assailant's right forearm and squeezed. The Prince's muscles and bones were genetically designed to be many times stronger than normal human tissue. He felt the man's forearm collapse and the bones ground together audibly as they broke. The man screamed and let go, falling to the ground.

With his left hand he grabbed that assailant's chest and his fingers dug in, piercing the skin. Ribs cracked in his grip and there was a rush of air as the pleural space was penetrated. The trauma caused a pneumothorax and the man made a coughing sound and began to vomit. He too fell away.

Sun then reached back and grabbed the man garroting him. No normal man could have done what came next. The two men holding his legs actually increased Sun's leverage. Using his tremendous strength Sun Koh put his hands around the man's neck and lifted him, throwing him overhead. As the man was passing over him upside-down, an angry Sun Koh twisted his hands. There was a sickening crack like a branch being broken. When the assailant landed on the side walk, his neck bent at an unnatural angle and he did not move.

The two men with the brickbats had to duck to avoid the flying body. When they came forward Sun Koh grounded himself and used the weight of the men holding his legs to his advantage. The man on his left was swinging the bat down on him. Sun used a left jab to deflect the blow and struck the man's face. The blow crushed his cheek and right jaw. It shattered the right side of the man's skull making his eye pop out.

The other man swung his club, but Sun grabbed it with his left hand and pulled the man in towards him and off balance. Using his own weight and that of the men on his legs, Sun delivered a right upper cut with all the force he could muster. It came up with tremendous force and tapped the man soundly on the tip of his chin. The man's head snapped back. The

Sun Koh knew that if he lost his footing it was all over.

blow was so rapid that neither the jaw nor the teeth were fractured. Instead, a rapid pulse of energy was transferred through the jaw into the lower portion of the skull. It created a shearing force that propagated a basilar skull fracture. The shear plane passed through the "Circle of Willis", a circular artery that received the blood from the internal and external carotid arteries and distributed it throughout the brain. This caused a massive cerebral hemorrhage. The man fell back unconscious and never woke up.

The Pugilist had stayed back hoping that the others would soften Sun Koh up for a thorough work over. He had brass knuckles on both hands and was wearing steel toed boots. He saw how the fight was going and charged in.

Sun Koh could no longer afford to be pinned in one spot. He had to move! With a war cry, he brought both of his arms down to strike the men on his legs. His left fist smashed into the top of the head of the man on his left cracking bone. His right hand glanced off the man's head and struck his right shoulder. It shattered the acromion process and the man's clavicle. At that point the pugilist was on him.

The man was a pro. In the confusion he went for a stunning body shot with his right hand and followed with a left to the head. Sun Koh absorbed the blow to his left chest and spun inside the left jab. He brought his right forward to strike the pugilist in the solar plexus and twisted out of the tangle of his other two assailants. He hit the ground, rolled and then flipped back to his feet. His opponent came in swinging. They traded blows, ducking and twisting. The boxer kicked at Sun's shins with the steel toes and hammered at his body. Sun Koh blocked his blows and protected his head. His moves were mostly defensive. He was angry. He had given this man every opportunity to break off and run, but the guy kept coming. He was either a dedicated pro or "punchy." Probably, he was a little of both. Sun determined that he would have to end this fight.

The boxer used a one-two combination that left his left lower chest exposed. Sun rolled away from the punch but then sent his right hand out to spear the boxer just below the xiphoid, the smallest and lowest division of the human sternum which is cartilage early in life but becomes bone-like during adulthood. The tip of his middle finger pressed into the skin tenting it up without breaking it. That finger made contact with the wall of the pugilist's heart and kept going. It struck the cartilage ring at the heart's center that supported the heart valves and tore it. The force of the blow also ruptured several papillary muscles and caused a sever contusion in the muscles of the left ventricle and the Purkinje conduction bundle.

The boxer staggered. He looked down to see if he had been stabbed but there was no blood or stab wound. He clutched his chest and turned white. The cardiac contusion and damage to the conduction bundle had set off a series of uncoordinated electrical discharges and the heart went into ventricular fibrillation. The big man fell like an old oak tree.

At that point, a barefoot Shani raced on to the sidewalk with the other three in tow. She had a concerned look on her face. She immediately assessed the scene. Sun Koh stood alone surrounded by prostrate bodies. Some of the fallen were moaning. Some were not even breathing. Sun Koh did not appear winded. His clothing was a mess and he had some facial bruises. Shani rushed to him and the other three surrounded them both with guns drawn.

"Are you all right, Sun Koh?" she asked.

He smiled at her. "I'm good. What kept you?"

•••

Everything had happened so fast that the management had not yet called the police. By the time they arrived, the men on the sidewalk were all gone and Sun Koh and his people were back in their suite. Shani insisted that he undress and let her examine his wounds. She was a trained Ayurveda physician. Shani had a look of urgency in her eyes.

Sturmvögel was the first to notice it and he grinned to himself. He signaled for Jan and Jim to come with him and leave Sun and Shani alone. Jim started to protest and Sturm rolled his eyes and picked him up bodily and carried him out. This was not lost on Sun Koh. Shani meanwhile was too preoccupied to notice.

She examined him thoroughly. He had several bruises and some abrasions, but nothing was broken. She had brought some soothing ointment to dress the wounds but marveled as they seemed to heal before her eyes. The minor bruises were gone. The more serious ones were smaller. The abrasions had sealed over and were already shedding scabs. Sun Koh should have been sore all over but he just looked tired. At this rate, by mid-morning, you would never know that he had been in a fight.

Shani looked at him quizzically. He shrugged. "I heal a lot faster than normal people. And in a healing trance, even severe wounds will rapidly resolve without scarring." His hard blue eyes, met her soft dark ones. Once again, Sun Koh felt the prickling of his danger sense. But he felt something else also; a stirring deep inside him. He could see that Shani also felt something. They had spoken very little to each other over the last few days. The attraction had been almost unbearable since the first moment they had seen each other. What words had not said, glances did. Now in private with her hands examining him, he no longer felt restraint.

Sun Koh spoke to her in the ancient Atlantean tongue. It was a brief poem of love and the invitation to intimacy. He sensed her heart racing and her face flushed. She faced him with a smile of joy and recited a Tantric love hymn:

Come to me, my beloved.
In my eyes, you are:
Like Shiva coming to Kali
Like Rama coming to Sita
Like rain coming to a parched earth
Like a ship coming to a warm safe harbor
My yoni longs for you
Your lingam is urgent for me
Ply your love for me here and now
Bring me *Satchidananda*
Free me from the *pashu* of unfulfilled passion
Maya conceals *prakriti*
One must rise by that by which one falls

They embraced and kissed. Shani removed her sari and he beheld her full womanhood. On her right arm she still wore the golden cobra. He asked her if she ever removed it and she shook her head and told him, "The very poison that kills becomes the elixir of life when used by the wise."

She completely undressed him and they drank in the sight, scent, and feel of each other's bodies. Sun Koh detected a heady musk from her that included pheromones which "cleanliness" suppresses in western women.

They came together like old lovers who had shared a bed over many incarnations and had known the other's pleasuring touch over millennia. Their urgency was matched by the depth of sensation. Their movements were slow, deep, and deliberate. They both approached climax around the same time and prolonged it as long as they could. It became a contest to see who could hold off the longest. The tension built up. Sun Koh finally could not contain himself and he began contracting. At that point, Shani released herself and they both plunged into ecstasy together. They contracted with pleasure over several minutes lost in themselves.

The flood gates opened for Sun Koh and the Akashic record flowed into him deeper than ever before. As it flowed into him, he saw a maelstrom in the flow that drew him in. He swirled around and around into a swirl of golden light. Then it resolved into two golden whirlpools that became the eyes of a man. A bronzed man with a handsome square face, and red-gold hair that gripped his head like a skull cap with a pronounced widow's peak. He could have been Sun Koh's brother. And then the golden eyes looked into his and he knew that he not only saw this man but was being seen by him. Sun Koh's danger sense charged through him like electricity. He pulled out of Shani and forced himself awake. Shani basked in the glow of post-coital bliss. She saw Sun's distress and reached for him. As she held him, he shuddered and told her what he had seen.

Outside in the sitting room, the smell of sex was embarrassingly obvious. The noises were less intrusive but even more disturbing. Sturmvögel smirked. Jan became uncomfortable and excused himself to go to bed. Alaska-Jim shook his head. A man and a woman. It was just biology. There was nothing surprising about it. As with most things, the Injuns never made that big a deal out of it and neither did Jim.

Minx had called right after they had left the two lovers alone. He had a feeling of dread during the ceremony and called as soon as he could. Sturm told him about the attack. Minx vowed vengeance on all who had done this and his voice deepened and became more resonant. When Sturm told him that Sun Koh and Shani were alone in his bed room, Minx quieted and said he would be back soon. When he arrived in suite the ambience was unmistakable.

This had been the greatest night in Minx's life as an adept, but he was crestfallen. What he had seen and feared had come to pass. Ashanti was his prince's woman. There was nothing he could do. To betray his prince would be to betray his discipline and he risked losing the great new power he had been granted. Nevertheless, he could not get Shani out of his mind.

•••

Shani and Sun Koh slept in each other's arms. At sunrise, they both awoke simultaneously. There was no embarrassment. What happened had been something they had both wanted. This had not been a proposal of marriage, but a celebration of mutual arousal. From that point onwards they would be lovers, but their future was unclear. Sun Koh was prince and marriage was a matter of statecraft for him. Ashanti was a devotee of Kali, Tantra, and the Left-Hand Path and the sex act was part of her discipline. Yet they both felt something more than the slaking of sexual desire.

This ambivalence kept a tension in the air. They embraced one last time and Shani went to her own room.

The whole suite had breakfast together shortly thereafter and they discussed the incidents from last night. No one mentioned the dalliance between Shani and Sun Koh.

After describing the fight, Sun Koh said, "Those men were not there to kill me, but to capture me. I am sure it is connected to that phone call."

"We need to take better precautions, Herr Koh", said Jan. "Maybe we should leave immediately."

"No. We are expecting the bank agent from Switzerland with our account books. Once that is done, we can move on. The police have not been by yet?"

"No, the front desk handled them."

"I have a premonition" Sun Koh said thoughtfully. "The police will come by this morning for a statement and we must be ready."

He was right. At 0900, the desk called up that a Col. Roch Peters and two of his men from the Bavarian *Staatspolizei* were on the way up. The officers were met at the door by Minx with Sturm and Jim standing behind him. They confirmed the police credentials and led them to the sitting room where Sun Koh waited.

Peters had a ramrod-straight posture and a crew cut. He was obviously ex-military. He introduced himself and then asked Sun Koh to give his version of the events of last night. Sun Koh said that he had been attacked by some toughs who seemed intent on robbing him and that he had fought them off. Peters made some notes and then pointedly asked Sun about the blood and vomit on the sidewalk. Sun Koh shrugged and said that the toughs must have been drunk and hurt themselves when they fell.

Peters nodded perfunctorily and looked Sun Koh in the eye. He said, "I think you and I need to talk, Prince Raimund. Alone." They both signaled their respective men to leave.

"That was quite a display you gave last night. My observer was impressed. I was not sure I believed his report until I met you. The British have been raising Holy Hell since you left London. They think you were one of our agents. My superiors were quite concerned. It took me a little while to piece together who you really were. Your new alias is a very bad pun." Peters said. "That forged passport of yours was very good. Nigel's work, no? The forger in Vauxhall?"

Sun Koh read his body language and responded, "Are you going to arrest me, Colonel?"

Peter's smiled. "*Nein*. You were just returning home. With all the other nonsense going on in this country, you are the least of my worries. I am charged with maintaining the security of a government that is teetering on the edge of collapse. The Americans have a saying: 'Rearranging the deck chairs on the Titanic.' That is what my superiors have me doing. Besides, you have very powerful friends, Prince Raimund, who can see beyond yesterday's politics to tomorrow's Germany."

Sun Koh realized he was referring to some of the local Thule Society members who were officials in the Bavarian government, but from the colonel's total body language it was more than that. Sun discerned that Colonel Peters was a Nazi sympathizer and that he knew about the planned meeting with Hitler.

"Look", said Peters. "You have created quite a mess that I am going to have to clean up for you. You can keep your forged passport. I will have a new one issued with your proper name, demographics, and date of birth. You will be able to use either passport as you choose. I have informed Berlin that you are one of my agents. I have also given you the honorary rank of Captain. A set of police credentials will also follow."

"That is very generous of you, Col. Peters."

Peters laughed, "My dear Prince, generosity has nothing to do with it. I will need to arrange all these things and pay off many officials. That will take money. About 50,000 Deutschmarks should do it. Agreed?"

Sun Koh eyed him for a moment and then nodded.

"Good." Peters handed Sun Koh a piece of paper with a long list of numbers and letters on it. "That is a Swiss Transfer Number. Give this to your banker and he will do the rest."

The Swiss Transfer Number was an ingenious invention of the banking gnomes of Zurich. It was filed at the Swiss National Treasury. Using this number, funds could be anonymously deposited and dispensed from one Swiss bank to another. After the transfer was complete, the number was deleted. No central records were kept. The money merely appeared and then disappeared. It was a zero-sum transaction and the books always balanced. The transaction happened on Swiss soil between Swiss institutions under the auspices of the Swiss government itself. The details of the transaction were treated as if they were a state secret.

Sun accepted the paper and then gestured. Col. Peters suddenly became glassy-eyed and unresponsive. Standing behind Sun Koh was Minx, his dark eyes glowing red. He had not left the room when the others did but had influenced the three policemen not to notice him.

"He is telling the truth, my Prince. He will accomplish all these things for you. Do you want me to dissuade him from demanding money?"

Sun Koh shook his head. "No. The worker is worth his wages. He will be quite useful to us and the money is a mere pittance. You would have to struggle with him to maintain his loyalty otherwise. But I do want to ask him some questions and I don't want him to remember me doing so."

Minx nodded and said, "You may proceed."

Sun Koh asked Peters, "Who do people say that I am?"

"Some of my Nazi friends say you are a rich eccentric. The police officials think you are an occult charlatan or a British spy. Most of the Thule members think you are the foretold heir of Atlantis."

"And who do you say that I am?"

Peters smiled, "I agree with the Director of MI5. You are Prince Raimund Sonnenkalb of Saxe-Coburg and Kohary, son of Prince Leopold and Princess Karoline. You were born in 1901 in Walterskirchen just north of here..."

Suddenly there was a pounding at the door. "Colonel Peters!" a voice cried out. "I must speak to you at once."

Sun signaled to Minx to bring Peters out of his trance. The Prince then opened the door. One of the policemen was there. "I apologize Herr Koh, but headquarters has just called, and they need to talk to the Colonel."

Peters spoke briefly on the phone and then informed Sun Koh that he was needed immediately at headquarters. "Another deck chair is out of line," he said. The two shook hands and Peters left with his men. Before he left he reassured Sun Koh that there would be increased security around and inside the hotel to prevent another incident like the one the previous night.

Minx said, "We must pass this new information on to Schreck in Berlin."

Sun Koh nodded. "That little bit of prompting has helped me pinpoint this mysterious Prince Raimund and his father. Do you remember in 1919 when the Weimar Constitution eliminated the legal privileges associated with all German noble titles? Shortly thereafter, it was reported that almost 1 billion Deutsche Marks had disappeared from the treasury and they were never recovered. This mysterious loss was one of the factors that contributed to the runaway inflation in 1923. It was suspected that the monies were embezzled by some of the nobility before they lost their privileges. Prince Leopold was one of the top suspects."

After lunch, Sun Koh had an appointment with an agent from Jan Mayen's Swiss Bank. The Prince was to go to the Bank's Munich office and fill out the necessary paperwork to deposit his share from the Alpine Cache. The same was to be done for Strum and Alaska-Jim. All the other of Sun Koh's associates already had Swiss Bank accounts. Minx remained at his Prince's side. Sturm and Jim carried concealed weapons. Jan Mayen came along to vouch for his friends. Shani remained in the suite in case Schreck or Peters called.

On arrival at the Bank building, Sun Koh and his men were taken to a conference room where a Swiss Bank manager from Zurich was waiting for them. When they walked into the room Sun and Minx both felt a sudden jolt. The Prince's danger sense started tingling and Minx caught a feeling of confusion and expectation in the air. Jan Mayen was surprised to see that the Bank had not sent his usual Bank Manager. Sun Koh took a deep breath and went into a mentalist trance. Time slowed down. He looked at the Swiss banker. He immediately saw that the man was looking at him as if trying—truly hoping—to recognize him. The manager came up to him and introduced himself as Jean-Batiste Clement.

Sun Koh replied. "Jean, why so formal? Have I changed that much?" He embraced the man to the surprise of everyone else in the room.

Clement looked at him trying hard to recognize the handsome bronzed face. "Is it really you Raimund? You have filled out! I know it has been five years, but your face and our voice are so different!"

Sun Koh read Clement's body language and played along. "I have been in hiding all this time. They would have killed me, so it became necessary to have my face changed."

Clement shook his head both in denial and amazement. "I must be sure, Raimund. Please." He then put his ear against Sun Koh's chest right over his heart. Sun Koh again made a quick assessment and he did something amazing. The Prince was a master ventriloquist and could not only project his voice but imitate very complex sounds. Through his Akashic knowledge, he recalled a Parisian medical professor who had been able to mimic a variety of medically significant heart and lung sounds in his own chest for the benefit of his students. He had trained hundreds of young doctors and the information about it was clearly available in the Akashic Record. Sun Koh mimicked a mid-systolic flow murmur over the pulmonic valve area with a fixed split in the S2 heart sound. This was far more detailed than was necessary because Clement was not a medical doctor, but it was enough to convince the banker.

A look of relief went across Clement's face. "Raimund, where have you been?"

Sun Koh smiled and his hard blue eyes began to soften and spin. He had already signaled Minx to reach out and touch the man's mind to make him more suggestible. Sun spoke in firm clear tones. "I told you. I have been on the run. During that time, I sought help from medical experts all over the world. I am now on medications that keep my problem in check. I have never felt better. Look at me! I can exercise now."

Clement laughed. "That is wonderful! Why did you not let me know you were back?"

"I had a few things to attend to first. I would have called you soon enough."

Clement shook his head. "More games and more secret bank accounts! I should not be making a new account for you, but if you insist. I guess that I ought to give this back to you now as well." Clement went to his brief case and extracted a small leather pouch with a label on it that read 'Raimund S. Kohart'. It was bound with rawhide ties and double sealed with wax impressions of the Bank's crest.

Sun then asked, "How did you know that I would be here?"

Clements looked sheepish. "I received a call from another client who said that he had seen you and suspected who you really were. I do not know the man's name, but my supervisor vouched for him. Somehow, he must have known that I had filed the missing person's report on you back in 1927. Two more years and your world have been declared dead and that package would have been given to your heirs."

Jean-Batiste processed the new accounts then gave each of the men their new bankbooks. When they finished, Clements gave each of them a card with his name and phone number on it. From thereon in, he would be their liaison with the Bank.

In the car, Sun Koh opened the pouch. In it was a single piece of paper with the letterhead of a Swiss bank branch in Zurich and a safety deposit box key. On the paper was typed: "In the event of my death, this key is to be passed on to the possession of my heirs as stipulated in my will." The note was signed over the typed name 'Raimund Sonnenkalb Kohart'.

"I suspect that this deposit box contains what our caller last night was looking for," said Sun Koh. He put the pouch and its contents into his coat pocket.

When Sun Koh and his entourage returned to the Four Seasons, there was an air of panic in the lobby. Uniformed police were everywhere. Sun Koh saw that Col. Peters was back as well. "It seems that a hooded man came in through the service entrance and burst into your suite. He

"I suspect that this is what our caller last night was looking for."

dragged off your Indian *freundin*. She put up quite a struggle. Two of my plainclothes agents tried to stop him here in the lobby and the assailant threw them around like children. They shot him at least twice with no effect. A car drove by and took him and your woman away.

Minx was astonished. "That little *freundin* would not have gone easily. It would take a very special kind of man to make off with her." Sun Koh ran up the stairs four at a time and found the heavy door to the suite splintered and ripped off its hinges. On the small table in the center of the room were the tiger's eye ruby and the coiled form of Shakti, the cobra.

Minx came in behind him. "My Prince, only an adept would be powerful enough to take Shani like that. But he has made a big mistake. Just because she is a woman, he has underestimated her. She is the Daughter of Kali. He will not be able to hold her in check for long."

Just then, the phone rang. It was Schreck calling from Berlin for Sun Koh. He insisted that Jan attached the scrambler to the phone before they talked.

"Herr Koh, I have some interesting news about this Prince Raimund. According to the official records, Princess Karoline of Saxe-Coburg, Gotha, and Kohary gave birth to her son Philipp Josias Maria Joseph Ignatius Michael Gabriel Raphael Gonzaga on August 18, 1901. What was not recorded is that Prince Philipp had a twin brother born the same day. There is a Photostat in the *Staatspolizei* files of a birth certificate for Raimund Sonnenkalb Maria Joseph Ignatius Michael Gabriel Raphael Gonzaga. Its authenticity has been questioned for many years now because the original is nowhere to be found. But my Gretchen found an old nurse midwife who attended many royal births and she was able to confirm the child's existence.

"It seems that Prince Raimund was very sickly. He weighed two pounds less than his sibling and had both heart and lung problems. It was not expected that he would survive the day. They sequestered him and only announced the birth of his healthy sibling. To everyone's surprise Raimund survived, but he was extremely ill, and they thought he would be crippled and retarded if he even lived. To reveal such a child at that point would have been a sign of weakness in the royal line and so they took him to a special clinic in Switzerland where the rich and the nobility send their 'problem' children, legitimate and otherwise.

"It turned out that Raimund was not retarded and his health improved over the years. Prince Leopold called in a Dr. Günter Asch who began a strict regimen of nutrition, education and exercise to strengthen the child.

Nevertheless, he suffered from a congenital heart condition which would limit his lifespan. Raimund was never very strong and remained thin and gangly even though he grew over six feet tall."

Sun Koh interrupted him, "It must have been an atrial septal defect. Such a problem causes a left to right shunt of blood may limit exercise tolerance, but it becomes more of a problem in middle age when it can lead to congestive heart failure and pulmonary congestion. Most people have few symptoms until their thirties. His must have been a large defect."

Schreck continued, "During those years, the anarchists had begun targeting members of the royal families all over Europe for assassination. They made an unsuccessful attempt on the Prince of Wales but succeeded in killing the Russian Czar Alexander II in 1881 after several attempts and the Austrian Empress Elizabeth in 1898. An American anarchist actually assassinated their President McKinley in 1901! Prince Leopold decided that he would keep his son Raimund safe in Switzerland as a guarantee of succession for his lineage. Raimund did not know of his true heritage until he was twelve. His father visited him periodically after that, but he never met his mother. Princess Karoline could not deal with his existence apart from her. He used the name Raimund Sonnenkalb Kohart while attending schools in Switzerland. I have picked the story on him from sources in Switzerland. That Jean-Batiste Clement was a bar sinister cousin of his who was raised in the same Swiss clinic.

"Rumors of Raimund's existence leaked out before the Great War but they were forgotten during the conflict. Afterwards, the German nobility were unpopular and no one cared. Meanwhile, Raimund attended the University of Geneva during the war and then got a law degree from the University of Lausanne. In the year 1922, he completed his law degree, and his father Prince Leopold died of a sudden stroke. You were right about the suspicions concerning Leopold and the mysterious disappearance of funds at the end of the War. At the time of his death, they still had no leads as to where the funds went.

"After his father's death, Raimund began traveling all over the world seeking out medical specialists to try and find a cure for his heart problem. It was never clear where he got the money for this. He went to England, France, Italy, Spain, the United States, and his mother's native Brazil. That was where he got into trouble. He made contact with some of his mother's family and word leaked back to Germany. The *Staatspolizei* started investigating and found the Photostat of the birth certificate which might or might not be genuine. They tried to question Raimund Kohart in Zurich, but he was a Swiss citizen and refused to cooperate. Then someone tried to kidnap him and it was apparently not German intelligence. Kohart fled to Africa. A scheduled airliner on which he was traveling disappeared over the jungles in 1927. No one has seen or heard from him since. That is all I have."

Sun Koh responded. "The pieces are coming together. Now I know what our phone call was all about last night, and why they took Shani."

"Who took Shani?" asked Schreck. "Were they crazy? She will kill them all."

Sun Koh filled Schreck in on what had happened and then they made plans to meet on Friday for the meeting in Berlin.

While he was on the phone, an envelope was delivered to the front desk for Sun Koh. In it was the ruby stud from Shani's nose and an unsigned note:

Prince Sun Koh:
Come alone to the top of the Chinese Pagoda in the English Gardens at midnight. No tricks, no tails, no weapons, no police. Bring the bankbooks and we will make an exchange. This is your first and last chance.

"What do we do, my Prince?" asked Minx.
"We do as we are requested," said Sun.

•••

The English Garden was a large park in the center of Munich. It was filled with woods and open areas. It had plenty of cover and concealment. The Chinese Pagoda was a circular tower with five levels that got smaller in diameter the higher you went. Each level was open all around. From the top, you have full visibility in all directions. It had been built in 1789 and was now a *biergarten,* which closed over the summer months at 2300.

Sun Koh arrived dutifully on the top level just before midnight. He was wearing a hunting shirt, and jodhpurs. As instructed, he came alone without weapons. There were lamps along the paths in the Garden, and his highly sensitive vision could see for over a hundred meters in every direction unimpeded. There was no way to sneak up on the tower.

At midnight, a hooded and cloaked figure appeared out the woods to the north and walked towards the Pagoda. At his side was Ashanti Garuda. Her hands were bound with an elaborate series of knotted cords. These were sacred Agarthan knots that allegedly could not be untangled. She was being pulled along by the hooded figure. When they arrived at the base of the tower, the figure leaped up and scaled each of the concentric roofs with a single bounding step, carrying Shani along with him.

The cloaked figure—his face hidden in the hood's shadow—mounted the top level and confronted the Atlantean Prince. Sun looked at Shani who appeared angry but unharmed. "Have you brought the bankbooks?" The voice was booming and deep as if electronically modified.

"Not exactly," said Sun Koh. "But I know where they are. They're in a safety deposit box in Switzerland along with documentation proving that Raimund Kohart was the legitimate son of Prince Leopold of Kohary. The only way to get them is for me to retrieve them. The bank manager believes that I am Kohart and he won't let anyone else into that box. Not even you, Prince Rákóczi. Or should I call you St. Germain?"

"Very good! I thought you might figure it out but not this quickly. The secret of human longevity is one that I have carefully guarded for almost a hundred and fifty years. Sadly, it has been hard trying to carry my wealth across the generations. There has been too much upheaval in the last century. That is why I need those accounts.

"I am surprised that you pulled it off with Clements. It was I who tipped off the Swiss Bankers about you. All I was trying to do was draw out some leads so that I could trace them back to Kohart's accounts. I have been waiting five long years to get my hands on those accounts. I never dreamed that you would be able to weasel your way into their confidence. Did you plan to do this all along? The similarity in your names must be more than a coincidence. The Agartha has always awaited Ts|un K!oh. Did you influence the naming of Prince Raimund SONnenkalb of KOHary in preparation for your return?"

Sun Koh shook his head. "Sorry. It was neither a coincidence, nor part of a plan. It was Destiny. I have arrived at a critical juncture in human history so that racial purity and genetic superiority may once again determine the fate of humanity. When the ice ages return, and Atlantis rises again, Germany will lead the way for the entire world."

The hooded figure responded. "You sound like that fool Hitler and his merry band of superstitious racist revolutionaries. Destiny! It is only planning and the heritage of the ruling class that can save Germany."

"I am surprised at you, Rákóczi. You had always sided with the revolutionaries in France, America, and even the Revolutions of 1848 in the German states. When did you become a monarchist?"

"I had hoped that you would figure it out." the hooded man said. "The Allied powers never intended to spread 'democracy' with their "Great War." Their sole goal from the beginning was the destruction of the German Empire and its ruling class. The German people had advanced politically, socially, and economically faster than any other nation in Europe. We had gone as far in twenty years as England had in a century! They feared us so they plotted our destruction. Everyone forgets that it was the Serbian government's carefully planned assassination of the heir to the throne of Austria-Hungary that started the war and that Britain, France, Russia, and the United States came in on the side of the outlaw state in Serbia! From the very start they were trying to destroy the monarchy to leave a political vacuum and breed anarchy in our lands. And then they had the nerve to force Germany to admit sole culpability for the war! Hypocritical mongrels!

"We need order! Not some 'new order' based on the fantasy of 'political equality,' but the hereditary order of a society where every man knows his place and functions within it. The Weimar Constitution is a farce and it has destroyed the natural order of our society by pretending that men have always been equal and that there is something wrong with those whom nature elevated to rule over others."

Sun Koh gestured in frustration. "The old order was even more corrupt than Weimar. Germany does not need to return to old errors but should look forward to a new future based on genetic superiority, not class struggles!"

"Sun Koh, we should not be fighting. Both of us want to return Germany to her greatness. Democracy is a total failure. We need a strong central leader. The time is ripe for such a leader to arise. Hitler is at best a comic opera troublemaker. The man who can really bring order to Germany is General Kurt von Schleicher."

Sun Koh was incredulous. "Schleicher? He is a conservative and a soldier. He has no broad appeal with the common people. If he comes to power, the Communists and the Social Democrats will go into armed revolt."

"You are wrong. He is a leader of men who know how to consolidate power. And I have been working on him, inculcating the idea of restoring a constitutional monarchy. This will solve our problems. The people will instinctively follow their natural leaders. We need the nobility now more than ever"

Sun Koh reviewed his knowledge of the previous century of European politics. He found no evidence that there were any 'natural leaders,' least of all among the nobility. Neither did he see any 'instinct' that made common folk follow noblemen. Modern commoners realized that accidents of birth do not make leaders. They were more likely to follow a dynamic man who emerged from their ranks than someone sporting a pedigree. St. Germain was mad.

"Prince Leopold was a visionary, Sun Koh. He took almost four hundred million Deutsche Marks from the treasury using Swiss Transfer Numbers and deposited them in his son Raimund's name. Since Raimund was a Swiss citizen, there was no way to trace the transactions. The Deutsche Marks were converted into gold and hard currencies almost immediately. Leopold did this to create a war-chest for the return of the monarchy. He also knew his son Raimund would never live long enough to abscond with that money. He entrusted it to him in secret. No one knew where Leopold had hidden the monies, nor did we know about Raimund's existence. Then Leopold had that damned stroke and he could tell us nothing before he died.

"When no one came looking for the money, Raimund thought he had inherited it free and clear. As he went around the world looking for a treatment for his heart disease, he also invested some of the money in foreign businesses. Even with the depression, the value of Prince Leopold's legacy must have doubled in value. As the world economy recovers, it will likely double itself again!

"I did not learn of Prince Raimund's existence until his visit to Brazil. That's when I put it all together. My agents contacted Raimund but he would have nothing to do with us. I told them to bring him to me alive or dead. The fools bungled their attempt to capture him and then sabotaged his plane. It exploded over the jungles in Africa and no bodies or wreckage was ever recovered. I will assure you that those cretins paid dearly for their stupidity!

"We lost the legacy again and had no leads as to its whereabouts. We would need to wait seven years before Raimund Kohart could be declared legally dead and his family would become heir to his assets. Then you showed up and I thought at first you were either Prince Raimund resurfacing or a scammer trying to get your hands on those millions. Instead, you turned out to be the real thing: a lost Atlantean prince. What's more, you have gotten access to the legacy that Prince Leopold intended for the Monarchists. Maybe you are right about Destiny after all."

Sun Koh responded, "I am sorry Count St. Germain, but Destiny has placed that legacy in my hands and I intend to use it to assist the National

Socialist German Workers Party in consolidating power. They will be the stepping stone to the re-establishment of the Ocean Throne and the Atlantean Empire. Herr Hitler is the key. He has a party based upon broad appeal but no depth of commitment. His will be a government of power wielded by elites and I will naturally rise to power over it and eventually the world itself."

"Your friend, Hitler, will never come to power. His days are numbered. I have decided to eliminate him. He will never attend that meeting on Friday."

Sun Koh stood tall and defiant. "And I will protect him from you. The power of the German monarchy is gone and I will keep it that way."

"Never!" shouted Rákóczi. He pulled out a huge naval saber with a thick heavy blade and struck Sun Koh on the chest. Sun was hit by the flat of the blade and it knocked him sideways. Rákóczi was *very* fast and *very* strong. But he took his eyes off Shani and that was a mistake.

With a quick movement, she deftly freed her hands parting the untyable knots and put all of her weight into pulling Rákóczi of balance. She grabbed and twisted his cloak to hamper his movements. The cloaked figure tried to pull free but then Sun Koh was on him. Holding down the figure's sword arm, Sun hammered blows at his head. Rákóczi was unfazed and spun around and out of his cloak. It fell away to reveal a figure covered in seamless golden chainmail from head to foot. There were no eyelets but instead there were two golden Chrysoberyl Cat's Eye stones that began to glow. Sun Koh realized that the mad Prince Rákóczi was trying to put him into a trance. But the Atlantean was impervious to such influences thanks to his mental disciplines.

Once again, Rákóczi made the mistake of ignoring Shani. Soft armor like chainmail might protect from penetrating blows and even attenuate the force of them, but it could not give support to joints like more traditional western armor did. The very flexibility of the chainmail allowed attacks against weak points on the human body. Shani put all of her weight into a kick to the side of Rákóczi's left knee. She then used the rope that had bound her hands to garrote his left wrist and use leverage to externally rotate his shoulder, exploiting the weakness of the smallest muscles in the shoulder. Rákóczi flailed wildly with his sword hand at Sun Koh who had grabbed one of the small benches and used it to block the attack. The blade became imbedded in the wood. Sun Koh dropped the bench then stepped back and leaped into the air kicking Rákóczi with both legs and his full weight. The top level of the pagoda was a small space and Rákóczi fell toward the railing. Shani put her full weight into a pull that on the left wrist that helped her lift the armored figure into the air and over the edge. Rákóczi fell out of the tower striking two of the lower levels before he hit the ground. He laid there unmoving.

Sun and Shani embraced and he took out her Tiger's Eye Ruby and placed it on her forehead where it adhered as if magnetized. Wordlessly they started down the stairs. When they reached the ground, Rákóczi was nowhere to be seen.

•••

The meeting between the Berlin Thule Society and the Nazi leadership happened that Friday at the Masonic Lodge in the Center of the City. Xaux and von Sebottendorff attended but Rákóczi did not. No one knew where he was. Hitler came with Rudolf Hess and Dr. Alfred Rosenberg who were both Thule members. Also attending as guests were Heinrich Himmler, Ernst Röhm, and Herman Göring. Just as Hitler was climbing the steps, a man ran towards him from the shadows with a pistol. From the roof across the street from the Lodge a burst of automatic fire cut the man down. Sturmvögel was on that roof as part of the security. There were no further incidents of violence.

At the meeting, Dr. Rosenberg introduced all of the participants. Hitler was very impressed with Sun Koh who appeared to be his ideal of the Aryan *Übermensch*. Hitler was not a mystic and would have found the story of Sun's traveling through time to be too farfetched to take seriously. Instead, Sun Koh identified himself as Prince Raimund Sonnenkalb of Saxe-Coburg, Gotha, and Kohary who had been raised under the training regimen of Dr. Günter Asch. Asch was well known to the Nazis and his ideas were incorporated into the training program of the elite SS members under Himmler who formed a special guard around *Der Führer*. Sun Koh told them that he had traveled all over the world seeking knowledge and the wisdom of the ages. In talking to him, it became evident that Sun Koh was knowledgeable in many fields. Hitler vowed that when the Nazis came to power, Sun Koh would receive the academic recognition he deserved. He would be Hitler's "right hand man". He also directed that Sun Koh should be made a Colonel in the SS effective immediately.

Hitler promised the Thule Society that when he came to power, he would authorize full archaeological investigation of the foundations of the Aryan Race. This agreement would lay the groundwork for the *Ahnenerbe* founded by Himmler in 1935. In future years, Sun Koh would assist these investigations to help uncover the remnants of Atlantean Civilization.

Hitler asked to meet the man who had saved his life earlier that night. Sturmvögel came dressed in his black fatigues. Hitler was told that Sturm had served with the irregular forces during the war. Everyone was surprised that Hitler knew Sturm by reputation. Sturmvögel had been one of the most decorated enlisted men of the *Reichswehr*. He had been cited several times for bravery in battle and had been awarded the Iron Cross. Yet he never rose above the rank of *Hauptgefreiter*, a senior corporal.

Hitler asked the man why he had never advanced to higher rank. Sturm answered that he was a soldier, not an administrator and that he craved to be in the midst of the action. Hitler smiled. He himself had received two Iron Crosses during the war and had been blinded by a gas attack. He too had refused promotions to stay with the troops at the front. They understood each other. Hitler directed that Sturmvögel should receive a commission in the SS as an *Oberleutnant* and be made Col. Koh's personal aide.

Ernst Röhm knew that Col. Gruber had marked Sturmvögel for liquidation, but there was nothing he could do. Sturm was now under Hitler's direct protection.

•••

Sun Koh and Minx eventually traveled to Zurich and retrieved the contents of the safe deposit box. It contained the true birth certificate of Prince Raimund and several signed affidavits from deceased government officials verifying its authenticity. It also contained several bankbooks, stock certificates and a ledger documenting all of Raimund Kohart's investments around the world. The value of the find was astonishing. It was greater than Rákóczi had guessed and it continued to increase in value as the world economy recovered.

Over the next year, Hitler became chancellor, the Reichstag was dissolved formally ending parliamentary democracy, and the Nazis systematically eliminated all opposition. They created a totalitarian regime in Germany under Hitler's direct rule. Socialism, Communism, and Monarchism ceased to exist in any meaningful way. Jews were brutally repressed. The only systematic resistance came from the Churches and this was too little, too late.

At Hitler's direction, Sun Koh was permitted to take exams in several academic fields. He was licensed to practice law and medicine and received honorary doctorates in several disciplines from German universities. Sun Koh made contributions to several branches of medicine and surgery. He and Jan Mayen churned out multiple patents together. The money kept rolling in.

When the Gestapo was founded in April 1933, Sun Koh was granted a commission with the rank of Colonel there. It would not be until April 1934 that the Bavarian *Staatspolizei* and the Gestapo came under unified command. During that interval, Sun Koh was an agent for both police agencies. He worked on several espionage and criminal cases, but he shied away from those of a political or racial nature.

In June 1934, a plot to overthrow Hitler involving the SA leadership was 'uncovered' which led to a bloody purge and the suppression of the SA. In that purge, Röhm, Gruber, and Schleicher were all executed.

The stage was now set. Sun Koh had defeated all of his enemies and was deeply entrenched in Germany society and politics. He was one of Hitler's favorites. He had an international reputation as a scientist and an adventurer. Shani had become his concubine and enforcer. Sturm, Schreck, and Alaska-Jim stayed with him as his permanent bodyguards. Minx was his advisor and mentor.

But still, nothing had been heard from Prince Rákóczi...

THE END

AS FAR AS THE EAST IS FROM THE WEST

Psalm 103:12 *As far as the east is from the west, so far hath he removed our transgressions from us.*

The light was on in a turret of a castle outside of Munich. It was midnight on a summer night in 1934. A radio transmitter in the turret sent out a scrambled audio message. To any ordinary radio receiver, the transmission sounded like static. Many miles away in the Swiss Alps, the signal was intercepted by a hidden antenna on a mountain top and transferred deep underground. A special radio receiver reconstructed the audio message. It was in a non-human language. The radio operator was a short, stout Neanderthal descendant whom the humans in the area would have recognized as a dwarf. He sent his own signal in acknowledgement.

Two days later, deep in the Königreich Mine in Switzerland, the miners were directed to a large cave where there was a large pile of unusual gold ingots which had not been there before. These ingots were taken to the surface, smelted down at the mine's processing plant, and recast into standard 12.5 kilogram bars. The total amount of gold was just over five metric tons. One week later, after they had cooled, the bars were loaded onto an armored train and shipped to Zurich. The gold was deposited there in a bank vault and their value was accredited to the Königreich Company account. The sole shareholder of the company was Raimund Sonnenkalb Kohart, a Swiss citizen.

This same Raimund Sonnenkalb Kohart was known to the world as Prince Sun Koh, the multi-millionaire adventurer and 'heir to Atlantis.' Sun Koh had been sent forward in time from 11,000 years in the past to claim his right to the lands of Atlantis when they re-emerged from the Atlantic Ocean during the next Ice Age. This story was too fantastic for popular consumption, and so Sun Koh had assumed the identity of the mysterious Prince Raimund of Saxe-Coberg, Gotha and Kohary and then claimed to be the reincarnation of an ancient Atlantean prince. In the popular attitude of the time, this was an acceptable foible. Only a handful of people knew the actual truth.

Since emerging on the scene in May 1932, Sun Koh had discovered a secret Atlantean cache of gold and other valuable materials hidden under the Alps. Using the old Königreich Mine he had purchased as a cover, he had extracted over thirty metric tons of gold and large amounts of other rare and valuable materials from the cache. He had also assumed the identity of Prince Raimund (b. 1901) and become heir to a secret fortune that Raimund's father, Prince Leopold, had left in his son's care. Prince Raimund had suffered from a congenital heart condition that included a severe Atrial Septal Defect. This defect would have ended his life before age forty. The prince had disappeared when his commercial flight over Africa vanished in 1927. Sun Koh had been able to mimic the heart condition long enough to convince Swiss and German officials that he was Prince Raimund. After that, he had allegedly 'cured' himself of the ASD using a combination of medications, herbal remedies, and yoga. The murmur in his chest (which he effected using ventriloquism) gradually subsided over the period of a year to the astonishment of the best heart specialists in Germany.

Sun Koh was a nearly perfect physical specimen and an intellectual genius. He had been genetically engineered in ancient Atlantis to be a perfect ruler. In the modern German press, he attributed these qualities to the rehabilitation program designed by Dr. Gunther Asch for Raimund which had begun in the prince's early childhood. In fact, Asch's program had helped keep the real Prince Raimund alive and active despite his congenital weaknesses.

During the destruction of his time ship, Sun Koh had been exposed to the Akashic Record that contained all human, non-human, and pre-human knowledge on Earth. This confusing jumble of information had no real index and parts of it were warded against casual perusal. But Sun Koh still had a virtually encyclopedic source of information stored in his memory on every topic. This wealth of knowledge he publically attributed to intensive studies all over the world during his formative years.

Sun Koh had thrown his support behind the Nazi Party and their platform of racial superiority and eugenic activism. He had helped Adolph Hitler achieve political power. In the election in late July, 1932, the Nazis had won several seats in the Reichstag, but they were still denied any participation in the Weimar government by von Papen and Schleicher. They began losing momentum. That was when Sun Koh pumped money and his personal support into the Nazi Party. Through his influence—and that of Ludwig Minx—Koh had convinced von Papen that Hitler could return stability to Germany and bring about a revival of parliamentary democracy. Koh had thus arranged for Hitler to be named Chancellor of Germany. Nothing could have been further from the truth. Hitler constructed a totalitarian state and concentrated all power in his own hands.

In thanks to Sun Koh for his support, Hitler arranged professional licenses for him in medicine, surgery, and law. The Atlantean prince had also taken several tests in other academic fields and scored well. For this—and at the request of Hitler—he had been awarded honorary degrees in many disciplines. Sun Koh also received the rank of full colonel in the SS, the Bavarian *Staatpolizei*, and the Gestapo.

Sun Koh had purchased a large forested estate in Bavaria centered on an old castle. He renamed the estate *Nibelungen* and the castle *Schloß Valhalla.* He enlarged and refurbished the castle as well as reconstructed its moat. In medieval times, moats were filled with sewage and kept foul to prevent enemies from crossing them. Sun Koh cleaned up his moat and filled it with crocodiles, poisonous snakes, electric eels, and piranha.

Using Minx' mental powers, the deadly animals left each other alone and were placed on heightened alertness for intruders. The castle itself was modernized with electricity, air conditioning, and every modern amenity. The dungeons had been further expanded into a large underground complex. The renovation included a huge private library, several specialized laboratories, and a secure radio station. It also had a modern gym with exercise equipment, a handball court, an indoor pool, and several garages. These contained a fleet of land vehicles of several types. There were tennis courts and a full-sized soccer field behind the castle. Elsewhere on the grounds was a mile-long private runway and a hangar large enough to hold a small dirigible and several aircraft.

The entire complex was surrounded by a deep forest that was kept stocked with small game. Within the forest, Sun Koh had imported several *tatzelwurms* from the Alps. These were ten to twelve foot snake-like lizards with vestigial hind limbs and forelimbs that sported a four-digit hand with an opposable thumb. These creatures were highly intelligent omnivores with a poisonous bite. They were capable of making and using simple tools and weapons. There were also panther-like sabertooth Scimitar cats and roving wolf packs which Minx kept restricted to the forest. Colonies of falcons were kept in woods with which Minx developed a special bond to help keep tabs on security on the estate. These birds could spot and track a mouse in the grass from 1500 feet up, even in low light. Minx was mentally linked to them so that he was made aware of any intrusion into the forest. At night, Minx used cave bats in a similar way. These nature based security measures were augmented with a variety of sensors and alarm systems.

In Berlin, Sun Koh owned an office building in Friedrichstraße near the *bahnhof* and not far from the government district. This was the nerve center of his economic empire. The 12th floor (by American counting, the 13th floor) was a penthouse complex and Sun Koh's headquarters in the German Capital. It contained a laboratory and a technical library. The Prince also maintained a mansion in the Steglitz-Zehlendorf district that had its own lake.

It was Prince Sun Koh himself who had made the radio call to the dwarves for more gold. He needed it to bolster his cash flow and allow him to purchase more stocks and bonds at the bargain prices for which the worldwide Depression was responsible.

Earlier that day, Sun Koh had performed a complex colonic resection at the University of Munich Hospital and had lectured later in the day on the newly emerging class of anti-bacterial medicines derived from fungi and other organisms. He decided to spend a quiet evening at home with his concubine, Ashanti Garuda, a trained assassin known as the Daughter of Kali. Meanwhile Ludwig Minx, the former stage magician known as Dr. Baphomet and the Prince's chief advisor and thaumaturge was still re-fining the night-time security system. Rudolf 'Sturmvögel' Rauhaar, Sun Koh's personal bodyguard and chauffer, was also in the castle sound asleep.

Sun Koh was planning to open a new clinic on the edge of the castle estate for the treatment of mental disorders. In reality, he wished to experiment with techniques for rapidly re-educating dissidents and controlling human behavior. Sun Koh had resurrected some techniques from ancient Atlantis that had been used to guarantee the loyalty of slaves and applied them to the domestic staff in his castle, some of the miners in Switzerland, and most of the private security force he maintained throughout his vast holdings. Just recently, a young researcher named Jonas Sown had shown him an interesting device that he claimed could influence the emotions of large crowds. Sun Koh hoped this machine could be harnessed to further the control of the Nazi Party over the German populace.

Sun Koh was a bronzed skinned, blue-eyed blonde giant standing nearly six foot seven inches tall and weighing just over two hundred eighty pounds. He moved with the subdued grace of a gymnast. His face was square-jawed with Aryan features. His eyes were a hard lapis lazuli blue which seemed to melt into swirling maelstroms if you stared deeply into

them. He had surrounded himself with competent assistants whose expertise in different fields complimented his own abilities.

Jan Mayen the detective and inventor was currently at his Austrian
mountain villa outside of Salzburg putting the finishing touches on the
secret *Schimäre* multirole aircraft in preparation for its first supersonic
flight. Rolf 'Schreck' Karsten, the private detective, was in Munich on a
case.

Another aide, Alaska-Jim Hoover, was in Canada where he worked as
an agent of the Royal Canadian Mounted Police. He was currently deal-
ing with Indian unrest. Since 1932, the League of Indians of Canada had
made strident requests to abolish specific sections of the Indian Act of
1876. Ill- tempered Canadian government officials had rebuffed them. The
Indian Act had created government appointed Indian Agents who controlled all areas of native life of Indian Bands and Status Indians. It had
isolated them on reservations and treated the Indians as if they were not
competent to manage their own affairs. This had led to impoverishment,
alcoholism, exploitation, and cultural decline among the reservation
Indians. The Indians even claimed that they were being kidnapped and
enslaved by some of the Agents. There were several episodes of violence.
Jim had his hands full.

Sun Koh had been disappointed with his visit to the University
Hospital. Many of the senior physicians had been Jewish but because of
the *Arierparagraph* laws enacted in April 1933, they were not allowed to
practice on non-Jews. Many had actually fled the country or were trying
to. He thought this was a waste of critical human potential. To his thinking the Jews were a subject race to their Aryan Masters and could best
serve them with their expertise in many fields. Sun Koh thought that these
prejudicial laws were only depriving Germany of the skills of competent
servants. It also convinced him that even Germany was not yet ready for
all the advanced technology he could provide. He shared with them only
what he thought would be beneficial and held back most of the information that could be used to build weapons.

After sending his radio message, Sun Koh was returning to the room
he shared with Shani, his concubine. Suddenly out of the shadows, Minx
appeared.

"My Prince, we have an intruder on the grounds coming from the
northwest towards the castle. It is a single man who seems to be unarmed
except for an edged weapon. How should I proceed?"

Sun Koh smiled wanly. "Why don't you bring him in to stay as our guest in the dungeon and we can interrogate him in the morning."

"It shall be done," said Minx and he vanished back into the shadows.

Several minutes later, deep in the forest, the intruder sensed that he was being followed. Local forest noises had ceased and the hairs on his neck were standing up. He thought he heard movement in the brush around him. Suddenly, there was a low mocking laugh that came from all directions. He stopped and crouched down looking around for the source of the voice.

"It will do you no good, my friend. We have you surrounded and there is no escape. Stand up with your hands over your head."

The man did not move. The hidden voice laughed again. A red glow bloomed in the northeast and in it was the silhouette of a man in a tuxedo with a cape and a top hat. He held a black cane with a multicolor glowing knob and he seemed to be floating several feet in the air. The figure lifted his head. His eyes glowed like hot coals. He had a goatee which gave his face a satanic look. This was Ludwig Minx in his stage persona as Dr. Baphomet. He saw the intruder in the red light. He was a man of average height wearing a multicolored tunic and sandals. Festooned on his garments were many shiny metal trappings and he had a short sword on his belt. His hair was cut in a bowl-shape very much like that of Mexican Indians yet his face was long and his features not like those of an Amerindian. Suddenly, the intruder began to glow with a bluish light and vanished. Minx was astonished. He could discern no trace of the man. He reached out to the bats, wolves, cats and *tatzelwurms* standing around him and found that they had lost sight of the intruder as well. Minx conducted a physical search of the area but could find no trace of the intruder. The man had not slipped past the animals around him yet he was nowhere to be found. Alarmed, Minx feared for the safety of Sun Koh. He immediately started back to the castle as quickly as he could.

Sun Koh lay down next to Shani. She opened her eyes and reached for him. Despite his fatigue, he responded to her ministrations and soon they were making love with Shani straddling him. Sun was drawn to climax rather quickly. As his body contracted, his mind was drawn into the Akashic Record updating its information to the present moment. Just as the orgasm ended he caught a brief glimpse of a glowing blue man at the end of the bed. In alarm, Sun Koh pulled Shani off him and rolled to the night stand. From the drawer he extracted a rectangular object about four inches long with a button and a dial on one face. He pointed it at the foot of the bed and pressed the button. A ball of white hot plasma shot from the object and exploded into electrical discharges. In the center of this small swarm of lightning bolts was a man in a tunic who fell to the floor unconscious.

Moments later, Minx knocked frantically on the bedroom door and Shani, wrapped in a silk robe, let him in. Right behind him in his pajamas came Sturm with a luger trained on the intruder. The tiger's eye ruby Shani wore as a tikala mark was glowing on her forehead. Sun Koh, also in a robe, was squatting next to the unconscious man.

"My Prince, I have failed you! This is the very same man I had seen in the forest who vanished before my eyes. I feared for your safety and rushed here. How could he have gotten here ahead of me? I ran as quickly as I could."

Sun shook his head. "You never could have outrun him. When he dematerialized, he could move effortlessly over or through any obstacle at high speed. He set you up, Minx. He drew you out of the castle to distract your attention away from me."

The unconscious man had black hair and an odd coppery skin-color reminiscent of an Amerindian. However, his features did not seem to belong to any known racial group. His tunic was made of an unknown cloth and the trappings were made of an odd yellow metal as was the sword that Sun Koh now held. The metal was some kind of alloy and must have contained gold, yet it was as hard as steel.

Minx remained distraught. "How is it that I could not see him?"

Sun smiled. "He went out of phase with our world and became a phantom in the halfway point between our world and paratime. It is a dangerous trick that only the madmen of the great underground world of the American Southwest could do in my day. Some of them just disappeared and never reappeared.

"He tricked you by appearing to be a mundane intruder. It took you off guard. Had he attempted to penetrate our defenses dematerialized, you would have had other warnings. This was very cleverly done. We have learned a lesson from this."

"Indeed, my Prince. I suspected that he had tried some kind of feint and came here immediately to protect you. How did you find him?"

Sun Koh smirked and cleared his throat while Shani looked away. "I was… immersed in the Akashic record when I saw him. These adepts make their entire body a single quantum mechanical object and they can smear it across a substantial volume of space-time simultaneously. It is only when they are observed that the body coalesces into a single location. The distance this one traveled is impressive. He must have done it in several rapid jumps."

Minx went down on his left knee, "My Prince, I failed to protect you. I await your punishment."

Sun Koh was within his rights to castigate Minx, but he shook his head. "Get up, Minx. Our defenses are new and we needed them to be tested. It is all right to make mistakes as long as you learn from them. No one was hurt. We will not speak of this again."

Minx arose and thanked his master. He then turned with anger on the unconscious intruder. "Shall I awaken this assassin, my Prince?"

Sun responded, "Oh, he is no assassin. He is a herald from the Abysmal Court of Ch'iny'n beneath the American Southwest. His clothing gives that away."

"But the sword!" said Minx.

Sun showed it to him. "You see, the point is rounded and the edge is blunt. It is ceremonial only. When he presents himself at his destination, he surrenders it as a sign of is peaceful intentions. And I do not sense any danger around him. He has a message for me."

"But why steal into your bedchamber in the middle of the night?"

"Well, for one thing, his dematerialization powers can be severely limited when the sun is out. Next year will be a maximum year on the Sun's eleven year cycle. For the last few years sun spot activity has been inordinately high. Remember the storm two years ago that destroyed my ship? He made the attempt at midnight because the sun is on the other side of the Earth and he is shielded from its effects. And I detect a sense of urgency. He felt he had to do this to deliver his message to me in person. Nevertheless, it was arrogant of him to barge in as he did. That is why I stunned him. I think he had a far too prurient interest in what Shani and I were doing. The Ch'iny'ns are a debased and morally degenerate people. Voyeurism is one of their most common vices."

Sun Koh gestured and Minx's eyes glowed again. The herald gave a start and opened his eyes. He rapidly moved to a crouch and frowned. His eyes went out of focus and he appeared as if his mind were in a fog.

Sun Koh spoke in a language that none of his associates recognized. The intruder responded in the same tongue. He stood unsteadily and bowed forward presenting the ceremonial sword to Sun Koh in both hands with down-turned eyes. The man then stood up straight and looked into Sun Koh's eyes. They stood like that for several minutes appearing to communicate non-verbally. Then the herald took out an envelope and handed it to the Atlantean. The non-verbal communication went on for a few more minutes and then Sun Koh made a dismissive gesture giving the sword back to him. The herald backed away. Sun told Minx to have the man escorted to the northwest edge of the forest and then released.

After the herald was escorted out, Sun Koh opened the envelope and read the letter inside of it. Then he turned to his people and said, "The Ch'iny'n herald came by a vessel that traveled in the shadow of the earth from North America to here. It was always midnight as it flew. He did so to avoid detection using their dematerialization technology and to protect it from exposure to the power of the Sun. He is returning home in the same manner.

"The Ch'iny'n people are masters of psychic powers and have a very old and complex technology. The particular type of psychic abilities they use can be affected by solar activity. They have perfected a form of diplomatic third-party telepathy which allows a herald to deliver a message without himself being aware of its contents. He could only do this around midnight because of the current solar storms.

"The diplomatic material he transmitted to me from his sovereign was quite alarming. He brought to my attention a serious problem that will affect not only the Ch'iny'n people but all mankind. The diplomatic message contained a series of disturbing photo-type images. The Abysmal Throne has no formal contact with any modern surface governments. The Ocean Throne of Atlantis had a non-aggression pact with them and the herald was invoking its provisions for mutual assistance."

Sun Koh held up the letter. "He brought a letter from Alaska-Jim. The case that Jim is now working on is directly linked to the Ch'iny'n problem. Jim has uncovered a particularly brutal prostitution ring and it looks as if some of the Indian Agents might be implicated. He has met serious resistance from his superiors in Ottawa who want the Royal Canadian Mounted Police to back off and let the Indian Bureau handle it. But Jim discovered that some of these Indian women disappeared into thin air. It appeared that they had been taken to an underground cavern in Asquith, Saskatchewan and were never heard of again. Jim began to search for evidence in the cavern when he made contact with the Ch'iny'ns."

Minx spoke up, "This is unprecedented! From what little I know of them, the Ch'iny'ns have always avoided contact with surface dwellers."

Sun Koh nodded, "I suspect that there are special circumstances here that I will not go into now. Among other things, the Ch'iny'ns who had purchased the women were wealthy and politically powerful. They re-

"The Ch'iny'n people are masters of psychic powers..."

quired fresh victims for private debaucheries that even their own people
would have found repugnant. So they bargained with surface dwellers to
supply them with untraceable women.

"At first they paid in gold, but later on the supplier's price got steeper
and they paid using exotic materials and technological information far in
advance of anything known to surface science. The Ch'iny'n bureaucracy
discovered that certain materials were missing and eventually discovered
the conspirators. They were made to talk. It appears that some of the materials and information used for payment could build weapons of tremendous power that could even be used against Ch'iny'n itself.

"If the panderers were Canadian government agents, that would explain why Jim is being forced off the case by Ottawa. They may be passing
these things on to London."

Sturmvögel sputtered, "The *gottverdammt* British! In possession of
such power, they could crush Germany. We cannot let that happen!"

"That is my concern as well," said Sun. We need to call Schreck and
have him check with *Abteilung Fremde Heere* in Berlin about any such
technology showing up in England. Meanwhile, the Ch'iny'n are threat-
ening unilateral action and Alaska-Jim can get no help from the Canadian
government. He is so disgusted that he is on the verge of resigning from
the RCMP."

Sun turned to Minx, "Ludwig, please call Jan Mayen and tell him
that we will have need of The Captain and *Schimäre* this coming evening.
Kameraden! Get a good night's sleep. Tomorrow, we leave for Canada!"

•••

The next evening, Jan Mayen and his crew arrived in *Schimäre* using
the new scintillating camouflage hull plates to conceal the plane in flight.
Schimäre was the multi-environment swing-wing flying submarine built
secretly by Jan Mayen based on the technology pioneered by his grandfather, Robur the Conqueror. The craft was capable of vertical takeoff and
landing. Sun Koh had made some design suggestions and it had been over-
hauled with four atomic "cold fusion" engines instead of two conventional
ones, an extended fuselage, as well as an active noise reduction system to
suppress the sound of the craft in flight. The hull had also been reshaped
to add lift and to deflect radar and sonar. There were now six 40mm automatic cannons in the nose and one in the tail for aerial combat along with
six pre-loaded torpedoes—four in the bow and two in the stern—for sub-

marine use. It also had other devices of an offensive and defensive nature with a comprehensive flying laboratory. Using its new engines, the craft should be capable of supersonic flight speeds and underwater speeds up to 200 km/hr. The *Schimäre* was quite formidable.

Schimäre was well known internationally as the vehicle of the mysterious man known as "The Captain" who traveled the world solving mysteries and seeking adventure. The Captain's secret identity was Jan Mayen. When in character, The Captain spoke English with an American accent while his various companions spoke other languages. He wore a stylized aircraft commander's uniform with a round dress cap and a domino mask to obscure his face. Tyrann, his copilot, wore a similar but less ostentatious uniform and mask. The two usually brought a crew from the technocrat Colony to assist them and this trip was no different. World governments officially considered them to be suspicious characters and potential spies or terrorists. Unofficially, those governments coveted the advanced technology in *Schimäre*.

Schreck had finished his business in Munich and planned to come with them. His gal Friday, Gretchen, had checked with German Military Intelligence and found that there was some excitement at MI5 over some samples of materials recovered from Canada under unusual circumstances, but there were no further details. Sun Koh knew from the Ch'iny'n herald that the materials in question did not occur in nature (at least on the Earth's surface) and that they had a potential use in weapons of mass destruction. Sun Koh briefed his people on the situation but withheld from them exactly what had been traded for the women.

Sun Koh packed several cases of special equipment for the trip including his new 9mm rapid-fire machine pistol, the *Schnellesfeuer*. It had a built-in silencer and used a 30-round clip. It fired hollow-point rounds at high velocity which had the impact affect of rifle bullets at close range, yet the weapon was small enough to wear in a shoulder holster.

Sun also brought the small *Strahlgewehr* energy weapon which he had used on the herald. It fired a phased energy pulse that could interact even with a dematerialized entity. He thought it might come in handy.

Schimäre landed on the bank of the South Saskatchewan River where Jim said he would be camping out. He had several saddled horses with him and a small truck. Jim was wearing his trademark buckskins and coon-skin cap with an RCMP badge on his chest. His features were rugged and he was of average height but husky. He looked like a mountain man. Jim was dark eyed and clean shaven. He wore two Colt .45 Peacemakers on his gun belt and carried a Model 1895 Winchester Repeating Rifle with a box magazine. He had had it specially made to accommodate an American .30-06 rifle bullet or a 7.62 mm shell from either Germany or Russia. Jim also kept a derringer in his cap. Previously it had been a two shot .40 Remington, but now, he carried a mini 5-shot .45 ACP semi-automatic that used special "hot loads" (which today we would call "magnums"). He carried several Native American weapons including a set of bolos, a razor sharp Obsidian knife, several metal blades, and a high-tech throwing tomahawk with a sharp metal head at each end. Jim was constantly chewing tobacco. Out of deference to Sun Koh's concerns about cancer, neither Jim nor any of the other companions smoked.

Jim greeted his friends and brought them up to date on the situation. About six months ago, some reservation Indian women were found in a brothel outside Moose Jaw. They claimed that they had been kidnapped, raped, and shot up with heroin to addict them before being transported to Saskatoon and parceled out to different houses of ill repute. They claimed that certain Indian Agents were involved in their abduction and that some of the girls were shipped off to Asquith to be taken into the underground caverns there. They suspected that many of the working girls who got "burned out" were sent into these caverns as well. No one knew why.

Jim's investigation had corroborated the women's story but before he could move against the Agents, they were taken into protective custody and he was pulled off the case. Jim protested and was nearly suspended. Instead he took a leave of absence and decided to investigate the Asquith caverns on his own. That was when he met a group of Ch'iny'n warriors.

The warriors had been searching the cavern for one of their own people who had been smuggling contraband into their realm. Jim found out that this fellow whom they called Tl'chiakp'no not only had brought in women, but alcohol, heroin, cocaine, and absinthe. His operation in Ch'iny'n had been discovered and his accomplices rounded up, but he had escaped with contraband materials of a dangerous type. It was also made clear that none of the surface women who had been brought to Ch'iny'n had survived.

The Ch'iny'n authorities feared that Tl'chiakp'no would use the contraband materials to gain asylum on the surface or even take revenge on them. The authorities were sufficiently alarmed that they had contemplated invading the surface to recover this material. That was when Jim told them about Sun Koh and they agreed to invoke the old treaties with Atlantis before taking more decisive action. They sent one of their heralds with a note from Jim to verify their story.

"They were awfully upset. The only reason they spoke to me was that they learned I was a policeman."

Sun Koh said, "That is not true, Jim. These people are paranoid, and they do not let any surface dwellers return who have discovered their realm. There was more to it, wasn't there? I could tell that from your letter."

•••

Jim nodded and sat down crossed-legged on the floor.

"They spoke to me because they sensed that I had once been amongst them. At first, they thought I was the man they were after. Soon, they figured out that I was someone else entirely. Someone who knew and understood their world."

Jim turned to Sturmvögel and asked him. "How old do you think I am?"

Strum shrugged. "You seem to be in your forties."

Jim laughed, "Not even close. I am 181 years old. I was born Jacob Huber in Darmstadt, Germany in 1753. I had been apprenticed to an ironsmith as a boy and was working at that trade in 1775, when I was conscripted into the service of the Landgrave.

"I was engaged to a beautiful girl named Lisle. The local burgher lusted after her and had me conscripted to get me out of the way. There was nothing I could do and no one to help me. I became one of the Hessians sent to America to put down the Revolution. In 1776, I was captured by Washington and his forces at the Battle of Trenton on Christmas Day. What kind of fanatic fights a battle on Christmas? I was held prisoner for several months and during that time I learned English rather well. I eventually escaped and found refuge with some Indians who were not very friendly to the colonists.

"I determined that I wanted nothing more to do with the war. So I was a deserter to the British and an escaped prisoner-of-war to the rebels. My only friends were the Indians. I have a flair for languages and I soon learned to converse with them. Eventually, the colonists would offer amnesty and a land grant to any Hessians who deserted, but not that early in the war. So I went west. There weren't many white people out there except for the French who didn't care for either side at that time and a few ambivalent colonists who were waiting to see how the Revolution seemed to be going before taking sides.

"My English got better. I even picked up some French and several Indian dialects. I found the country amazing and so I did some trapping and hunting along the Mississippi. I met the last remnants of the Cahokia Indians who had made the great mound city near St. Louis. They are all gone now.

"I spent some time in New Orleans but I preferred the open country and was curious of what there was further west. There were lots of rumors about gold and the 'Seven Cities of Cíbola y Quivira'. I ran into the Spanish in Texas and New Mexico during the time when they were at war with the Nomadic tribes of the plains, especially the Comanches. I stayed with the Pueblo Indians and helped them and the Spanish fight the nomads.

"From some prisoners, we learned that the Nomadic tribes were being incited to attack by men from within the Earth that they called *Xinaián* who hated the brown robed Franciscan Monks who had been opposing the native gods and religions of the Indians. When the brown robes moved in, the influence of the old gods went away and somehow this weakened the *Xiniáns*. So I fought on the side of the missionary Indians.

"During a battle on the Old Spanish Trail I was seriously wounded and took shelter in a cave in the mountains. The cave turned into a clearly man-made tunnel in which the floor followed an inclined spiral down deep into the Earth. I travelled on it a short way until I had lost so much blood I could go no further. It was then I felt invisible hands pulling on me and I blacked out.

"When I awoke, I was in Ch'iny'n. It was a damnable place of weird machines and monsters. The people were human but not of any race I knew. It was their custom to welcome visitors from the surface, but to never let them leave. They were morally bankrupt and totally degenerate. I had been healed to be a plaything for their amusement.

"They learned all they could from me, and then they made me participate in their debased social customs. I rebelled and demanded to be released. They imprisoned me and made me fight in the arena against men, beasts, and horrible things of their own creation. The Ch'iny'ns were impressed with my fighting skills and so they let me live and spared me the torture they usually inflicted on uncooperative outsiders.

"They kept me healthy and regenerated my wounds so many times that my body began to heal spontaneously. They had tried to teach me their mind tricks, but I was never any good at them.

"Then in 1786, there was a major volcanic upheaval. I later learned that Mt. Shasta had erupted and that there had been some eruptions as far north as Mt. St. Helens and Alaska. There was utter chaos in Ch'iny'n. The eruptions were apparently an attack by something from even deeper in the Earth that was trying to break through.

"In the confusion I escaped and made my way to the surface somewhere in northern Arizona. Again, I was rescued by Indians. I had spent over three years underground and my fighting prowess was now quite formidable. I decided that I wanted to put as much distance between me and the Ch'iny'ns as I could.

"I went south and traveled in Mexico, Central America, and all the way down South America to Tierra del Fuego. It took me thirty years, but I saw everything the continent had to offer. I learned new languages including Portuguese, Italian, and even some Japanese! I met lost tribes and learned their languages and histories just before they died out. I climbed plateaus in the Matta Grosso where horrible monsters lived. Literally flying dragons! I visited lost cities that even modern archeologists haven't yet found. I was the first white man to see Machu Picchu, almost one hundred years before Bingham.

"I made and lost several fortunes. But since being in Ch'iny'n, I was changed. I had stopped aging. My skin was thick and leathery and immune to sunburn and minor cuts and scrapes. I never scarred. My skin would not hold tattoos. I healed rapidly and could survive serious wounds and even poison. I could regenerate body parts. I could even control my bodily functions such as beard and nail growth. But I am not immortal. I have been close to death too many times to fool myself about that. I've just been lucky. My senses are acute. My nerves are steady. I have enhanced strength and stamina. I also have a perfect photographic memory and my talent for languages has become almost preternatural.

"I came back to the United States and lived as Jacob Huber for many years. I couldn't stand the cities, so I traveled around and lived in the wilderness while a man still could. I visited all the Indian tribes that I could find. I shied away from the plains of the southwest to keep away from Ch'iny'n. But I discovered that they had many portals all over the west even here in Canada. I changed my name a few times and moved around. Sometimes I was a man with no name at all. I fought at the Alamo but left prudently before the end. After that, I avoided wars. When they struck gold in 1849, I went to California and roamed throughout the west.

"The Civil War was a terrible time for the US so I spent several years up north in Alaska and Canada. I not only learned about the Eskimos and the Northern Indians, but I learned to speak Russian as well. After the war, the US bought Alaska and I decided to live there. The contrast in climates and the changes in the length of the days were inspiring. I took over an old abandoned Russian Orthodox Monastery *Sviatoyi Sofiyi* (St. Sophia) on top of a mountain and started to fill it with mementos, books, and keepsakes gathered over a century of life. I had stored these things all over two continents and I finally brought them together there. When I signed the homestead papers for the place, I used the name James Hoover. That is how I came to be known as Alaska-Jim.

"I traveled around the western US and Canada and lived as a mountain man, a lawman, a farmer, a cow poke, even an Indian scout. Then the big Alaska Gold Rush started in 1893 and I went back to my home on the mountain to protect it. I've spent most of the last thirty years in the northern territories and I've spent twenty years in the RCMP. I'm getting bored now. It is time for a change. I need a new frontier: what Herr Hitler calls *liebensraum*.

"The wilderness that I love is almost gone. The trapper's lifestyle is an anachronism. Everything is citified now and under government control. A man can't live free anymore. I have learned to survive in forests, jungles, deserts, swamps, coastlines, rivers, mountains, lakes, and in the arctic. My hobby has become collecting the folklore of Native Americans of all types before they fade away."

Jim shrugged, "That's my story. I have never told anyone about this, except my wife who died almost twenty years ago."

"So that is why the Ch'iny'n trusted you," said Sun Koh. "You had escaped them but you had not betrayed them."

Jim nodded. "They said they would let me keep my freedom if I helped them find this Tl'chiakp'no and recovered the things he stole from them.

"I believe that Indian women are still being abducted into prostitution, though no more are being sent to Ch'iny'n. The tribal elders do not trust the government authorities. But they do trust me. I want to catch the abductors and trace them to their network in Saskatoon so we can shut it down."

"Meanwhile," Sun Koh said, "We need to try and find this Tl'chiakp'no fellow. He is likely still in Saskatoon under an assumed name. From the sound of things, he has been importing traditional liquor into the area as well as other exotic contraband: heroin, cocaine, and absinthe. There is only one criminal organization that could provide all of those things: the French gangs out of Marseilles. They are the primary heroin source for Europe and the Americas and absinthe is a distinctly French vice."

Alaska-Jim concurred, "The Dubois gang out of Montreal is behind a lot of the vice trade out here. I can get you some leads."

It was decided that Sturm and The Captain would join Alaska-Jim out at the reservations while Sun, Minx, and Schreck would travel to Saskatchewan to hunt down leads on the prostitution ring and the Indian Agents that were involved. According to Jim, the agents were being held in protective custody somewhere in the city. Sun wanted Shani to come with him, but she elected to go out to the reservations. She thought that she would be better able to interact with the Indian women. Tyrann would stay with *Schimäre* and keep it safe under the river along with the other crewmen.

•••

Alaska-Jim took his group into the reservation area. He explained that the Indian women were mostly abducted from local saloons, theatres, or other public places probably by being drugged then taken off to be raped repeatedly and then brought to Saskatoon to be shipped to the various brothels. Shani volunteered to act as bait in the local town. She would frequent several of the salons in disguise and see if anyone tried to molest her. Jim was quite concerned about this. He thought that Shani might be hurt and opposed it. But The Captain thought it was a great idea.

"You underestimate our Shani. I have worked with her before. I feel sorry for any fool that tries to trifle with her."

It was settled. Shani dressed like a local Indian woman and left her pet cobra with The Captain. She took her Tiger's eye tikala from her forehead and placed it on the back of The Captain's right wrist. It stuck to him like a magnet.

"As long as the eye glows its normal red, you will know I am in no danger. If I find something of interest the eye will glow with a golden light. If it starts flashing on and off that is the signal to close in. If it goes black, I'm in trouble." The Captain had her swallow a capsule containing a small radio transmitter. He would use it to track her location.

Shani went into town that evening and frequented several saloons and public places drinking very little. She used the name Shani Eagle. As a devotee of the Tantric Left Hand Path, she had strong premonitions about the various men around her. She knew who was harmless and who was dangerous. In one salon, her senses tingled. There was a man looking at her with a combination of sexual and aggressive desires. She chatted him up. During their conversation, she saw him slip something into her drink. She tasted it and recognized chloral hydrate: a "Mickey Finn." Shani smiled and finished her drink. She took a deep breath and drew the oxygen into her blood where it combined with and neutralized the drug. She then feigned symptoms of intoxication. Her companion signaled and another man came over. They took Shani to a small truck and strapped her down in the back and gagged her. The Mickey Finn should have kept her out for at least an hour. They drove off.

Sturm and The Captain prepared to follow in their own car. Jim tried to come with them but Strum stopped him.

"You are a policeman, Jim. We may need to do some things that you may want no part of. Let Jan and I handle this. We will alert Tyrann and the hit team in *Schimäre*. Let us take it from here. You keep the Indians calm."

Jim balked, but then he looked into Sturmvögel's eyes and agreed. Sturm drove, and The Captain kept track of Shani's radio signal. The ruby on his wrist glowed bright yellow for a while and then went back to its normal red.

After about a ninety-minute drive on back roads, they arrived at an old house just off the road north of Saskatoon. It was isolated with no nearby neighbors. There was a generator in the basement that powered electric lights.

Shani was kept bound and gagged as she was manhandled inside. They brought her to a large room in the center of the house with no windows. There was a table and chairs and an elevated pallet with a polished leather mattress. The head of the pallet was close to the wall. The room smelled of sweat and bodily fluids. Off to the side was a bathroom with a shower stall.

One abductor was a tall man with pock marks on his face. As he wrestled with Shani he said, "She has some spirit. I like it when they kick and scratch."

The affable one who had been in the bar with her smiled. "I get off so much better when they are fighting me. The more they try to hurt me, the better the rush."

The third man was short and ugly. He started undressing. "It's my turn first. I'm tired of sloppy seconds. I want to feel her while she's still tight. Good thing there are only three of us this time."

"Well, she'll be gone tomorrow with the others when Randy gets here. He'll be sorry he missed this one tonight. But we have her all to ourselves until the morning. I like it when we get them here early."

Shani was untied, and her gag was removed. They stripped her naked as she struggled. The tall man grabbed her arms and pulled her back on to the pallet. He held her down with his back against the wall. The af-

fable one had his pants down around his ankles and was stroking himself. The ugly one was already aroused. He moved in between her legs and entered her roughly. The other men howled and laughed. But suddenly, it all changed. There was a strong musky smell in the air and it made the men feel sluggish. They all developed solid erections. This was caused by a pheromone that Shani was releasing. Suddenly the ugly one screamed. He started twisting around inside her, yelling that it was too tight. He kept trying to pull out but he couldn't. Shani kept thrusting and gyrating her hips as she moaned in ecstasy. The ugly man gave a final wail of agony as Shani climaxed. Then she brought her feet up against his chest and pushed him out of her.

The ugly man tumbled back, and they saw his phallus. It was bent at a sharp angle and swollen to twice normal size. It looked severely bruised and it pulsed, getting larger with each beat of his heart. Blood was seeping from skin tears and abrasions on its base. He moaned in pain.

The other two men were stunned and confused. Shani twisted her arms loose with ease and turned around on her knees to face the tall man. She looked at him with eyes the color of death, her pupils dilated wide. There was a horrible smile on her face: the rictus of Kali, goddess of death.

The tall man tried to get away, but she slapped him back like a cat toying with a mouse. She batted him back and forth with rapid blows that moved so fast, he could have sworn she had six arms! Then she began raking him with her finger nails. Shani treated all of her nails to harden them and then she sharpened them until each one was like the tip of a dagger. She pummeled his face and ripped through his shirt, gouging out ribbons of flesh with each rake of her fingertips. She then clawed off his ears and gouged out his eyes, all the while beating him back and keeping him from escaping. There was blood and flesh everywhere. The man howled in humiliation and pain. Finally, with one sweep of her right hand she tore out his throat. Carotid arterial blood spurted over her as he fell to the ground, his breath gurgling in his throat. Shani climaxed again and wailed with animal pleasure.

She turned around and licked the blood off her lips. She now faced the affable fellow. He had stood paralyzed with fear watching with horror as she tore the tall man to pieces. Shani moved toward him. She was naked and dripping blood from her hands, face and breasts. She had her head lowered and her mouth open. He could swear her canine teeth were elongated. The rictus on her face was even more horrible and frightening than before.

Suddenly, the affable fellow became tumescent and tried to get away, but the old saw is true: A woman with her skirt up can run faster than a man with his pants down. Shani was upon him. She picked him up and threw him into the wall. As he rebounded back she grabbed his right arm executing an overhead judo throw. As he flew through the air, she twisted his arm expertly and dislocated his shoulder with a snap. He screamed as he landed. He rolled over and tried to lift himself with his left arm, but she kicked his left collar bone shattering it. He fell to the floor writhing in pain.

Shani rolled him on his back and straddled him. She positioned her hips over his manhood and her loins sucked him up inside her. She began to squeeze him with her perineal muscles and rotate her hips. He was helpless beneath her. She made him erect with her body and began forcing him in and out of her with thrusts of her pelvis. It was damnable. He felt violated and it hurt every time she thrust up and down on him. He felt his pulse rise and his breathing speed up. He was nauseous, and his head throbbed like it would explode.

Shani writhed on top of him in obvious rapture, moaning with arousal and pleasure. She was enjoying this. She picked up the pace and her victim screamed in agony begging her to stop until he could speak no more. Then he felt his climax coming. It mounted with heat and pain in his member. He fought it but to no avail. When he finally let go, it was not an orgasm but a thanospasm: a death paroxysm. It felt like a wave of intense pain as if he were being electrocuted. The spasm caused a seizure, stopped his heart, and choked off his breathing. Blood vessels ruptured in his brain. He ejaculated not just semen but a copious amount of blood as well.

Shani then climaxed a third time. With each contraction of ecstasy, she slammed down on his pelvis. On the third contraction there was a loud crack as his pelvic bone fractured. On the fifth contraction, his pelvis collapsed.

Shani then stood and turned to face the ugly man. Blood and semen were dripping down her legs. The man had dragged himself over to his clothes and now pointed a pistol at her.

He yelled at her, "Satanic bitch!" and started firing.

Shani's beautiful face was still twisted into a horrible visage. She started to laugh and stalked towards him. It seemed as if she was moving in slow motion but she dodged each bullet he fired until she was on him. She grasped his gun hand by the wrist and squeezed until he dropped the weapon. She then reached down and grabbed his swollen member and twisted it. The ugly man screamed. Shani wrapped her legs around his abdomen and scissored them together. This was the Python Crush from *Mallayuddha* wrestling. Every time the ugly man exhaled, her legs squeezed tighter. He could not inhale. His face got darker and his tongue swelled. He struggled pathetically but she pulled tighter and tighter until he finally passed out. Shani continued constricting him until his heart stopped. At that instant, she had her fourth orgasm and in a sudden spasm her legs twisted his trunk breaking his lumbar spine with a loud crack.

Shani surveyed the room. It looked and smelled of death. Blood and flesh were everywhere. She went to the bathroom and showered. There was actually hot water! In the shower she started crying and sat there for several minutes letting the fresh water cleanse her. The shower had a douching set so she could clean herself out. In the medicine chest were hypodermics and vials of heroin. After the rape, they had planned to shoot her up and start her on the road to addiction as a means of controlling her later.

She dressed herself in her clothing. It had not been stained but it was torn. She searched the rest of the house and found six women chained to cots in the basement. At that point she concentrated and the ruby on The Captain's wrist started flashing on and off.

The next morning around 10 o'clock, Randy arrived with a medium sized van. It would he his turn this morning for a quickie with one of the women since he missed out the previous night. He mounted the stairs to the porch when he was struck in the chest by something heavy. It was Alaska-Jim's bolos thrown by Sturm. The spinning weights wrapped him in leather cords which pinned Randy's arms and threw him to the ground. The Captain, in full uniform, came out of the house. He rapped Randy on the chin.

When Randy woke up he found himself tied up on the floor of the rape room facing his three dead compatriots. His heart was racing and he was very frightened. The Captain had given him a sub-cutaneous injection of epinephrine to heighten his fear.

The Captain came in and spoke to him. "Your only hope is to tell me everything. Do not be fooled by the uniform. I am not a policeman and I don't play by the rules."

Randy cooperated.

Schimäre arrived later that morning. The women were taken back to the reservation by Shani in the truck the Captain and Sturm had used. Meanwhile a powdered accelerant was sprayed around the house and The Captain ignited it, burning the house to the ground. Randy's van then started out for Saskatoon.

At 3PM, the van was driven to a warehouse on the outskirts of Saskatoon. It appeared that Randy was driving. The van was brought into the warehouse and the doors closed. Suddenly, a cloud of tear gas was released from the back of the van, and out came five men from *Schimäre's* hit team dressed in body armor and firing freely with silenced *Schnellesfeuer* machine pistols. They shot anyone who moved. Two men tried to escape to the outside, but Sturmvögel dropped them from his vantage point on a roof across the street.

The driver had been the Captain disguised to look like Randy. He wore a gas mask as he got out of the truck. When the fumes cleared, he then put on his domino mask, round cap, and uniform great coat. The hit team searched the building and found empty pens where the women would have been kept. There were also pallets of liquor and cigarettes. They also found a series of written records detailing various transactions. And finally, they located a man cowering on the second floor who was well dressed and obviously the head mobster of this operation.

The man was bound hand and foot and brought before the Captain. "Do you know whose place this is? You men are all dead," he spat. "DuBois will hunt you down and kill you and your families!"

The Captain's face was hidden behind his domino mask. In perfect American English he said, "Do you recognize me?"

"You are that Captain fellow who has made trouble for us up north."

"Indeed. Your threats mean nothing to me. Meanwhile your traffic in human misery offends me."

"Go ahead! Turn me in to the police. I am not saying anything more."

The Captain shook his head. "It's the uniform. It always fools them." He lifted a sawed-off shot gun and emptied both barrels into the hoodlum's abdomen. The man collapsed to the ground but did not lose consciousness.

The Captain said, "I believe this is the trademark of your local competitor, Giles Macgregor. You will not live long enough to tell anyone otherwise. Hopefully a gang war will cripple both of your organizations."

With a gesture, the strike team and the Captain went to the roof where *Schimäre* was waiting. The scintillating hull plates made the aircraft difficult to see. They picked up Sturm and then flew off.

Phase one of the mission was completed. The Captain raised Sun Koh on the radio and informed him of what had transpired.

•••

Schreck had been hitting various dives in the rough parts of town for the last 2 days. He affected a reasonable Canadian accent and his every-man face made him both un-threatening and forgettable. People spoke freely to him and around him. Later in the evening he, Sun Koh, and Minx exchanged information.

"Jim was right," said Schreck. "The two big dogs in this town are Dubois and Macgregor. It was Dubois' mob that was running the abduction and prostitution ring. It seems they were also bringing in drugs and alcohol. They used to export the booze to the US during Prohibition, but for the last few years, they have been running firewater and drugs to the Indian reservations with the help of crooked Indian agents.

"I found out that recently they have had some client here in town who has bought cases of high class hooch. I even confirmed that Absinthe was brought in. I still don't know who the buyer was. There was some mention of a weird looking half-breed who used to hang around with our two Indian agents and seems to have been involved in smuggling. This guy had been recruiting local muscle over the last few years, but no one has seen him in weeks."

"Not bad for two days work," Sun Koh said. "We have been casing the hotel where they are keeping our two Indian agents, Fawkes and Brightman. They are kept in a suite on the 10 floor with three detectives: one inside the suite, one in the hall way, and one in the lobby. They have had them there for 2 weeks now. So far as we can tell, MI5 has still not interviewed them."

Minx nodded, "Jim said they gave themselves up after the samples they sent were analyzed. Why is MI5 taking so long?"

"The Labour Government in England is in disarray," Sun said. "Their Prime Minister Ramsay MacDonald is a pacifist and in failing health. It is unlikely that they will move swiftly on such a matter. Frankly, I think what they were sent was still very advanced for British scientists to understand. Our Ch'iny'n friend was taking a real chance smuggling that stuff out of the cavern. The Brits may not know what to do with it and they are a conservative lot. It will take them a while to decide what to do. We can use that to our advantage."

"What did Tl'chiakp'no bring out exactly?" asked Schreck.

Sun Koh sighed, "The herald said that three different materials were missing. There were ingots of pure Uranium 233, an isotope unknown in nature because of its short half-life existence. Also, there were ingots of Element 94 isotope 239. This element is unknown to surface science and was probably artificially produced.

"There were also several liters of heavy water—water that contains heavy hydrogen or deuterium. Modern surface science doesn't know it yet, but these are the necessary components to build powerful atomic bombs. All that would be needed is the technical information on how to assemble these weapons and Britain would have a monopoly on the most powerful explosives imaginable. Whole cities the size of London or Berlin could be flattened by one bomb! I am sure this Tl'chiakp'no fellow can provide the necessary data."

Sun Koh did not say so, but he himself knew how to assemble such weapons and had samples of similar materials in the Atlantean cache in Switzerland. He had never shared this information with his aides as he considered it too dangerous.

"Meanwhile, the materials have to be handled carefully. Improperly stored, they could result in an atomic chain reaction and premature detonation."

"Well, how do we find this stuff?" asked Schreck.

"The radioactive metals give off radiation unique to their nuclear composition. I have a detector that we can use to trace them, but they are probably stored in shielded containers and we would need to be right on top of them for the detector to work. Our best bet is to locate Tl'chiakp'no and have him lead us to the stuff. I am sure he is using his psychic abilities to monitor Fawkes and Brightman. When they have concluded a deal with the Brits, they will arrange a hand-over of the materials and the technical plans. We need to get to them during the daylight hours when the sun storms interfere maximally with Tl'chiakp'no's psychic powers. Then we can set a trap for him.

"Tl'chiakp'no's people in Ch'iny'n are very anxious to arrest and punish him so I assume that he plans to leave North America and seek asylum somewhere else in the Commonwealth. That is our ace in the hole. Tl'chiakp'no will be anxious to leave as soon as possible. If he thinks his deal is going through he may get careless. We should not underestimate him. The herald said he is a powerful psychic."

Minx said, "My Prince, we are also quite psychically powerful and our technique is not affected by solar activity."

"I hope so. Shani, Sturm, and Jim will be linking up with us tonight. Tomorrow morning we will interview the Indian Agents."

Around 10 o'clock the next morning, a well-dressed man in a goatee and a tall, tanned man in sunglasses came to the hotel and proceeded directly to the suite where Fawkes and Brightman were. They presented I.D.

"My Prince, we are also quite psychically powerful..."

cards to the policemen in the hall identifying them as Dr. Otto Frisch of Birkbeck College in London and Thomas Barrett of MI5. They presented a letter of introduction from the British Secretary of State for War, Douglas McGarel Hogg, 1st Viscount Hailsham. It requested full cooperation with them. (The documents were all forged by a local printer whose shady proclivities Sun Koh learned about from the Akashic Record.) The senior policeman complained that he had not been informed of their arrival. The bearded Dr. Frisch (Minx in disguise) was able to "convince" him and the other guards that everything was in order. Agent Barrett (Sun Koh) was there to provide security.

Minx and Sun Koh were permitted to interview Fawkes and Brightman in private. The two agents were haughty and arrogant. They had been caught distributing booze and drugs to the Indians in their charge and also were complicit in suborning Indian women into prostitution. They showed no remorse. They repeated their demands for £10 million, full executive clemency for any alleged wrong doings, and passports with immigration visas to Australia for themselves and their accomplice whom they called Fletcher Pinto. Minx and Sun interrogated the two men but found that they seemed to know very little about the atomic material or the whereabouts of their accomplice.

During the discussion, Sun Koh picked up subtle variations in word order and syntax and in their overall response to questions. They even had certain physical tics when questioned on certain matters. He glanced at Minx who glanced back knowingly. These men had their minds altered by a psychic surgeon of great skill. They had been programmed to respond in certain ways. No doubt attempts to threaten, torture, or coerce them with drugs would be doomed to failure. In fact their minds might disintegrate under such duress.

Sun Koh, acting as Tom Barrett, told the Indian agents that Dr. Frisch was a physicist who had been sent to inventory and verify the contents of the offer. Once this was done and everything was found to be satisfactory, their demands would be met. He asked them how they could get in touch with Pinto who had the materials. Fawkes said that Pinto would contact them. He recommended that Dr. Frisch be ready that evening to do his verification. Sun Koh made it clear that he would have to accompany Dr. Frisch and that they would be bringing technical equipment with them. He insisted that this was not negotiable. Fawkes paused for a moment staring straight ahead. He then said that he would see what he could do when Pinto called. In any case they should be in the suite by 10 PM ready to go.

Sun and Minx left after carefully implanting a suggestion to the police guards that none of this be reported to their superiors. It was a post-hypnotic suggestion that might only last for a day or two. That would be all they needed.

At the 7PM guard change, Minx identified the policemen as they came into the lobby and got into the elevator with them. By the time they had reached the 10th floor, he had them under his influence.

Sun and Minx entered the suite at precisely 10 PM with a large suitcase. The agents told them that Pinto had called and that a van would come to pick them up at 11 o'clock. They were to bring no radios or weapons. The van would take them to the location of the materials and they had until dawn to perform any tests they wanted. They were not to be followed. Sun and Minx agreed to this. While there, Minx subtly influenced the guards and fogged their minds ,slowing their response times for the rest of the night.

At 11PM, a dark van pulled up to the hotel. Sun Koh and Minx were frisked by two burly men in overalls and then blindfolded. The suitcase was searched and nothing suspicious was found. Sun recognized the men as two local toughs well known to the Saskatoon constabulary who had dropped out of sight over the last several months. The men seemed well muscled; more so than Sun would have expected from the pictures in his Akashic memories. He also noticed the dead look in their eyes and their lack of affect. He had a sudden chill.

These men were *yom'bhi* automatons. Their minds had been essentially wiped clean of all humanity and volition. They were obedient slaves to their psychic master. They felt no pain and spent their off time exercising and training for new tasks. They were not intelligent enough for complex behaviors, but they could drive vehicles and operate simple machinery. They made perfect guards since they did not require much sleep and could focus entirely on their assigned task. In total, there were three *yom'bhies* in the van, including the driver. A powerful adept might be able to control about a dozen of them. This was going to be an interesting night.

The van drove around for almost ninety minutes clearly attempting to confuse the passengers about their destination and foil any pursuit. But Sun Koh had a natural sense of his exact location on the face of the Earth with extreme precision. He was not confused. He knew exactly where they were at all times.

Finally, the van pulled up to a barn on a farm south of town. As the van stopped both Sun and Minx felt a telepathic probing of their minds trying to verify their identity. They had been prepared for this. Both men had constructed a "persona" based on the men they were impersonating. The real Otto Frisch was an expatriate Austrian-Jewish physicist who had defected to England the year before. The real Tom Barnett was an MI5 operative whose file Sun Koh had access to through the Akashic Record. The two men had used the type of immersion into character that many actors did in preparation for stage roles. They were able to create such in-depth portraits that it was hoped they would pass even a moderate telepathic perusal.

The one creative addition to Sun Koh's persona was a torrid affair with an Indian woman. He kept directing his thoughts back to her. This would hopefully seem to be nothing more than extreme infatuation but in fact it allowed Shani to track him. She, Sturmvögel, and Alaska-Jim were maintaining a long-distance tail on the van.

The telepathic probe had been relatively brief but thorough. When it was over, Minx and Sun Koh were taken out of the van while still blindfolded. They were taken to a cellar door in the floor of the barn and directed to climb down a ladder.

Sun Koh had a preternaturally keen sense of smell and had detected many odors on the trip. There were the scents of several men, women, *and children* in the van all in a state of fear. In the barn, he smelled these scents again with others. The stink of sex, death, and dismemberment permeated the place. Sun's eyes narrowed. Unspeakable things had happened here very recently.

Sun Koh also smelled lubricating oil, ozone, and other odors consistent with a workshop in the building.

When they reached the bottom, the cellar door closed and electric lights came on. The blindfolds were removed and Sun Koh and Minx faced a moderately tall man who looked about forty-five years old. The man had coppery skin like an Aztec Indian but his facial features and anthropometric proportions were not Amerindian. He did not fit into any surface world ethnic group. His long black hair was drawn back in a ponytail and he wore a beaded Indian headband. He was dressed in jeans, cowboy boots, and a denim shirt. The illusion was to make him appear to be a half-breed of partial Indian extraction, but Sun Koh recognized him as a member of the upper class that had ruled in Ch'iny'n for thousands of years. His eyes were bloodshot and there was a dissolute cast to his features. Behind him stood a very tall man in the shadows and the two *yom'bhies* who had escorted them from the van. They heard footsteps above them that were of two more yom'bhies on foot. Sun Koh's danger sense started to tingle.

Sun counted six *yom'bhies* all together: Three in the van (two of whom accompanied him and Minx into the cellar), two in the barn itself, and the big one who had been in the cellar with Tl'chiakp'no. He did not see or hear anyone else, but Sun Koh was certain that there had to be more of them. He heard the van moved so that one of its tires rested on the closed cellar door. No one could leave until the van was moved.

In the night sky above, *Schimäre* was circling and scanning the landscape with infrared viewers. Shani had directed them to the farm and was in constant telepathic contact with Sun and Minx. The viewers showed one man stationed on the roof of the barn and one on the pinnacle of the Farm house tower. Four others were circulating around the grounds.

That made twelve *yom'bhies* in all. As the Daughter of Kali, Shani recognized that these were not ordinary guards but a form of the walking dead which she knew as the *Bhūta*. These undead humans are virtually impervious to pain and have berserk strength. Some of them had augmented abilities such as night-sight or a poisoned bite. They would need to be dealt with swiftly and decisively.

The big *yom'bhi* with Tl'chiakp'no came out of the shadows. He was a well-muscled, bald-headed black man who was well over six feet tall with a knife scar across his face from his left cheek across the bridge of the nose to his right forehead. His eyes were not as blank as those of the others. Sun recognized him from the Akashic Record as an American cowboy named Rapier X who had fled to Canada to escape from murder and robbery charges. His signature weapon was a twelve inch triangular bladed dagger with which he could kill a man quickly but silently with one puncture to head, chest, abdomen, or neck. He had been missing for several months. The other two were petty toughs known to the police, but not seen in a while.

The Ch'iny'n spoke up, "I am Fletcher Pinto. You can see on the ground behind me two hundred closed boxes. Each shielded box contains a 10 kilogram ingot of radioactive metal. On your left are ninety-eight boxes with Uranium isotope 233 and two empties. On your right are one hundred boxes with Eka-Samarium—Element 94—isotope 239. Neither of these substances occurs in nature so these are the only known specimens in the world. Along the far wall are six ten-gallon drums of pure deuterium oxide—heavy water. This is the purest heavy water on Earth."

He then held up a notebook. "In this notebook are the technical details on how to assemble these materials into atomic explosives. Using either of these metals, you can build a bomb that is thousands of times more powerful than its weight in TNT. With a little more complex structure which includes deuterium, you can build an even greater bomb that is a thousand times more powerful than that! With this material, Britain will have a monopoly on atomic weapons."

Minx, playing his part as Dr. Frisch, asked, "But where did all of this come from? How did you obtain materials that do not exist in nature?"

Tl'chiakp'no dismissed his question with a wave of his hand. "It came from a lost civilization living right under this continent. They are so absorbed in their own pursuits that they care nothing about what happens on the surface. With these weapons in your hands, you can be sure they will leave you alone."

Pinto pointed to an eight foot long cylindrical object along the right wall of the cellar.

"This device you see behind you was built by me. It is why there are only ninety-eight ingots of Uranium. I took two ingots and used them in this machine. The first was shaped into a cylinder and put in the breach of a large bore gun. The second was formed into a round concave target. If I fire the gun, the bullet will be shot into the target causing a nuclear chain reaction. The device will explode with the force of 10,000 tons of high explosive. The resulting explosion will destroy half of Saskatoon and kill thousands of people. What is worse, the explosion will likely cause some of this other nuclear material to partially detonate enhancing the explosion and vaporizing the barn and everything in this room. Highly radioactive debris will be spread by the winds over most of central and eastern Canada. Thousands more will die slowly of radiation poisoning."

There was a mad, sadistic leer on Pinto's face as he described this horror. Sun Koh was revolted. His people always considered the Ch'iny'ns to be racially degenerate sensualists, but this man was disgusting. He had the stink of death all about him and over his whole farm. Many people had recently been tortured and killed here for this man's pleasure. Now he was talking of mass murder with a wistful gleefulness!

"This is my insurance policy," the mad man said. "If you pay me what I am asking, you will receive this bomb prototype which you may test at your leisure. If you refuse, I will detonate this bomb, destroying myself and most of this nation. I really think you have only one rational choice, but that choice will benefit you much more than it will me. I am giving the British Empire the power to rule the world."

Sun Koh nodded and said, "We need to evaluate this material and verify its authenticity."

Sun put the large suitcase on a table in the cellar and opened it up. He removed two rubberized lead aprons, two pairs of lead-lined gloves, and two industrial dust masks which he and Minx put on.

They went to the water canisters first and siphoned off a small sample from each. They then tested a drop of water from each in a Refractometer. They measured the index of refraction of the specimen and used it to calculate the specific gravity of the liquid. Plain water had a specific gravity of 1.000 at standard conditions. Each sample they measured gave a reading consistent with a specific gravity of 1.107 ± 0.005 at standard conditions. This confirmed that the liquid in each container was pure deuterium oxide.

They then went to the uranium boxes and opened them. Each contained an ingot as described with black streaks of corrosion on it. Two of the boxes were empty. Drawing a metal file along the surface of the ingots caused sparking and flashing. Uranium was a pyrogenic metal. Minx brought over a Geiger counter and measured the radiation from the ingots. It was highly energetic and consistent with the radiation energy of Uranium 233. The boxes were made of a light material that seemed like wax. When the lid was snapped closed, there was no radiation leakage at all. It even seemed to stop neutrons. It was a far more effective radiation barrier than lead at a fraction of the density.

Minx asked, "What are these boxes made out of?"

Tl'chiakp'no snorted. "After you buy them, you may analyze them yourself."

After they had verified that the Uranium ingots were authentic, they moved on to the Eka-Samarium side. Each box was opened. There was a lustrous silver ingot in each box marked with yellow oxides. Again, the Geiger counter verified that the metal was radioactive and that its radiation level was consistent with Element 94, Isotope 239.

While they were doing this, Shani, Sturm, and Jim were released downwind of the farm along with the six-man hit squad. Each had on an infrared visor and projector. They kept in touch with each other and the ship using portable radios with small headsets and microphones. The Captain maneuvered the silent camouflaged *Schimäre* to a vantage point in the air about a mile away. He took aim with his 40mm cannons. Shani kept Sun and Minx in the loop by telepathy. In the middle of their analysis of the Eka-Samarium, Sun gave her the signal and she relayed it to *Schimäre*.

The Captain opened fire on the house top and the barn roof. The explosive shells ripped the two *yom'bhies* apart. He then directed his fire to the ground and targeted the infrared signature of the other human automatons on the grounds. He hit two of the remaining four. That was when the ground party entered the farm grounds from the opposite direction. As the *yom'bhies* sought shelter behind the barn, they were picked off by

9mm machine pistol fire. The assault team then entered the barn and engaged the *yom-bhies* on the ground floor in a fire fight.

In the cellar, Tl'chiakp'no was immediately aware of the invasion, but Minx concentrated on fogging the Ch'iny'n's mind and preventing him from communicating with his *yom'bhies*. The *yom'bhies* had limited ability to respond on their own to a change in plans and so it was hoped that the ones in the cellar would be unable to act. The two *yom'bhies* who had come down with Sun and Minx stood still as if catatonic. But Rapier X sprang into action and started towards Minx.

Sun Koh was stunned. He thought that Minx's attack would have paralyzed all three of them, but Rapier X seemed to have some greater measure of autonomy. Sun had moved to get himself between Tl'chiakp'no/Pinto and the bomb. He now had to move quickly to save Minx's life.

He collided with the huge black man and they went tumbling among the boxes of ingots. The boxes were knocked around but remained closed. Rapier X rolled onto his feet and pulled out his dagger. There was a blur and Sun Koh by reflex twisted around. Still he felt the tip of the dagger graze his lead apron. The man had moved faster than any normal human should have. In fact the blur was not from a rapid movement but was the superimposition of possible quantum states for Rapier X's arm. The black man had used some psychicportation abilities.

Rapier X struck again with his dagger. It blurred again and struck in the middle of Sun Koh's chest. Sun meanwhile had controlled his breathing and focused his *prāna* for an "Iron Shirt" *ki-gung* defense. The dagger point penetrated the lead apron and his shirt but was stopped—barely—at his skin. He grabbed the black man's wrist with both hands and held on tight. As long as they were in direct contact, the man could not use quantum superposition for another attack.

Sun wrestled with Rapier X, keeping him off balance. The combatants tripped over the boxes and started to fall to the ground. As they fell, Sun squeezed hard and he could feel Rapier X's wrist bones grinding together. When they landed, the dagger was knocked away. Rapier X jabbed at Sun Koh's head with his left hand. Sun rolled under it and pushed the black man off of him. He grabbed one of the boxes and hit Rapier X in the temple with it. The *yom'bhi* staggered and Sun grabbed his neck and tried to use the paralyzing *tharouk* neck pinch. To his surprise, it did not work. He realized that the *prāna* flow in the *yom'bhi* was altered. Before he could adjust, Rapier X spun around and dove for his dagger.

Sun Koh had had enough. He came down hard on the black man's back and put him in a Full-Nelson grappling hold. He then concentrated his *prāna* against the base of his opponent's brain. With his fingers touching the hilt of the dagger, Rapier X convulsed for a few seconds and then lay still. Sun had induced a mild seizure that completely shut down the *yom'bhi's* brain. He would remain unconscious for several hours.

The sudden release of *prāna* momentarily disrupted Minx's concentration and Tl'chiakp'no took that fraction of a second to dematerialize. Minx lost sight of him and the link broke. Suddenly the other two *yom'bhies* were on him. There was no time for mind tricks. Minx exhibited exceptional strength throwing them off and engaging them in fisticuffs. He was no mean fighter himself!

While this was happening, Sun Koh dove for the Geiger counter, popped open a panel and pulled out his phased-ray *Strahlgewehr*. He set it to stun on a wide dispersion and fired in the general direction where Tl'chiakp'no had vanished. The plasma wave caught the Ch'iny'n and stunned him into re-materializing. Sun then turned to the two *yom'bhies* and blasted them as well. They staggered and he fired once more. They finally went down.

Then Tl'chiakp'no started to dematerialize once more, but Minx again fogged his mind and stopped him. By then, the Ch'iny'n was at the control panel of the atomic device. He kept trying to dematerialize, but it was useless. Minx kept that power restrained. Tl'chiakp'no used all of his psychic power to resist Minx and retaliated as best he could with a counter assault on Sun Koh. This gave him enough time to get his finger on the firing button.

Sun Koh linked with Minx and together they fought back against the psychic assault. Sun realized that Tl'chiakp'no was going to detonate the weapon. He was able to slow the flow of time for him and Minx. In an instant he flashed a message to Minx and together they lifted the suppression of the Ch'iny'n's dematerializing power just as his finger hit the button. By an act of will, Sun and Minx extended the dematerialization to encompass the bomb as well. Both Tl'chiakp'no and the device vanished from sight.

There was a quivering effect like ripples distorting a reflection on a pond's surface. Even the assault team staggered slightly on the floor above. The effect was only noticeable for about one hundred yards from the barn. The *yom'bhies* who had still been fighting staggered and the assault team finished them off. Of the original twelve, only the three in the cellar were still alive.

Sun Koh sat on the ground with his head in his hands. The battle was over.

•••

Later that night, a nondescript man (Schreck) struck up a conversation with the guard in the hotel lobby. He offered the guard a cigarette laced with opium. The policeman promptly fell asleep.

Schreck then approached the desk clerk. They were alone with the sleeping policeman. Schreck asked for a key and gave a false name. When the clerk bent down to check the register, Schreck tapped him nonchalantly with a sap and knocked him cold. He took the man's keys and locked the lobby doors. He then took out a handheld radio and said into it, "Time to go."

Above the hotel, *Schimäre* hovered quietly and several armed men climbed down a rope ladder to the roof. The men were led by the Captain. They went down the stairway. Meanwhile, Schreck took the elevator to the 10th floor. He went down the hall towards the suite where the police guard stood. The guard was groggy. Schreck quickly put the man in a hammerlock and held him until he lost consciousness. Quietly, he pulled the limp guard down the hall.

The Captain and his hit team came to the unguarded door of the suite and planted an explosive charge in front of it. The charge went off with a loud bang. The Captain tossed in three combination concussion/flash grenades which went off in rapid succession. The police guards were taken by surprise and were momentarily confused. This was followed by a tear gas grenade. The hit team in light armor and gas masks overpowered the cops and restrained them with their own handcuffs.

Fawkes and Brightman were in the sitting room waiting for the alleged British agents to return. They were also overpowered and restrained securely with five-point shackles linking their neck, wrists, and ankles together. The men had to hunch over and were prevented from running by the chains on their legs.

The Captain addressed them, "I hereby arrest you for crimes against humanity in the name of decent people everywhere." They were lead to the elevator and taken to the top floor. From there, they were dragged up to the roof and taken aboard *Schimäre* along with the hit team, the Captain, and Schreck. The craft floated into the sky and then with a scintillating flash, it disappeared from sight.

•••

Two days later, one of the *yom'bhies* was taken to Asquith Caverns and sent down into the Earth with a message written in the script of Ch'iny'n.

By then, the farmhouse and barn had been emptied of all remaining Ch'iny'n materials and burned to the ground using the same accelerant they had used on the other house.

One week later, at high noon, a delegation of Ch'iny'n warriors and deformed pseudo human giants appeared in the caverns at the place where Tl'chiakp'no used to drive his vehicles full of alcohol, drugs, and human slaves for transfer into the underground world.

One of the Ch'iny'ns identified himself as the officer in charge. Sun Koh offered him an empty machine pistol with an open breach as a sign of his peaceful intentions. They conversed telepathically. Sun had insisted that this meeting take place during the daytime when the Ch'iny'n psychic powers were at their lowest ebb to prevent them from double-crossing him.

The officer explained that the detonation of the atomic device in its ethereal state had wreaked havoc on dematerialized people and certain technological devices in Ch'iny'n. With no substantial barrier to prevent it, the ethereal energy pulse from the explosion had penetrated through the Earth with impunity. As a result, they were now fighting off an incursion by monsters from the deeper darker realms.

Sun Koh explained that Tl'chiakp'no had resisted capture and deliberately detonated the device while dematerialized. He did not apologize for what happened but expressed regret that lives were lost. The annoyed officer was upset that Tl'chiakp'no was not available to be punished. Sun Koh assured him that three of Tl'chiakp'no's accomplices —Randy, Fawkes, and Brightman—were being turned over to Ch'iny'n for judgment and punishment along with one of their *yom-bhies*. Except for the two Uranium 233 ingots used in the detonated bomb, all the other materials were being returned intact. The officer accepted this and seemed very excited at the prospect of having three victims to blame for the devastation of his world. He assured Sun Koh that they would suffer for their crime. The materials and the bound men were removed from the van and carried away by the giant pseudo-humans.

It was clear to Sun Koh that the officer had been instructed to either kill or capture any surface dwellers that had been involved in this affair, and so he laid it on thick about the mutual non-aggression treaties made between Ch'iny'n and Atlantis. That and the fact that Sun Koh's people were well armed and strategically placed (including Minx at the full height of his mental powers) persuaded the officer that discretion was the better part of valor. He returned the pistol to Sun Koh, made a kind of salute and backed away before striding off into the depths of the cavern.

Outside the cavern, Sturmvögel voiced his disappointment.

"I still do not see why we had to give that all back to them. Germany could have used such powerful weapons."

Sun Koh shook his head, "We could not risk it, Sturm. The Ch'iny'n would have come after that material and they have far more terrible weapons. It is best to placate them and keep them in their own world. Besides, atomic weapons are far too powerful and dangerous. They are almost as deadly to the user as to the recipient. Explode an atomic bomb in France and within days the residual radiation will be killing German schoolchildren. We are lucky that Minx and I got the bomb dematerialized before it went off. Any remaining radioactive debris from the explosion will have sunk deep into the Earth by now and poses no threat to the surface."

The Captain spoke up, "Herr Koh, do you think you can really rehabilitate that big Negro in your German facility?"

"We can try. He suffered some brain damage from Tl'chaikp'no's fiddling with his brain, but not as much as the other Yom'bhies. He had amazing abilities taught him by his master that Minx and I want to study. Meanwhile we may find him useful."

Shani had been somewhat withdrawn and reflective for the last week. Even when she and Sun made love, she seemed to be holding back. Sun Koh was aware of what she had done to those rapists. He found it both laudable and disturbing. Of all the people she had killed, these had been the most horrific executions. The two of them would have to work it through.

Schreck sat down next to Alaska-Jim. "So you are coming home with us to Germany?"

Jim nodded. "I am taking an extended leave of absence from the RCMP. I reckon it's time for me to look up my family and see what's happened to them over the last one hundred and sixty years. Maybe it is time for me to retire and move on."

Schreck chuckled sympathetically. "I miss my Gretchen. We still have several cases pending and I have been gone far too long." He shuddered, "Besides, I don't feel safe here in Canada. I long for the comfortable security of the Third Reich."

THE END

The Triumph of the Will

The hospital orderly pressed the alarm button in the security wing. Immediately, all security doors were locked down and armed guards surrounded the building covering all exits. It was in the evening of 3 August 1934. The Gutrune Neurosurgical Hospital was on the grounds of the Munich estate of Prince Sun Koh, international adventurer and Heir Apparent to the Ocean Throne of Atlantis. The hospital had been named after the daughter of Gibich from the Ring Cycle whose potion had caused Siegfried to forget his true love, Brünnhilde. It was an experimental neurosurgical facility where severe brain injury patients were brought and treated. It also had other 'special' patients selected by Sun Koh, the facility's senior physician, for experimental treatments for a variety of neurological and psychiatric diseases including criminal tendencies. It was those patients who occupied the security wing.

This was not the first time that a security lockdown was activated. Over the last few weeks this had happened several times. It was always because of the same patient: Mordechai Absalom Jonathan. He was a six-foot-five-inch Black American cowboy who was the grandson of former slaves. He had been captured in Canada and brought to Gutrune Hospital for study. Wild West stories were very popular in the German pulp magazines in the 1920s and 1930s. Very few Germans knew that around one quarter of the men who had worked cattle drives in the Old West were Blacks, many of whom were former slaves. Mordechai's father, Clarence, taught at Tuskegee Institute but had been a Buffalo Soldier in his youth. This was the nickname that the Plains Indians used to give black cavalrymen because their kinky hair reminded the Indians of the curly mane of the bison.

Mordechai was the "black sheep" of the family. Legend had it that he was descended from an ancestor who was part of an educational experiment during the Revolutionary War and who had later escaped from slavery to become a world renowned soldier-of-fortune. Because of the turmoil in black family life during the dark days of slavery, this was impossible to prove. But the family he knew had all shown exceptional intellectual skills.

Mordechai's grandfather, Clarion, while he was slave at the Johnson Plantation in Virginia, had taught himself to read and became an accomplished blacksmith, artisan, and inventor. He eventually led a slave revolt during the Civil War and had escaped with his family to the North. He volunteered for the Union Army and served in the Cavalry towards the end of the War. Eventually he settled in Baltimore and owned an iron foundry. His son Clarence was educated at the Baltimore Normal School which had been founded in 1865 to teach colored students and train black teachers. Clarence had an adventuresome streak and so he went out west serving in the US Cavalry during the Indian Wars. Clarence had become interested in Indian culture and western folklore. He started up correspondence with noted experts in the field who at first did not know he was black. They recognized his erudition and encouraged him to publish papers. He eventually became a guide for visiting scientists including paleontologists looking for dinosaur fossils. They recognized his intelligence and assisted him in getting a job teaching at Tuskegee Institute. He married the daughter of another instructor and they had several children of whom Mordechai was the oldest.

Mordechai's younger brother, Steven Daniel Jonathan, had been a child prodigy. He had been educated at Tuskegee and received his bachelor's degree at an early age. In 1934, he was doing graduate work at Harvard in education. Steven was both a scholar and a seasoned athlete. While at Tuskegee he participated in numerous track events. When he was at Harvard, they tapped him for the Decathlon team which was a major breakthrough for a black athlete. At that time the Decathlon was considered an event for older, more seasoned athletes who had already made their accomplishments in single events. Steven hoped to complete his doctorate and then train full time as a decathlete for the 1940 Olympics that were to be held in Tokyo.

Mordechai had been bright but always got himself into trouble. He was a rough and tumble child who often got into fights. His father had enrolled him in both boxing and fencing at school to work off some of that aggression. He boxed in the heavyweight class and remained undefeated. But he preferred fencing and Mordechai became accomplished with the rapier. Combining his boxing and fencing skills, he was fascinated with knives and knife-fighting. It also got him into trouble more than once. His father worked hard to keep it quiet. But Mordechai couldn't stay in school. It was just not for him.

He ran away to New York and became a professional boxer using the alias "Jack Holligan." Mordechai was undefeated in his division, but then his supposed manager put pressure on him to "take a dive." He refused. Suddenly, fighting venues started to disappear and Mordechai realized he had been set up as the fall guy in a crooked boxing scam. He still refused to give in. At that point his life was threatened and "Jack Holligan" disappeared.

When the United States entered the Great War, Mordechai used his real name and volunteered to join the Army like almost 370,000 other black Americans. Six infantry divisions were composed of black soldiers, but fewer than ten percent of these men saw combat. They were mostly relegated to support roles. Mordechai Jonathan lucked out. He became attached to the 93rd Infantry Division before he was shipped to France.

White American soldiers treated the black troops badly. In some places, the white troops wantonly opened fire on unarmed black American soldiers killing and wounding many of them. To prevent further incidents, black units were kept separate from white units. The 93rd Division was integrated into the French 4th Army and fought with distinction on the front lines.

Unlike the American military, the French welcomed the black troops with open arms. These troops fought so well that whole units were decorated by the French and 171 black Americans were awarded the *Croix de Guerre,* France's highest military honor.

Many black soldiers received field promotions to officer ranks during the conflict. The black troops discovered that the racist prejudices that hampered them in America did not exist in France. They were treated as equals by French men—and women—especially in Paris. Captain Mordechai Jonathan proudly wearing his *Croix de Guerre* and several other decorations had been the toast of Paris after the Armistice. Then he returned to the United States and became a second-class citizen again.

He could find no decent work despite his war record and he needed to avoid the mobsters who still held a grudge against "Jack Holligan." In his frustration, he went out west to work as a cowboy on cattle drives. This was the one place in America where blacks suffered little discrimination and were paid and treated as equals by whites.

Mordechai Jonathan was a rough character known for drinking and brawling. In a drunken knife fight, he received a scar that went from his left cheek across his nose to his right forehead. There had been accusations of him being involved in robberies. There had also been several men killed in fights in which cause of death had been a single deep puncture to vital organs. Mordechai was a suspect in these deaths. He was known to carry a stiletto and have a bad temper. He became a wanted man and had to leave the United States, fleeing to Canada.

He dropped the surname "Jonathan" and replaced it with "X." An 'X' had been branded on his grandfather's upper arm when he was a slave as an identification of his servitude. Mordechai decided not to carry a slave-owner's name into posterity and used the surname "X" to protest the loss of his true African Heritage and the abuse his grandfather had suffered. (His decision became legendary and it inspired a young member of the Nation of Islam to do the same thing twenty years later.) So he changed his name to Rapier X. His friends called him Rap.

In Saskatoon, Rap had been hired by one Fletcher Pinto to act as muscle for his smuggling operation. Pinto had actually been Tl'chaikp'no, a powerful psychic from the underground civilization of Ch'iny'n who had tried to telepathically "pith" Rapier and turn him into a human automaton known as a *yom'bhi*. Such pitiful creatures were literally walking dead men with no personality and no volition who obeyed their master's orders implicitly.

But Rapier X was different. He retained some of his autonomy and in fact manifested natural psychophysical skills which Pinto enhanced with special training. These skills had intrigued Sun Koh and so he had brought the black man back with him to Germany to study.

Since he had arrived, Rapier had been a problem. He was very adept at picking locks and in escaping from confinement. He was six-foot-four, very strong, and very fast. He spoke very little at first and only in English. He seemed quite withdrawn, but over several weeks his awareness improved and he began talking to the staff in halting American-accented German. He did not carry on long conversations but responded to simple questions. It seemed that his brain was repairing the damage done by Pinto and that he was recovering his memories. He also began trying to break out almost routinely.

Today he had overpowered an orderly during the evening meal and gotten out of his cell. Luckily, Sun Koh had installed television monitors in that hall way and the staff was able to lock the facility down. Even so, it would take two hours, five injured orderlies, and several hundred Deutsche Marks worth of damage before they were able to subdue and sedate him.

At that time, Sun Koh was in Berlin for an appointment with top government officials on providing security for the National Socialist Party rally in Nuremburg that September. He was in his office complex on *Friedrichstraße* when he received a phone call about Rapier's latest escape attempt. With him was private detective Rolf "Schreck" Karsten, one of his associates. Sun Koh was a bronzed giant of a man standing two meters high. He was blond with classical Aryan features and lapis-lazuli blue eyes. He moved lightly on his feet for a man of his size and was so well proportioned that he did not appear as large as he was until you got close to him. His voice had a deep resonance and his diction was perfect. He instructed the charge nurse over the phone to keep Rapier X sedated until he returned the next day.

Sun Koh hung up and shook his head. He told Schreck about the problems they were having with Rapier X.

"It is almost unbelievable. The mind-wipe technique of the Ch'iny'ns is usually quite thorough and irreversible. Even their own regeneration methods can't bring back the mind of a *yom'bhi*. Yet Rapier is recovering spontaneously, almost by an act of will. And even without full cognitive function he is fighting to get free!"

Schreck spoke, "Herr Koh, might I make a suggestion?"

Sun Koh nodded. "Certainly."

"In my career I have known many criminals who could not stand being incarcerated. Prison drove them crazy. These men would do anything to keep from going back. Some would kill to cover up a misdemeanor so that they could avoid further imprisonment. Many of them would rather die than go back.

"Maybe this Mordechai Jonathan is like that. You have said that he has great powers which will increase as his mind heals. He also does not seem to want to stay locked up. If you keep trying to restrain him, he might seriously injure or kill someone. He might even decide to kill himself.

"When I was boy, I had a dog at our farm. My mother insisted on chaining him to the house so that he would not run away. When she did this he pulled the chain out to its full length and constantly strained against it. One day, the chain came loose and he started running off. I thought he was running away, but he stopped after going a few yards and came back. He stayed in our yard. He did not want to escape. He just did not want to be chained."

Sun Koh reviewed his extensive knowledge on the psychology of prisoners. He had in his mind a stored version the Akashic Record, the sum total of human knowledge. It was a complex set of memories without a real index and with many hidden secrets that were hard to tease out. But he could see that Schreck had a point. He returned to Munich in his private plane that night.

The next day, Rapier X woke up just before noon. He was no longer in a cell, but in a large comfortable bed in a guest room in *Schloß Valhalla*, Sun Koh's castle elsewhere on the grounds. He did not know where he was. He searched the room and found clothing that would fit him. He washed in the adjoining private bath and dressed. He went out of the room and started to search the castle. He met the butler and asked him in halting German for the way out. The butler answered him in halting English and directed him to the main gate. Rapier walked across the drawbridge and onto the road leading away from the castle. No one stopped him. He walked down the road into the forest until he was just out of sight of the castle. He stopped and looked around. Then he walked back to the castle, found the butler, and asked if there was anything to eat.

Rapier X settled in as the guest of Sun Koh.

•••

Rapier X had not fully recovered his faculties. At first, he was functioning at the level of a ten-year-old child but he improved every day. Sun Koh spent time with him at least twice each day talking to him and helping to improve his German. Rapier was a good student. After a week, Sun took his guest to the gym and they exercised together. Sun exercised for at least one hour per day and Rapier tried to imitate him, but he could never quite match the Atlantean's performance. They boxed and wrestled several times and Sun Koh's superior strength and anatomical knowledge gave him a distinct advantage. But Rap was a formidable opponent. He and Sun Koh's bodyguard Lt. Rudolf "Sturmvögel" Rauhaar even sparred a couple of times. The seven-foot German soldier—an expert in hand-to-hand combat—had been hard pressed to keep up with him.

During one particularly rigorous sparring session with Sun Koh, Rapier stopped boxing and looked at the prince in a strange way. He had been having memory flashbacks more frequently as his mind healed. Sun stood by and watched the look of recognition in Rapier's face.

The black man reached out and grabbed Sun's elbows and said to him, "*Danke schön*. Thank you so much for rescuing me."

Sun Koh smiled and nodded. "*Bitte,*" he replied.

Then they went back to sparring.

One day, Sun Koh and Sturm practiced fencing with rapiers in the gym.

Sturmvögel was seven feet tall and had a long reach. Sun Koh was only slightly shorter but much faster. Rapier observed them for a while and then asked if he could try. Sun Koh agreed and he and Rapier squared off. Almost immediately, Rapier began showing expertise that could only have come from prior experience. He also started moving in a strange "blurry" way that was far faster than any normal human could. Sun Koh was hard pressed to keep up with him, but he still won each of the first three rounds. Rapier X got frustrated and in the next round he came on so rapidly that the eye could not follow him. He tagged Sun Koh immediately. The Atlantean prince was surprised and with an effort won the next tag after several minutes of prolonged sparring. The two squared off for the third and final point and went at it. Forty minutes later they were still dueling fiercely.

At that point, they were interrupted by an urgent phone call from Berlin. Sun Koh, sweating and breathing deeply excused himself to take the call. Rapier looked around to see if Sturmvögel wanted to fence, but the bodyguard was hurriedly accompanying his prince.

"*Scheiße,*" the tall soldier said, "He is quite a swordsman." Sturm scratched the old *renommierschmiß* dueling scar on his own cheek.

"Yes," said Sun Koh, "He has mastered techniques of psychoportation and psychometabolism to a degree that I have rarely seen. He was taught well by Tl'chiakp'no, but some of his capabilities seem to be innate. In Atlantis long ago, we were never able to subdue the Africans. They were incredible warriors even with primitive weapons. The best we could do was to plant a few colonies, mostly on the coastline. The one large inland colony we founded was over a mineral deposit rich in gold. The Africans had no use for the stuff except as ornaments and as long as we did not disturb them, they left us alone. Lots of strange things happened in Africa that to this day are not very clear to me. Hidden cities, lost cultures, weird animals: there were more of them in Africa than anywhere else on the Earth!"

"Are you learning anything from him, Prince Koh?"

"Indeed. His mind is still that of an adolescent but his adult memories are starting to come back. He has discussed some of the training that Tl'chiakp'no gave him. I am trying to duplicate some of this. Sadly, he was never able to master the dematerialization trick. But those quantum-jump arm jabs and the 'blurry' superimposition movements are very interesting. I will need to work on them."

The phone call was from Heinrich Himmler who had become the head of all the police agencies in the Third Reich. A new security matter had arisen with regard to the Nuremberg *Sechste Reichsparteitag* planned for next month. There would be a briefing in Berlin tomorrow and Sun Koh was instructed to attend. Sun Koh held the rank of a full colonel in the Gestapo and in the 1st *Schutzstaffel* Division, *Leibstandarte SS Adolf Hitler.*

The next morning was August 1st. The meeting was held in a small conference room at Gestapo Headquarters on *Niederkirchnerstraße* in the old School of Applied Arts. Present at the meeting were Adolf Hitler, Himmler, Sun Koh, Reinhard Heydrich the chief of the Main Office of Reich Security, Dr. Goebbels the minister of propaganda, a tall well spoken civilian academic wearing tortoise shell glasses, and various other high party officials.

The academic was a brilliant neurologist and psychologist from Heidelberg who was using the alias of "Dr. Johan Gesät" to conceal his true identity. He had been working with the NSDAP officials over the last month to prepare a field test at the Nuremberg Rallies of a new conditioning technique designed to control large masses of people. The heart of the project was a complex machine that he had designed to project a state of euphoria and receptivity into the crowds. He alleged that his device could actually induce emotional surges of hatred, anxiety, and fear. He claimed that it could even inculcate such fully-formed ideas as patriotism, party loyalty, and conformity to specific party principles but only in conjunction with other conditioning stimuli.

Dr. Gesät had been working on this device for many years. He was well traveled and had become acquainted with several oriental scholars and wise men that he credited with inspiring his system of conditioning. Apparently, the Chinese Emperors for many centuries had used sophisticated conditioning techniques that included some psychic influences to keep control on the masses in their empire. Some of these methods could be traced back to the legendary Emperor Ashoka who had ruled over most of India in the 3rd Century BC. Ashoka allegedly had started a secret society of learned men to preserve knowledge in all fields, including Psychology. Gesät had been able to obtain information from this society and he applied it in conjunction with modern western scientific principles.

Dr. Gesät had perfected an electronic device that he had used on small groups to influence behavior in the laboratory and at certain select venues. But this would be the first field test of the device on a large scale. If it worked at the 6th Party Congress, such devices could be used throughout the country to control the German populace.

But there were even larger plans. He hoped to use the device to influence the people of other nations to support German National Socialism and even to stir up similar political movements in those nations. He also wanted to use it to sow despair among the enemies of the Reich, but so far the experiments in that regard had been less than successful. The device could spread fear very well, but was less capable of spreading apathy and lassitude. Subjects who were aware that they were being influenced could resist by an act of will. For this reason, it was most important to keep the device utterly secret. At that point, less than two dozen people in the entire Reich knew about Dr. Gesät and his *Projekt Lotosesser* (Lotus Eater). Most of them were in the room.

At a signal from Himmler, Dr. Sown stepped to the podium and signaled for the first slide. It was security warning that the following images were from *Projekt Lotosesser* and classified as Top Secret, Eyes Only. The contents of this briefing were not to be copied, drawn, or otherwise divulged or discussed with anyone not in the briefing. The next slide showed an unusual device that looked like a wide-mouthed, squared-off megaphone attached to large complex electronic device.

"This is the Lethe device. We have two of these at the Nuremberg stadium and another two in trucks that will be driven around the city. They appear to be loudspeakers but that trumpet is actually a wave guide that concentrates and directs the Lethe-effect. The devices are designed to be portable so that they can be removed and taken elsewhere in the country for use. The operators of the device have been told that it is a hygienic device used to prevent disease in crowds. They have also been sworn to secrecy about its use. We have guaranteed their compliance with this cover by using the Lethe device on them.

"These devices are difficult to make, extremely delicate, and use large amounts of power. We have people working on miniaturizing the various components but because of the sensitive nature of the project this is being done by separate laboratories. Each lab deals with only one component and none of them know exactly to what kind of device their component belongs. Most of them think that the complete device is a radar system. Herr Dr. Koh has been instrumental in integrating and assembling the various components into the final design. It is hoped that by next year, we will have a device that will be no bigger than a large cabinet radio which will be able to blanket an area the size of a small city. Using such a device, we should be able to successfully eliminate from 90 to 95 percent of dissident activity."

Sun Koh said nothing, but he thought that those figures were far too high. Similar devices in Atlantis, which was a far more technologically advanced civilization, had been barely able to control 75 percent of the population, and even less if the masses were under stress or not favorably disposed to government policies. He also knew that too strong a projection beam or the use of too many projectors could lead to psychological confusion and unpredictable mob behavior. The Lethe-effect was at its best when it was subtle and just one stimulus among many others which were mutually reinforcing.

With subsequent slides, Johan Gesät discussed several technical matters with regard to the planned use of the Lethe devices at Nuremberg and the various other conditioning cues built into the Rally *programm* which were designed to bring about the desired results of bringing the nation into conformity with the National Socialist agendas and of influencing foreign dignitaries to support the NSDAP government..

Then Gesät put up a slide of a triangular headed man with a full head of hair styled in a marcel wave and a thick mustache.

"This is the electrical engineer and inventor Nikola Tesla. He is an ethnic Serbian who was born in the Austro-Hungarian Empire and who immigrated to America and currently lives in New York City. He is one of the greatest inventive geniuses in the world and has many electrical patents to his name. He is the inventor of alternating electrical current. The standard unit of magnetic flux density—the 'tesla'—was named in his honor in 1906. The list of his achievements is impressive.

"Mr. Tesla has been in deep negotiations with the Americans, the British, and the Russians to develop an energy projecting weapon. This has been confirmed by agents in New York and London. He was quoted in a *New York Times* article published on July 11th of this year as claiming to have created an electrical projection ray that would work just as efficiently in air as it does in a vacuum. Recent correspondence between Tesla and political leaders in Eastern Europe have been intercepted by our agents. They confirm his talks with the Russians and the British and indicate that that he has already achieved a working prototype of his ray. They further confirm that he is planning a public demonstration of his device for potential buyers. Such a ray he claims can destroy large numbers of aircraft or ships or buildings even at a great distance from the weapon itself. Rumors have been floating around among counter-revolutionary circles that there will be a major disruption of the Nuremberg Rally involving a "new technology" and Tesla's name has been mentioned in connection with this.

"Tesla is a political opponent of National Socialism and of our Chetnik Serbian allies. We suspect that he will attempt to use his projection ray device at Nuremberg to disrupt the 6th Party Rally and possibly assassinate the Fuehrer. It is my belief that his ray is not quite as deadly as he portends but I think it may be powerful enough to disrupt electrical power and interfere in many ways with the Rally. He could induce waves of heat into the crowds or cause some other deleterious medical effect on them. His ray seems to work on principles very similar to those in the Lethe device. This means that he too may be trying to influence the emotions of the crowd. The presence of such a ray therefore might interfere with the Lethe devices and defeat our plans. I think it is also unlikely that his ray will work from a long distance. It will have a range similar to the Lethe device and so it will have to be within Nuremberg itself.

"If Tesla succeeds in disrupting the Nuremberg Rally, he will likely receive large amounts of funding from the United States and Britain. He may also get some support from the Judeo-Bolsheviks in Moscow. Meanwhile, he will almost surely disrupt our plan to exercise large scale control over the German people and foreign governments through the use of the Lethe device at this rally. There will be important people there from all over the Reich. We are counting on the Lethe effect to help us eliminate the last remnants of political opposition and to begin preparing our people for the long struggle ahead."

Gesät sat down. Hitler was visibly agitated and burst into a long tirade. He charged the security people with gross incompetence and told them that they were being held personally responsible for preserving security at the Rally and for foiling this new Jewish plot. He stated flatly that the Rally could not be canceled and that he was willing to sacrifice his own safety and that of every man in that room so that the Lethe project would succeed. After ranting for over forty minutes he stormed out, ignoring the cries of "Heil Hitler" from the other men in the room.

Himmler spoke quietly but definitively. "The Fuehrer has given us our instructions. We will not fail him! Herr Koh, what are your thoughts on this matter? What solution do you propose to this problem?"

Sun Koh stood and spoke carefully. "Tesla is a formidable electronics designer. He is seventy-five years old: too old to come to Germany. He will send an agent to do his dirty work. He once created a relatively small device that stored millions of volts of electricity. He had charged it using only commercial power sources. With such an accumulator, he could build up portable power reserves for a very powerful device making it independent of outside sources of energy. I think it is unlikely that he will try to influence the crowds emotionally. Tesla is not a neuroscientist and does not have the expertise to perfect such a device. But his device could interfere with the Lethe-effect and his agent might discover our own machine's operation and choose to interfere with it. I think it is more likely that he will target the Party leadership at a critical point in the ceremonies and strike boldly and publically to embarrass us. I think it is also likely that his machine will self destruct after it has been used so that the design will not fall into our hands. He would not be so foolish as to try and have his agent escape with a functioning device after we had been alerted to its existence. The agent himself, though, will likely try to escape.

"In any case, we must locate the Tesla device *before* it is used and attempt to capture its operator if possible. Likely, the operator will have to test the device to make sure it is functioning before the Rally. That will be the time when we will be most able to detect it.

"We should immediately set up electronic detectors in Nuremberg—at least three for triangulation—and remain vigilant. We need to check the identity of all foreign nationals who have entered the Reich in the last year to see if any of them are known Tesla associates. Meanwhile, we need to step up security around the main events in the Rally and do a continuous round-robin sweep through the nearby buildings looking for anything suspicious."

There was further discussion and an assignment of particular responsibilities to various parties before the meeting broke up. Sun Koh spoke briefly with Dr. Gesät about the final set up for the Lethe devices before they both left.

•••

As he walked to his staff car, Sun Koh's face remained impassive but he was seething. A major security threat was uncovered, confirmed by multiple independent sources. Instead of taking control of the situation, the "Leader" throws a temper tantrum, provides no constructive input to the situation, and passes the buck to his subordinates with threats of personal reprisals if they do not solve the problem for him. And then that backstabbing coward Himmler turns to Sun Koh and passes the responsibility to him! What kind of leadership is this? "Delegate blame; accept credit."

Sun Koh realized that this matter had been dropped in his lap and that if anything went wrong, he would be blamed. This was not leadership. It was rule by intimidation. This also was likely Himmler's revenge for Sun Koh's refusal to get involved in Gestapo cases involving politics or racial

Sun Koh spoke briefly with Dr. Gesät about the final set up...

issues. Sun's interest was more in Kripo cases and those involving operational security. Sun Koh understood the necessity of strong social controls to combat the anarchy that had reigned under Weimar and prevent the communists from gaining a foothold here.

Sun Koh continued to ruminate. Look at what that psychopath Stalin was doing in Russia! Their economy was on the way to inevitable self-destruction. It might happen in ten years or fifty years but it was inevitable. Russia had been the major nation hardest hit by the Depression and there was no chance of its recovery without outside help. The horrible genocide committed in the Ukraine! Sun estimated that eight to ten million people had been systematically starved to death by Stalin's fiat. This could not be allowed to continue. With the proper timing, a solid war plan, and a little luck, Germany could eliminate the Bolshevik threat and open the vast wilderness of the Soviet Union for *lebensraum*. The NSDAP would show those Bolshies how to manage an economy!

Sturmvögel was behind the wheel of the staff car. He took Sun Koh to the *Friedrichstraße* office building that was his headquarters in Berlin. Sun did not speak during the trip. When they arrived, he went straight into the elevator that led to his top floor offices. Frau Gertrude Reinhardt née Shumann, his receptionist and office manager, was a middle-aged *gnädiger frau* who had been a government secretary for twenty years. She ran a tight ship and could be trusted to hold down the fort in a crisis. She was the daughter of an Admiral, the widow of a battleship Captain and the mother of four sons, each of whom was in a different branch of the military: *Abwehr, Reichsmarine, Reichswehr*, and *Luftwaffe*. She also had two daughters who had married military officers. Gertrude had the highest possible security clearance for a civilian civil servant. She also had no sense of humor and a frown that could turn a basilisk to stone. She greeted Herr Koh and informed him that there were several messages waiting for him at his desk and no further appointments for today.

Sun thanked her and went into his office. It had a large teakwood desk intricately carved with the likenesses of various animals. Sun looked through his messages and saw that there was nothing urgent, so he called Schreck's office. Schreck's secretary Gretchen Schulmann answered. She said that Rolf was out "on a case" and in a seductive voice asked if she could be of some assistance. Gretchen was a petite, well-formed blonde with an upturned nose, a sprinkle of freckles on her cheeks, and bedroom-blue eyes. She was not a classic beauty but was very pretty in a glitzy way. She wore her hair short but full bodied so that it covered her head like a large helmet. She wore tasteful jewelry that was carefully matched to her outfits. Gretchen dressed well everyday and paid almost obsessive detail to every part of her body and clothing. She was always manicured and pedicured with pink nail polish. Her clothes fit her just snuggly enough to show off her figure without being risqué. She wore dark hose with a seam down the back and preferred open toed shoes with a short sturdy heel and cut long enough to show some toe 'cleavage.' Her makeup was lightly applied and always bright. She checked and refreshed it frequently. She was always smiling. Gretchen was very conscious of how she moved and how she affected men. Her voice had a musical quality and her laugh was like a tinkling bell.

Gretchen was also a terrific typist (120 words a minute), took short hand, spoke seven languages (German, English, French, Dutch, Italian, Spanish, Portuguese), and was the best documentary research analyst in Germany. She could get her hands on any information that was to be had in Berlin or anywhere else in the country. She was the mistress of libraries, government files, military records, bank records, and even medical records. The men in the security sections of the government were always happy to assist Gretchen in her research work. She was also familiar with information sources in London, Paris, Madrid, Rome, Lisbon, Brussels, Bern, and Amsterdam.

Quite frankly, Sun Koh found her very attractive and competent. In his earlier days in Atlantis 11,000 years ago he might have been tempted to bed her. But she was the long-time mistress of Schreck Karsten and Ashanti Garuda, the Daughter of Kali, was already Sun Koh's concubine. In the modern world of 1934, it was not seemly of a gentleman to be so licentious. Besides, he really had deep feelings for Shani and he would not want to do anything to undermine their relationship. Shani was no prude, nor was she the jealous type. In fact, their affair was an odd mixture of affection and convenience. But Sun Koh with his Akashic knowledge now knew how much sex truly affected a woman, and he cared about Shani's feelings. He was a very different man in the 20th Century than he had been in his own time.

Sun Koh made a decision. He did not trust the bureaucrats to do a thorough check on foreign passports in such a short time. But Gretchen always came through without fail. She had a knack. Because of security issues she could not be told about *Projekt Lotosesser*, but she could be asked to look for suspicious people from outside Germany who might be Tesla's agents and saboteurs. He instructed her to attach the scrambler to the phone, and then proceeded to give her a secure briefing. She gave him a musical laugh and said that she would do her very best.

Sun Koh then did an inventory of the pieces of advanced technology he had brought with him from the past. Most of these devices were running low on power and—except in a few cases—he had not been able to repower them. They had suffered damage during the solar storm that had destroyed his time vessel. He did not have access to the necessary technology to repair them. In a few decades, he should be able to fix them but not now.

One of the devices he could not repower was his armored flight suit. That was too bad because the sensors in it could have been helpful in this case. His holographic plasma blade had also failed. He had been able to recharge the *Strahlgewehr* hand-held ray projector, but it was not working at peak efficiency and he had no replacement parts for it. Basically, he had nothing that would be helpful to him in this situation. He would need to depend on what he could cobble together using available materials.

At that point Ludwig Minx, the former stage magician and now personal thaumaturge to Prince Koh, was announced by Gertrude and ushered into the office. He wore a three-piece suit with a carnation, suede gloves, a fashionable men's hat with a narrow brim and a feather, and a prominent watch fob with an occult talisman on it. He carried a walking stick with a large polished steel knob. He was dressed immaculately at all times. On his ring finger was a gold ring with an iridescent opal stone that reflected a rainbow of colors. He had dark eyes and a goatee that emphasize the sharpness of his chin. Minx was a trained Agarthan adept whose power had been enhanced by the gift of the opal ring from his liege, Sun Koh. He was Sun's most trusted aide after Shani, but even he did not know about the Lethe devices. None of Koh's aides knew of them.

"There is something troubling you, my prince. How may I assist you?" He had the mellifluous voice of the consummate performer. With a flourish the walking stick vanished, and he took off his gloves seeming to make them vanish into thin air. He removed his hat and it too vanished.

Sun briefed him on the intelligence report about the Tesla weapon and its possible demonstration during the Nuremberg Rally. Minx nodded.

"My prince, I bring you some equally serious news. There have been rumblings of dissatisfaction in the occult community. The direction the country is going has many of the *Thule-Gesellschaft* members upset. Von Sebottendorff wrote that abominable book *Bevor Hitler kam* trying to disassociate himself from Hitler. It has now been banned and he has been 'encouraged' to return to Turkey. Xaux, the Agarthan representative, has gone back to Shambala, and the erstwhile Comte de Saint-Germain has not been seen since your duel in the English Gardens two years ago. Hess and Rosenberg have strongly politicized the Thule Society and its focus on esoteric knowledge has been redirected into radical racial and political theories. Herr Hitler has snubbed this community more than once and I do not think we can call on them for support."

Sun Koh sighed. He had thought the Ch'iny'n legends that claimed man had come down from another planet over five million years ago were far-fetched. But the Blavatsky woman who had so influenced Hess and Rosenberg had man originating hundreds of millions of years in the past! In Atlantis, it had been well known that modern humans had their origin within the last 100,000 years and that all known human civilizations could be dated to a migration out of Africa a mere 25,000 years before Atlantis' high point. There was talk of starting an official archaeology section in the SS and Sun Koh was worried that they would waste their time on these fantasies instead of recovering the real stories about Atlantis, Lemuria, Mu, and the First Age of Man.

Sun Koh said, "We have less than five days to uncover Tesla's plan before Hitler leaves for Nuremberg. Let's hope that Gretchen and the Security people can get us some leads. Meanwhile, we will need Jan Mayen and his technical expertise. I have been working on a machine to detect electronic devices—a counter-radar system—that will allow us to find and target enemy radar stations. The prototype is crude but it can be used to detect anomalous electrical activity and may help us find Tesla's weapon. We should also get hold of Alaska-Jim down in Hesse to assist us."

"What about Shani, my prince?"

Sun Koh became uneasy. "I am concerned for her safety in Nuremberg. The city will be teeming with 200,000 National Socialists of Nordic descent. Even though she is a true Aryan, they might find her a little too… dark. Besides, someone needs to keep an eye on Rapier X. He is experiencing a mild adolescent crush on Shani and she can keep him occupied until this matter is over. The last thing we need right now is for a knife-fighting Negro to be wandering around in Germany!"

Sun Koh sent a scrambled radio message to Jan Mayen asking him to go to *Schloß Valhalla* and use Sun Koh's tri-motor cargo plane to bring the anti-radar rig to Nuremberg. He gave strict instructions that Shani was to remain at the castle to mind Rapier X.

He then called Alaska-Jim Hoover on an open phone line and requested his help on an urgent matter in Nuremberg. Jim agreed to come right away by train.

Sun Koh had already booked a suite for himself at the *Hotel Deutscher Hof* near the train station which was where Hitler was staying during the rally. There would be plenty of room for his crew. Also, Sturmvögel's mother lived in an apartment in town and could accommodate some guests if need be. He decided to fly to Nuremberg that night and begin a serious canvas of the city.

•••

Sun Koh flew with Minx, Sturmvögel, and Schreck in his "flying wing" transport prototype *Todesfalke* which had five pusher engines, could accommodate eight people, and travel at over 350 knots. They would expect Jan Mayen with the equipment later that evening.

Sturmvögel was especially excited. He had grown up in Nuremberg and his widowed mother still lived there. This meant that he could visit with her while Sun Koh was in town.

The National Socialists considered Nuremberg to be the "most German of German cities" dating back to the old imperial days of the Second Reich. For this reason, Hitler had decided to start holding the annual NSDAP conferences in the town in 1933. Albert Speer had been given *carte blanche* to create a suitable place to hold the conferences. On a site on the southwest side of the city he began construction of the *Parteitagsgelände* complex. At the time of the 6th Party Rally and he had completed one part of the overall plan including *Zeppelinfield,* the Luitpold Arena, and a temporary enclosure where mass party meetings could be held indoors.

Helene "Leni" Riefenstahl was a German film actress who had directed, produced, and starred in a fantasy film *Das Blaue Licht* based on German fairy tale. Hitler had been enchanted with that film and Leni herself had been mesmerized by Hitler's oratory and his book *Mein Kampf.* The Fuehrer asked her to make a film of the 5th Party Rally in August 1933. It was called *Der Sieg des Glaubens* (The Victory of Faith) and was officially released on December 1, 1933. She was given very little time to prepare for the filming and a limited budget, but the results so impressed Hitler that he gave her an unlimited budget to make a true spectacle on the next Party Rally in 1934. She spent over seven months in preparation for the Rally and was instrumental in choreographing and scheduling Rally activities around her filming. She used over one-hundred-seventy people in her film crew including thirty-six cameramen. There was a strict schedule of filming both day and night from several angles on every day of the Rally.

They anticipated getting anywhere from fifty to seventy-five hours of film which was to be pared down to a feature film length. It was the most ambitious film schedule in history.

The opening sequence would show Hitler flying to Nuremberg and then driving through the streets to the *Hotel Deutscher Hof* while standing in an open car. Sun Koh reasoned that this was the most likely time that a directed energy weapon would be used against the Fuehrer. He would be passing by hundreds of buildings in the medieval town center, any one of which could house a sniper.

The entire crew—including Alaska-Jim in his trademark buckskins and coon skin hat—traced over the route that would be followed by Hitler. It was a nightmare from a security standpoint. Sun Koh resolved that they needed to change the route or at least pick some alternate route at random on that first day to foil any potential attack. When he suggested this to the SS Security officer in charge, the man turned white and said that this would be impossible. Leni would not permit it.

Sun Koh was flabbergasted and resolved to speak to the filmmaker himself. She was on location at the *Zeppelinfield* supervising the final placements of the cameras for the events there when Sun Koh found her. This was a large open arena dominated by Albert Speers' massive stone dais the *Zeppelintribune* which was overshadowed by a huge five story metal eagle supported by eight steel girders.

Leni Riefenstahl was an athletic former show dancer who had starred in several mountaineering films as an adventurous heroine. She had short dark hair, long legs and the lithe build of a track star. Sun knew that Dr. Goebbels, the minister of propaganda, had tried several times—unsuccessfully—to seduce her. When she first saw the tall bronzed blond Atlantean, Leni caught her breath. Sun could see her nipples coming erect through her blouse and he was assaulted with the scents typical of female sexual arousal. Sun Koh had a sense of smell rivaling that of a brown bear and it allowed him to detect fear, hatred, and other emotions in people that were otherwise obscure. He also had a very well developed vomeronasal organ in his nasal septum that could detect pheromones and other complex chemical signals. That and the look in her eyes let Sun Koh know that *his* sexual advances would not be rebuffed.

Sun Koh tried to keep things professional and spoke frankly to Leni about the need to alter Hitler's route to the Hotel. At that she came unglued and argued vehemently that she had heard this nonsense before from the SS *schläger*. The route was set, the camera angles chosen, and the matter was closed. She had spoken to Hitler himself and he backed her judgment fully. It would be the job of the security forces to make that route safe.

During this tirade, Sun Koh could tell that she had become even more aroused. The difficult part about vomeronasal sensation is that it goes almost directly to the thalamus in the brain and can initiate sexual arousal. He took a deep cleansing breath, made his apologies, and withdrew as quickly as he could. It was obvious that there was no way he could argue with her and he did not have time to deal with another amorous female.

Sun had been the target for sexual advances from many women since he arrived in Germany. He had even been approached by the wives of high party officials! In Atlantis, there had been courtly sexual intrigues but high-born women were never so overt towards men of the same class. They always had specially prepared eunuchs to service them if need be. Courtly love "affairs" might go on for years without there ever being any physical consummation. But most such women were either the wife or daughter of some important figure and it was dangerous to trifle with them and endanger the purity of their offspring's paternity. There were always concubines, courtesans, and low-born women available and Sun Koh had taken his pleasure there in the deep past. But he had become very leery of any sexual entanglements in this new world and he had remained faithful to Shani since he had taken her as a concubine.

In any case, the route to the hotel could not be altered. They would need to maintain extremely tight security and hope for an intelligence break.

That break came that afternoon. Gretchen called from Berlin. She attached the scrambler set to her phone and reported an important finding.

"I decided to widen the passport search to include known European colleagues of Nikola Tesla, especially those with anti-National Socialist tendencies. His nephew, Sava Kosanovich, has been politically active in opposition to the Chetnik party in Serbia. He came into Germany six weeks ago by train and stayed in Frankfurt. It was noted when he came into this country that he had recently visited America in April. American visas had been stamped in his passport. He vanished a month ago and it was assumed that he went home to Serbia and was just not recorded at the border. Then, three weeks ago he showed up at the *Hotel Am Josephsplatz* in Nuremberg, and his passport was recorded. He was there for five days and then checked out."

Sun said, "He must have gotten a room in a boarding house. They do not register passports there. Do we have any pictures of him?"

Gretchen sounded apologetic. "No, Herr Koh. But they might be able to give you a description of him at the *Am Josephplatz*."

Koh put Schreck on the job. The private detective had an everyman face that was hard to describe and easy to forget. He was a master interrogator and was as talented as any police sketch artist. After a brief visit to the *Hotel Am Josephplatz*, he returned with a detailed sketch showing a clean-shaven man with hair cut short like a military officer. The man had a long thin nose and deep-set, haunted eyes and wire spectacles. Sun Koh's Akashic memory recalled Kosanovich's passport photo. It showed him as having long hair parted in the middle, thick eyebrows, and a bushy mustache with thick black horn-rimmed glasses. There was a decided resemblance between Schreck's drawing and the photo, but at casual glance, the two did not look alike. It was a good disguise and certainly confirmed that the Serb had tried to change his appearance.

The Security people were sent door to door along the motorcade route, especially to boarding houses with windows facing the route. At first, no one recalled seeing the man in the drawing. Then, they got another break. One of Leni Riefenstahl's camera men noticed the picture and recalled seeing a man like that in the same building where they had installed a camera. It was a rather tall apartment building that faced down a one-kilometer length of a main thoroughfare which curved just in front of it. Hitler would be traveling in his open car down that very street towards the apartment along with several other cars in the motorcade filled with NSDAP dignitaries. It was both a cameraman's—and a sniper's—dream.

It was the evening of August 2nd, and Jan Mayen finally arrived in Sun Koh's modified Junkers tri-motor cargo plane with the equipment cases. His assistant Gunther Raus was his co-pilot. Sun was at the hotel when Jan and Gunther arrived in a closed Mercedes limo. Jan and his assistant got out sheepishly followed by Shani who was wearing a red and gold sari with a prominent swastika on her chest. Her pet cobra, Shakti, was coiled around her right upper arm and a red Tiger's Eye ruby as a tikala mark was on her forehead. Her finger and toe nails were polished with a shiny red varnish. Embedded in the varnish on each of her thumb and great-toe nails were golden swastikas.

Following her out of the car was a giant dressed in a crusader's mail armor with a turban and a pointed helm with a steel visor. He wore mail gloves. His features were hidden by the visor and turban. There was a 7 cm diameter swastika on the forehead of the visor. The giant wore the

German War Ensign as a mantle. It was a flag with three even-sized stripes in red, white, and black going from top to bottom with a white-bordered black Iron Cross in the center. He was armed with a rapier and a stiletto and looked like a medieval warrior monk. The armored figure followed Shani like a bodyguard. Sun Koh knew immediately that Shani had bullied Jan into taking her along, but she had also dragged Rapier X along as well. Sun rushed them up to their suite and locked the door.

"Shani, are you crazy? I told you not to come here. And then you drag along Rapier X. This is not a safe place for you."

Shani looked at him with mild disdain. "Sun Koh, I am probably the only true Aryan in this whole city. I am not a fragile courtesan who must bathe in goat's milk every day to keep her skin soft and hide from the gazes of strange men. I have been to Nuremberg more times than you have! And Rapier X is supposed to be free to come and go as he pleases according to your own instructions. He insisted on coming with me so I made sure he was properly disguised. I explained to him that he needs to keep his identity a secret."

She looked up at the giant figure. The crusader outfit was from *Schloß Valhalla*, and between the heavy boots and the conical peaked helm, Rapier looked almost seven feet tall.

"No one will bother him. They will think he is part of some honor guard for the Fuehrer."

Sun shook his head helplessly. "I will have to vouch for him as one of my personal security staff. He will have to remain in this suite and away from prying eyes."

Rap spoke up from under his helm in his gruff but much improved German. "Do not worry, Herr Koh. I am only here to protect Shani. She told me you were worried for her safety, so I thought I would just tag along to keep her out of trouble."

Sun smiled resignedly. "All right. You two manage the phones in case we get any word from Gretchen. She is continuing to check out recent foreign visitors looking for any other Tesla agents. If you find out anything, call me on the small portable radio. Is that clear?"

Shani nodded, but Rapier executed a stiff armed National Socialist salute and cried out "*Jawohl, mein Herr!*"

Sun Koh gave Jan Mayen a withering look and then they proceeded to assemble a portable electronics detector that they could take to the apartment building the next morning.

•••

Parking just down the street in a small truck, Sun and Jan surveyed the building with the detector. They found a hot spot of electrical potential in a tenth floor apartment. They moved the van twice to triangulate the signal and confirmed its location. The camera crew was located in an apartment two floors above that. Sun Koh radioed the location of the apartment to an SS security team armed with Bergmann submachine guns. They entered the building from the rear and covered the lobby, all exits, the elevators, and the stairwells. An assault team took the stairwell to the 10th floor. They approached the apartment where the electronic signature was located.

An SS lieutenant knocked sharply on the door and said, "Open the door please. This is *Schutzstaffel* security."

There was no answer so he knocked again. There was a sudden whining hum and a loud crack. The door exploded into flames. There was a palpable tang of ozone in the air. The lieutenant fell back and lay still. The SS men opened fire with their *Machinenpistolen*. The apartment door expelled a continuous stream of white hot blobs of plasma that tore through the walls. The blobs were about 6 cm in diameter and exploded on contact with solid objects. Between the extreme heat and the concussion, flames and wall debris were flying everywhere. Several of the SS men were burned or wounded. They retreated to the stairwell and a dark figure in rubberized coveralls, gloves, and a protective helmet with visor chased after them. The figure was carrying a one-meter-long metallic tube with a pistol grip in the middle that had an umbilical line connecting it to a thrumming back pack.

The man entered the stairwell and ran upwards to the roof. The buildings were close enough together that he was able to leap to the next rooftop. He did this several times, working his way down the block with the SS troops in hot pursuit. They fired at him only sporadically for fear of hitting civilians. He had been hit several times but did not slow down. Meanwhile, he returned fire with plasma pulses, blowing holes in roofs and chimneys. His back pack hummed loudly whenever he fired.

The roof tops got progressively lower and the fugitive made some spectacular leaps that the SS men were afraid to duplicate. They could not understand how he could jump from such heights and not be injured. He reached a particularly old building that was unoccupied and went down through a trap door on the roof. Shortly after that, the humming increased to a crescendo followed by a loud explosion. The building seemed to expand and then collapsed into a heap of flaming rubble. Troops surrounded the site and cordoned it off. The fire brigade came and put out the blaze. When they inspected the burnt-out wreckage, it seemed that a large volume in the center of the building had literally disintegrated. They surmised that the plasma weapon had malfunctioned and exploded, obliterating itself and its operator. They could not find any recognizable human remains.

The management of the apartment complex confirmed that this furnished apartment had been rented by Sava Kosanovich five weeks earlier. He had paid in cash for three months in advance. Inside the apartment they found tools and evidence that some electrical device had been assembled there recently. There was a suitcase and minimal personal effects.

The SS security team reported to headquarters that a potential sniper attack on the Fuehrer had been averted. The details of the matter were kept secret. Hitler was called directly by the *SS-Oberführer* in charge of security. At the Fuehrer's request, he spoke to Sun Koh and congratulated him. Sun was promised a fitting decoration for uncovering the sniper's nest.

Sun Koh thanked Hitler, but he remained troubled. Immediately after the old building had collapsed, his danger sense had started tingling. It had not stopped. He decided to set up the three triangulation sensors: one at the Hotel *Deutscher Hof*, one at the Rally grounds, and one in the van.

•••

Sun Koh slept that night with Shani snuggled against his chest. They did not make love. Shani just wanted him to hold her. Shani was a strong woman and a trained assassin. She had killed many times before and was wanted by the British for terrorist activities in India. But she had a strong emotional reaction after she killed the rapists in Canada with her Tantric powers. She understood that it was a necessary part of her mission as had Sun Koh. She had used her sexual powers against men before, but she had never killed with them. Sun knew that it was irrational for a trained killer to be affected in this way—especially when the targets so richly deserved what they got—but human beings are not completely rational, nor are they mere machines. Shani was human, after all. But she was also well-trained and she had chosen to be what she had become. Sun Koh had no doubt that if she needed to, Shani could use the Left Hand Path to kill again. And the second time would be easier.

Sun was actually pleased that she had defied him and come to Nuremberg. She was asserting herself as part of his team and she needed

Sun Koh slept that night with Shani snuggled against his chest.

that right now. It showed she was becoming her old self. But even more important, Sun had missed her.

But this disturbed Sun Koh, especially after his physical reaction to Leni Riefenstahl. Exactly what was Shani to him? Indeed she was a concubine by their mutual agreement but in this crazy world there were no women of rank equal to him. All the Atlantean high-born families had disappeared in antiquity and, with his detailed knowledge of history, he realized that the concept of "nobility" was an accident of birth usually stemming from some unremembered event in the distant past. Whereas he had been the product of careful genetic engineering, the various royal lines in all subsequent cultures were the product of political alliances and expediency. Genetically, noblemen and peasants were indistinguishable, and Sun knew that the inbreeding among the European nobility had actually resulted in hereditary genetic defects such as hemophilia, porphyria, and mental instability.

The beautiful and competent woman lying next to him was formidable in herself. She clearly was of sound breeding stock and she had the gravitas to stand beside him as a queen when he came to power. So far, he had not met any woman like her, even in old Atlantis. Why should he not marry her? What did it mater that she was not of royal lineage?

At least there he had to agree with the official policies of National Socialism. There should be only one people, not a whole spectrum of castes or classes: one people, one nation, one law, and one leader. Look at how much the NSDAP had accomplished in less than two years based on that philosophy! The economy was back on track, poverty was being eliminated, and the German people had a restored sense of pride and destiny to help guide their future.

But there had been great costs. The continued racial hatred extending even to other whites was irrational. It is one thing to say that Germany should be for Germans. It was another to say that Jews, Gypsies, Blacks, and Slavs could not also serve the Reich in their proper place. And large amounts of resources were being diverted from civilian use to build up the military far in excess of the need for mere defense. Spontaneous acts of violence in the streets were not only excused but encouraged as a means of social control. This last made him fear for Shani's safety and that of Rapier X.

He mused again for the umpteenth time what a burden the Akashic knowledge was to him. As an Atlantean prince he had been spoon-fed his father's royal opinions as if they were the truth. He now knew that his world had been far more complex than he had imagined 11,000 years ago. Maybe the warnings of the old prophets should have been heeded. This world today was even more complicated. Try as he might, it was getting harder for him to accept the simplistic racial views of Hitler, Goebbels *et al*. Sun Koh accepted that Hitler's regime was a stepping stone on the path to a proper government based on real genetic superiority, but he began to question whether his own original Atlantean ideals made sense.

Sun finally closed his eyes and forced himself to sleep.

•••

The next morning, Gretchen called from Berlin with an urgent message. She asked to speak directly to Sun Koh. She had discovered something disturbing. Just five days earlier, an American engineer named Pyrrhon Quick had left Germany and flown to England where he had boarded a ship bound for the USA. What was disturbing was that he had come to Germany four weeks earlier and been working in Nuremberg for Leni Riefenstahl. He was a Hollywood based consultant recommended by Agfa, the Belgian film manufacturer, to be a technical advisor for the use of their special night film during the rally.

Gretchen had not been told about Quick previously because he had been "cleared" by Goebbels himself. But she had been thorough enough to not only check people recently arriving from America but also those recently departing for it. Gretchen had tried to confirm this man's credentials. The people at the Agfa company offices in Brussels said he had been recommended by some of their Hollywood clients but she could find no phone listing for the American address given in his passport. It was far too early to talk to anyone in Hollywood about him, but she had a bad feeling about this man. She wanted to alert Sun to start looking into his activities over the last month. He thanked her and told her to continue her investigations.

Sun mused over the name Pyrrhon Quick and found no record of him in his Akashic memory. That did not mean much since that memory had no index and it was far easier to pick out widely known or published information than it was to track down individual details. He then analyzed the name itself and had a sudden epiphany. If he was correct there was a very serious problem. Sun instructed Schreck to do some snooping about the mysterious American engineer's activities there in Nuremberg.

Then Sun Koh went to the film crew's main office and confronted

Leni's office manager about the man Pyrrhon Quick. He was flanked by Sturmvögel and Alaska-Jim who had very intimidating looks on their faces.

The manager started sweating. Miss Riefenstahl was not in the office and like many Germans he found it frightening to be interrogated by Gestapo agents. Sun Koh held the rank of full colonel in the secret police.

"You must understand, mien Herr," the manager sputtered. "We needed special film for the outdoor night sequences and the only source for it was Agfa. They had developed this nighttime film for American film makers from Hollywood. It is highly sensitive to the upper reaches of the infrared and with some additional lighting in that part of the spectrum we get a sharper picture with better clarity and contrast in the background. If we use increased lighting in the visible range it bleaches out the background and blurs the foreground. The film had been used several times in the USA and Agfa recommended that we hire an American consultant to help us set up the shots."

"What exactly did this Mr. Quick do while he was here?" Sun asked.

"He set up the various lighting sets for the night filming and tested them. There are shots scheduled for the downtown area, *Zeppelinfield,* the Luitpold Arena. All of the light sets needed to be augmented with special infrared lamps which he brought from America. They had been specially designed to be used with this film. The light systems are delicate and tend to overheat. Herr Quick made sure everything was working perfectly. The systems included their own step-down transformers that were needed to integrate the lamps with our own power sources. He spent the last two weeks getting everything right and training our technicians. "

"Why did he not stay for the filming itself?"

"Sadly he had other obligations back in America for a large film production. But my technicians tell me he did a wonderful job setting things up and training them. They said he was a virtual wizard with electricity."

That last comment confirmed Sun Koh's suspicions, but it did not show in his face.

"I wish to examine these light sets"

"Of course, Herr Koh! Whatever you want."

Sun called Jan Mayen and had him meet them outside the *Hotel Deutscher Hof* to examine the lighting set up. There were several sets of klieg lights around the entrance. In each set there were some smaller kliegs with red bulbs. These connected to a special transformer that was hidden out of sight of the cameras. The unit was a cube approximately 1.5

meters on a side. Jan had brought safety equipment including visors, rubber suits and gloves. Carefully, Sun Koh removed the access panel looking for booby traps. There were none. A quick glance inside the cube told him that this was more than a mere transformer. Sun Koh asked one of the electrical engineers who was running the lighting system about that. The man shrugged.

"It is typically American," he said. "It is over-built. A much simpler German system could do the same job in one quarter the space. Mr. Quick insisted on using these power sources and Fraulein Leni backed him up."

Sun poked around carefully, still worried about booby traps. Much of the inside of the cube was not immediately accessible without a welding torch and power tools. He did find a small plaque on the inside indicating that the transformer had been manufactured that year in the USA at the Telefunken Wireless Corporation in Sayville, Long Island. That clinched it.

Sun pulled his head out of the cube and told the electrical engineer. "This transformer is defective. It must be replaced at once. All transformers of this model must be replaced."

The engineer was very hesitant. "Fraulein Leni will never permit this. We had told her that we did not need these American monstrosities, but she refused to listen to us."

Sun Koh looked at the man with his swirling lapis-lazuli eyes. *"Mein Gott,* man! We are Germans! We have no need of gross foreign power sources. These things are dangerous and unreliable. We must replace them and we will! Hasn't the Fuehrer proven that we Germans can do anything! We need to get rid of this monstrosity and replace it with sound German technology! I will speak with Fraulein Riefenstahl myself. Please start disconnecting this thing immediately."

The deep blue eyes of the bronzed giant were very compelling and the engineer did as he was told.

Sun and his men returned to their hotel Suite. Sun began changing clothes. He had a look of resignation

Sturm said, "I don't understand. What did you find? Who was this Pyrrhon Quick?"

Sun nodded, "The manufacturer of that cube is Telefunken Wireless, a company owned by Tesla. Those machines are not just power sources. They must be part of this plot. They must be removed from Nuremberg and taken as far away as possible to some wilderness area."

Minx chimed in, "My prince, how did you know that Pyrrhon Quick was Tesla's agent?"

Sun smiled wryly. "It was his name. In America, most people use ordinary Christian names like John, Joseph, or William. But there are fanatics on both ends of the religious spectrum who choose more unusual names. Those who are overly religious tend to use biblical names like Ichabod or Gomer while the overly irreligious tend to use classical names of famous persons like Socrates or Tiberius. Pyrrhon is such a classical name. Do you know who Pyrrhon was?"

Minx reflected thoughtfully, "He was a philosopher. Sometimes he was called Pyrrho. Wasn't he the father of skepticism?"

"Indeed he was," said Sun. "Among the religious in America, Pyrrho is looked upon as one who questioned things excessively. They have a euphemism for that: a doubting *Thomas*!

"And the name Quick comes from an English word that means *schnelle*. There is another English synonym for *schnelle* that is very important here. It was the nickname given to a certain young man named Thomas who was very fast on the uptake in school. He became a clever inventor and had many adventures chronicled under this nickname as a teenager. Later on, he served in the Great War and received another nickname for his inventiveness in using an old piece of artillery in repelling an attack. Later in the war he fell in with a group of equally intelligent companions headed by a remarkable young man who was a polymath. They are still compatriots to this day. This 'doubting Thomas' is both an electrical engineer, and an inventor. He has worked and studied with all of the great American electrical geniuses including Edison, Steinmetz, and *Tesla*!"

Both Jan Mayen and Alaska-Jim understood immediately. They had lived in America and were familiar with the person to whom Sun was referring.

Sun Koh addressed Jan and gave him a phone number there in Nuremberg. "This electrical supplier should have the proper power sources to replace the Tesla cubes. I am putting you in charge of hooking them up. The Fuehrer arrives tomorrow and they will be doing night filming at that time. We must have all the cubes replaced before then. You will commandeer the power sources in the name of the SS. Take Sturm with you in uniform. They will not question you."

"But, Herr Koh, what about Leni Riefenstahl?"

Sun sighed, "I fear that we do not have time to argue with her. More drastic measures will be necessary. I will handle it personally."

Sun Koh located Fraulein Riefenstahl at the main rally site running a dress rehearsal with her camera crews. Leni was very highly agitated and had been berating the crews for their sloppiness. Sun strode towards her purposefully. She caught sight of him and was once again smitten. There was something almost menacing in the way he came towards her which excited her even more. Sun came up to her and just looked at her. His lapis-lazuli eyes gazed right into her and the seemed to swirl like maelstroms. She felt herself drawn into them as if she were falling. She became aroused again and her pulse quickened.

He spoke to her, "Fraulein Riefenstahl... Helene. I know you are very busy, but I have urgent business to discuss with you. It really cannot wait. Is there somewhere we might go to speak in private?"

His voice had a depth and smoothness that cut through all of her tension. It made her skin tingle. She thought of a hundred objections. There was so much to do and not enough time to do it in. But she heard herself say, "Of course Heir Koh. My trailer is over here."

She excused herself, and she and Sun Koh went to her trailer. She locked the door. The workers grinned among themselves and got back to their jobs. Over the next two hours Leni and Sun were left undisturbed. The trailer rocked and shook, sometimes violently. In the end, Sun Koh came out, slightly disheveled but with a look of satisfaction. Leni did not emerge until almost an hour later. She had changed clothing and redone her makeup. She was calm and relaxed and she remained so for several days. Sun Koh had told her about the need to replace the power sources and she called her chief assistant to authorize it. She sighed. Whatever Sun wanted, Sun would get.

The three American power Sources were loaded onto a flat car in a special military train. It was taken 130 kilometers north of Nuremberg to an abandoned side track deep in the Frankenwald Forest just west of the Czech border. The area was cordoned off by the *Reichswehr*. No one was allowed within 20 kilometers of that flatcar.

Sun Koh returned to the hotel and immediately went in to change clothes and shower. He avoided Shani as he made his way through the suite to their room. He had done what was necessary to foil the Tesla plot—whatever it was—but he still felt guilty. It had been the first time that he had been with another woman since meeting Shani. He wanted to dismiss these feeling as mere bourgeois morality, but he knew better. He had not only broken faith with his woman but with his own honor. In Atlantis, he would have done this without compunction or regret. He was, after all, a prince of the blood. Who had the right to stand in judgment of his actions? But he had become aware from the Akashic record of what the sexual act really meant. He could no longer deceive himself. He had not only betrayed Shani but Leni as well. For the first time in his life, Sun Koh actually cared about the feelings of the women he had bedded. But he would have to deal with this later. For now, he would wait for Schreck to report in.

Meanwhile, Sun Koh placed himself in a trance and began sorting through the new information that he had gleaned from the Akashic record during his dalliance with Leni. It was only during orgasm that he could update the records. He did this with a feeling of urgency, for despite all the actions he had taken today, his danger sense was even more highly stimulated. The threat had not been averted. It felt as if it had gotten even more severe.

•••

The next day, Hitler flew in from Berlin. Camera crews in the air and on the ground filmed the historic journey. After landing at the airfield, Hitler drove to his hotel standing up in an open car. The motorcade drove slowly through the downtown streets. On both sides of the route, people stood cheering him and giving the one armed National Socialist salute. There were tricolor-striped German banners and red flags with the Swastika flying everywhere. Leni Riefenstahl's film crews documented it all from several angles. Smiling, Hitler gave his floppy one-armed version of the salute to the crowds. When he arrived at the *Hotel Deutscher Hof*, he went in immediately and consulted with his staff. Sun Koh was called to the Fuehrer's suite and Hitler congratulated him on successfully foiling the Tesla plot.

That night, there was a rally outside the Hotel which was also filmed. Other sites in the downtown area were also filmed. In many cases, the shots were staged with actors following a predetermined script, but the enthusiasm of the crowds was genuine. The Hotel façade had been festooned with light bulbs and just above the entrance the words "Heil Hitler" were spelled out in lights. The infra-red lamps functioned perfectly using the German transformers.

Sun Koh and his men were circulating in the crowd looking for problems. None occurred. Shani and Rapier were part of the hotel festivities that night. They mingled with some of the foreign dignitaries that attended. These included representatives from Italy, Hungary, Austria, and Japan. Rapier remained in costume and carried a large shield with a Maltese cross on it which he had brought with him from *Schloß Valhalla*.

He spoke very little, but he was quite decorative, and Hitler complimented him on his costume. They were even filmed together shaking hands by Leni's camera crew. Minx had been ordered by Sun Koh to place a strong mind block on Rapier to keep him on his best behavior and in the hotel for the duration of the conference.

The next day, the party Congress opened officially at the Rally Grounds. Many speeches were given by Hitler, Hess, and other party leaders. There was extensive filming outside and indoors at the makeshift meeting hall. That night, the SA held a rally and torchlight parade in Luitpold Arena which was also filmed. Once again the infra-red lamps worked without any difficulty. At this meeting the new SA figurehead Victor Lutze rededicated the loyalty of the SA to the Fuehrer. No mention was made of the former SA chief, Ernst Roehm who had been executed together with many other SA leaders only a few weeks earlier in the "Night of the Long Knives."

The rally was an amazing spectacle. Around 200,000 people attended. There was a complex choreography involving thousands of people moving in unison in several events. These had all been planned by Leni Riefenstahl and the Ministry of Propaganda. Some of the events had to be re-staged and re-filmed specifically for the planned documentary. Surprisingly, the great masses of people cooperated with little or no problems. This was due in no small regard to the Lethe Devices which were being used in all of the major events of the rally to control the mind and will of the crowds.

The third day of the rally saw more elaborate spectacles involving the Hitler youth, and the *Reichswehr* along with more speeches. That night a large torchlight ceremony was scheduled for the *Zeppelinfield*. With the back drop of a giant German eagle held up by eight steel girders, Hitler standing on the *Zeppelintribune* would address all the party leaders and representatives from around Germany at mid-night. Albert Speer arranged for a "Sea of Flags" with every delegation carrying several NSDAP flagpoles. The arena would be filled with thousands of the swastika banners held high. All the major party figures would be at this speech. Every important NSDAP leader would be at that rally.

It was 2330 that evening when a powerful electrical source became active in downtown Nuremberg. It was housed in an old disused building next to the dilapidated Henkersteg (Hangman's Bridge) over the Pegnitz River. The tower of that building used to be the home of the city hangman and would have been just on the edge of town in the Middle Ages. The populace did not like having the hangman actually living in town near them but they needed his services, so they did not want him too far away either. This location was chosen with deliberate irony. The tower was only a block away from one of the main underground power cables that fed the electrical needs of the city.

A small device had been set up in the tower with no connection to the power cable. One of Tesla's discoveries was that it was possible to establish an electrical potential field in the ground itself that could conduct electrical energy. This device was linking itself wirelessly to that power line and hence to the whole Nuremberg power grid. It was a briefcase-sized box containing a circular metal coil—a Tesla coil—that was connected to another box of electrical components with dials and meters on it. Next to the box stood a tall figure dressed from head to foot in a suit of golden chainmail armor. He had a backpack on and a 1-meter metallic tube with a pistol grip was attached to it on the right side. He also had a large naval saber in a scabbard on his left hip. There was no opening or visible seam in the suit. Where the eyes should have been were two golden Chrysoberyl cat's eye gems. The figure seemed to be watching the meters on the box. While he had no visible expression on his face, his posture was tense and concerned.

This was the Comte de Saint Germain (aka Prince Francis Rákóczi of Transylvania) the two hundred year old Agarthan adept who had battled Sun Koh two years earlier. In that battle Rákóczi had been thrown to the ground from twenty meters above the English Garden in Munich and seriously injured. He had barely escaped and it took several months to recover. During that time he watched as Hitler with Sun Koh's assistance consolidated power in Germany. Rákóczi was convinced that only the restoration of the German monarchy could give the proper political stability to Germany. He watched with distaste as Hitler ran roughshod over the claims of the hereditary nobility.

As he recovered Prince Rákóczi plotted to overthrow Hitler and his National Socialist Party. But it became increasingly difficult as the NSDAP became more powerful. They had political leaders all over Germany and it became apparent that if Hitler were eliminated, there were numerous equally onerous replacements waiting in the wings. Rákóczi toyed with the idea of inducing a power struggle among the different factions as a way of destroying the regime when he saw the news reels of the 5th Party Congress from 1933. All of the major NSDAP leadership were there along with a large number of their local representative and even foreign supporters. Hitler was determined to make the next annual congress even bigger and better.

Rákóczi decided that the 6th Party Congress would be the ideal time to strike and completely decapitate the National Socialist government. If he could arrange a means of mass destruction to strike the Congress, he could kill, cripple, or discredit the whole party and the government would collapse.

There was only one man in the world who had been openly working on weapons of mass destruction who had any hope of achieving that end: Nikola Tesla. Tesla had been toying with the idea of projected energy weapons since the turn of the century but he always ran into obstacles. His knowledge of electrical phenomena was greater than that of his contemporaries and Rákóczi was convinced that the Serb genius was somehow unconsciously tapping the Akashic record. He had ideas that the meager technology of his day could never test, let alone exploit. He was like a caveman trying to build a space ship using stone-age tools.

Tesla had learned how to broadcast power through the ground and how to start and maintain an orbiting standing-wave of electrical energy just above the atmosphere. He had also discovered "non-hertzian" scalar waves which were a complex coordination of extremely low frequency electromagnetic waves and a kind of subspace faster-than-light phenomena that could tunnel through even solid objects and conduct electrical potential without resistance. The three limitations that prevented him from exploiting these discoveries was a lack of fine-tuned control (i.e. computers), an inability to project complex shaped three-dimensional fields as wave guides (i.e., holography), and lack of money. Tesla was chronically broke.

Rákóczi visited Tesla in New York in the fall of 1933 posing as a wealthy Serbian businessman: Slobodan Rado. He flattered the scientist and pumped him for information concerning his weapons research. He also met Tesla's nephew, Sava Kosanovich, who was visiting his uncle.

Using his powers as an adept and playing on his host's distaste for the Chetnik fascists in Serbia, Rákóczi convinced Tesla to disrupt the NSDAP 6th Rally using a prototype of one of his projected energy weapon. Because of technological limitations, the weapon could not be directed from America to Nuremberg, which was 5500 miles away. But Tesla came up with a plan. If he could plant certain devices in Germany, they could be controlled from New York using his scalar waves and create a lightning storm in Nuremberg fed by a standing wave he could generate above the atmosphere. All he needed to do was place a resonating antenna in the vicinity of a major power line and create a scalar wave that would open a conduit for the power from the stratosphere to the surface. The same antenna could then create a conduction conduit deep into the Earth to draw the electrical discharge into the ground. If he placed accumulators on the ground near his desired targets, they would act as lightning rods to attract the lightning bolts where he wanted them to go. The one danger was that if the accumulators were not online, the lightning would be attracted to the power grid itself, especially to the largest transformers and the places where power was being maximally used. That would draw lightning strikes all over the city which would level it to the ground.

For this reason, Tesla needed a good electrical engineer to set up his devices in Germany. There was only one man he trusted with this job. He was a fellow with whom Tesla had worked on several projects and who was a bit of an adventurer in his own right. He had already fought the Boche in the Great War and had no love for a resurgent Germany. The ideal cover for the mission had fallen into Tesla's lap.

When Leni Riefenstahl called Hollywood for technical help with the Agfa night film, the movie industry, which had many prominent Jewish leaders, was at first unwilling to help her. But Tesla had been involved in designing the required infra-red lamps and power sources needed for the special film. He was able to convince some of the Jewish executives to go along with what he billed as an espionage mission into the Third Reich. If they would vouch for the pseudonymous "Pyrrhon Quick" it would be a great blow to the Nazis.

Quick was well known in Hollywood. He had experimented with electrical cameras and other devices for the motion picture industry and he knew enough about movie cameras to pose as a film production engineer. The American film executives vouched for Quick and gave him a sterling recommendation. Quick contacted her and told her what he would need. Leni agreed to let him have carte blanche and allowed him to bring whatever he needed from America. The rest was easy.

But as the plot unfolded, it was clear that Tesla would not able to keep a lid on the matter. In private correspondence with several people abroad, he hinted about a demonstration of his "latest weapon" and he quite frankly told the American, British and Russian governments to watch the Rally. Quick was unaware of the old scientist's indiscretion, but Rákóczi became concerned for mission security, and so he traveled to Germany using a fake Serbian passport in the name of Tesla's nephew. This allowed him to observe Quick and surreptitiously assist him. He mostly distracted the German security people and he helped to cover up Quick's several absences by fogging the memories of key people. It was he who also convinced the passport security people that Quick was above reproach. But just in case Berlin became aware of the Tesla plot, he planned a red herring to throw them off the scent.

Rákóczi built a plasma gun based on a design he had discussed with Tesla. It was a relatively simple device but it was also literally decades ahead of anything available in 1934. He revealed himself to the security forces in his disguise as Sava Kosanovisch then staged the chase across the roof tops and the illusion that he had been blown up in that abandoned building. He hoped that would convince the Nazis that they had foiled the Tesla plot.

It probably would have worked if not for that damned Sun Koh! The man was a menace. He and his team were far too thorough. They had discovered the accumulators and managed to ship them away with Riefenstahl's consent! But they had not known about the resonating antenna. As long as that was active, the plot was still viable.

He watched for several minutes. He knew from surreptitiously observing the tests that Pyrrhon had done that the Tesla coil should be resonating with the scalar waves being transmitted from Long Island in the United States. These waves could pass through the crust of the earth itself allowing straight line communication with any point on the globe. The coil would create "convection" conduits in the ether for electrical flow from the stratosphere and then ground it several miles into the earth. Being connected to the main power grid wirelessly, the coil would induce resonances at points of high electrical use and that would attract lightning. This would turn the entire power grid into a field of potential lightning rods that would attract massive electrical discharges to the ground.

He knew that at the same time, Tesla was projecting a standing wave front through the upper stratosphere that was circling the globe at the speed of light. The wave circled the globe around seven times a second. With every pass, the wave picked up more energy from the solar activity. The Earth only received about one billionth of the total output of the Sun which still amounted to hundreds of billions of megawatts per second. The amount of energy that the atmosphere and the Earth's magnetic field deflected away from Earth was staggering. Tesla was merely siphoning off a negligible fraction of that in his standing wave and holding it in a stable wave front above the atmosphere. He hoped that he would build up a total energy of ten to eleven billion megajoules before the Tesla coil started drawing lightning to the Nuremberg power grid. This would be

It was a relatively simple device decades ahead of anything available in 1934.

the equivalent of two to three million tons of high explosive. When that happened, the scalar convection from the grid would begin conducting huge amounts of electrical energy to the lower atmosphere each time the standing wave passed overhead. This would create wave after wave of super-lightning unlike any ever seen on Earth. It would be at least a hundred times as powerful as any natural storm and would continue until the resonance antenna self-destructed. Single super-lightning bolts could be so powerful that they might pulverize an entire city block.

Tesla's original intention was to use the transformer cubes to direct the vast majority of that lightning to the Rally point and the hotel where Hitler and his staff were staying. When the lightning finally destroyed the cubes, it would automatically shut down the resonator which would then self destruct. But since the cubes were now over a hundred kilometers away and could not be linked to the grid, the lightning would be much more indiscriminate. The large number of lightning strikes would still occur at the rally in *Zeppelinfield* and no amount of regular lightning rods could siphon off all the resulting energy. There was an entire building filled with transformers on the Rally grounds just behind the *Zeppelintribune* and that would attract a lot of lightning which would ground itself by sending charges though the power lines to the Tesla coil. In fact, the *Zeppelintribune* with its eight upright steel girders and six flagpoles would receive multiple strikes almost immediately and be reduced to dust and ashes. All the hundreds of little flagpoles among the delegates would just be accessory lightning rods that would attract secondary discharges into the crowd. That would only be a small fraction of the total energy output. Nuremberg itself would be struck by thousands of super-lightning bolts. Whatever was not destroyed by lightning would burn in a raging firestorm. All electrical power plants and power stations would be burnt out along with telephone and radio communications. In one fell swoop the entire National Socialist leadership would be annihilated. Unfortunately, so would most of the half million people occupying the city of Nuremberg.

All this depended on that small Tesla coil creating a proper deep grounding while getting the power grid to resonate. For some reason this was not happening. The energy in the coil was building up and it was starting to get hot, but something was suppressing the scalar wave transmissions and preventing resonance with the grid.

Rákóczi sensed scalar wave interference emanating from somewhere in the city to the south east of him. This meant that the electrical energy could not be drawn down from the standing wave. It was coming from the direction of the *Hotel Deutscher Hof*. There was no question about it. Someone was deliberately jamming the signal and suppressing resonance.

Saint-Germain seethed. That someone could only be Sun Koh. The hotel lay on a straight line from the Hangman's Bridge to the Rally grounds.

The golden mailed figure realized that it was time for him to leave. It was no longer safe for anyone to be standing so close to the Tesla coil. His job here was done. He had kept watch on the coil until it was fully charged. At this point the coil would be safe from any interference. Now his job was to destroy the source of the jamming so that the power grid could achieve resonance.

•••

The golden figure emerged from the tower and began moving rapidly towards the *Hotel Deutscher Hof*. He moved in a straight line leaping from roof to roof with no apparent effort. The Golden mail suit enhanced his physical powers and would protect him from small arms fire and shrapnel. The Chysoberyl gems enhanced his vision so that he could see everything around him in a 360° sphere. His vision was enhanced directly in front of each of the two gems with a 90° angle of peripheral vision. Outside of that, he had limited vision but it extended all around, even directly above, beneath, and behind him. As he approached the Hotel, he saw the van with the electrical detector and a large trailer truck from which the jamming signal was coming. Rákóczi grabbed the metal tube and activated the controls on the plasma weapon. He came over the rooftop across the street and prepared to fire when he was hit by a beam of phased energy.

The blast momentarily blinded him and caused him to tumble off balance. He fell to the ground, dropping the tube but was able to land on all fours and cushion his fall. When he did, he heard Sun Koh call out to him. As with his vision, the armor enhanced his hearing as well.

"Hold still, Saint-Germain." The deeply resonant voice of Sun Koh commanded obedience and Rákóczi found himself fighting its authoritative power. He knew that Minx must be nearby backing up his master. Rákóczi slowly stood up, holding his hands out open at his side. His backpack hummed with restrained power. A large bronzed figure emerged from the shadows holding the *Strahlgewehr* ray projector in his right hand.

"It's over," said Sun. "Your plot has failed."

The golden figure laughed quietly. "I should have known. How did you know that the accumulators were not the only part of Tesla's weapon?"

Sun shrugged, "I am familiar with this technology. It is a primitive duplicate of machines we used have in Atlantis to draw down free energy from the upper atmosphere. It was never enough just to have an accumulator. You needed a grounding field to draw the power down. Schreck found out that Quick had spent a lot of time touring the city especially in the days before he had left. It was logical that he had hidden the grounding device somewhere away from the primary target areas. As long as that device was not turned on, we would never be able to find where Quick had hidden it. Once it was turned on, it could use the entire city power grid to act as a lightning rod. So I set up a jamming device that would prevent any resonance between the grounding field and the power grid. When your field generator came on line, we detected it and started jamming."

Sun Koh did not mention that the jamming device was actually one of Gesät's Lethe Devices. The good doctor had a fit at first but Minx had "persuaded" him to cooperate. The device was mounted inside the trailer truck and was connected by cable to the city's power lines. Sun had reasoned that if Tesla's device could interfere with the Lethe effect, it might also work in reverse. His gamble had paid off.

"So, what do we do now, Herr Koh?" asked the golden figure.

"You will drop your weapons, take off your armor and come with me as my guest to Bavaria."

"To Gutrune Hospital? I think not." The golden man shook his head. "Come on, Sun. You know what is happening here. Local gang violence has replaced police enforcement. The extent of the persecutions are expanding. It is not just Jews and leftists, but intellectuals, Christians, Freemasons, and anyone who interferes with the regime's plans. These *Nazi* bastards are even betraying their own kind and killing them."

Rákóczi said the word "Nazi" with a distinct Bavarian accent. Some Bavarian journalists had begun using the word as a contraction for National Socialist and it had caught on for a while despite the fact that a more typical contraction in German would have been "Natso". That was when Himmler—who had been raised near Munich in Bavaria—got wise to its real meaning. In the Bavarian dialect "nazi" was derogatory slang for "fool," "jerk," "bumpkin," or "simpleton." Hitler, a native Austrian, was enraged when he found out and ordered his inner circle never to use the term themselves and to officially — but quietly—discourage any one else from doing so. He did this to avoid the embarrassment of admitting that his enemies had put one over on him. He always used the term "National Socialist" as did other party officials.

Sun Koh spoke up. "Germany has suffered greatly at the hand of her enemies and the fatherland needs strong leadership to recover its rightful place in the world. Theft, violent crimes, and social disruption used to be out of control. The city streets had been unmanageable by the police. Even the *Reichswehr* could not keep order. Now the population polices itself. The economy is booming. Unemployment is down and poverty is being virtually eliminated."

"But at what expense? Personal liberties are eroding more each day. The best minds are leaving the country. Jews and other ethnic groups are persecuted. The degree of racial polarization is worsening. How can you support this?"

Sun replied, "Is Germany the only nation on Earth that is racially intolerant? Look at how the British have acted towards Negros in Rhodesia, and South Africa. Or towards the peoples of India; many of whom are true Aryans. Or towards the Welsh, the Scots, and the Irish!

"The Belgians literally mutilated the natives of the Congo if they did not make their work quotas. They were so vile to the natives that it is still difficult for a white man to be safe there.

"And what about the Turks and their genocide against the Armenians? They killed one in ten of them. Over one and a half million people were slaughtered.

"Look at America! They point their fingers at Germany for persecuting Jews, but in their country, they ration the number of Jews that can go to profession schools. They are not tolerated in polite society. They cannot join professional societies or private clubs.

"And Negros in America are treated much worse. Dozens, hundreds of lynchings happen every year and everyone from local governments to the White House turns a blind eye. They can't vote. They can't be served at the same restaurants or ride in the same public transport as white people. And don't get me started on the American Indians! Even the Canadians are guilty of mistreatment of them! And what happened in Central and South America was close to genocide."

Then Sun Koh sighed and his voice got lower but more intense.

"And if you are so concerned for human rights look at what the Bolsheviks are doing in the Ukraine. Stalin is starving ten million of his own people to death! Not just Jews. The press all over the world has turned a blind eye to it, but we are adepts. We cannot be fooled. "

"Sun, that is what will happen in Germany too if the Nazis are not stopped. It is inevitable. It cannot be avoided."

"So you would punish men for what they *might* do? I am sorry. Every major regime on Earth has practiced ethnic or racial intolerance in its own self interest. It seems to be part of the growing pains of nation states. But nations are made of men who have free will and can choose what they will become. It is not for us to judge the German nation any more harshly than other nations. Germany has not acted any differently than Britain, Belgium, Turkey, France, America or Russia. Until Germany has committed some crime as a nation that singles it out from the rest, it remains just one developing nation among many.

"Hitler has shown us that we can have anything that we have the will to possess. He has taken away the stigma of the unjust Treaty of Versailles where Germany was forced to admit sole responsibility for the Great War. Even though it had actually been started by the Serbian government when it assassinated the heir to Austria-Hungary's throne. The Russians, French and British came in on the side of the assassins and then blamed us for the war. Germany merely fought to defend itself against unjust aggression and interference in our internal political affairs.

"The German people, like every other nation on Earth, will have to decide who they are and what they want their future to be. We have had enough 'help' from the castrating 'great powers.' We will choose our own course and will our own destiny. And thus Germany will be solely responsible for what it wills itself to become. That will be our triumph: the triumph of the will!"

Sun Koh gestured with his left hand. "Enough talk. Loosen your sword belt and let it drop. Then remove the back pack."

Saint-Germain shook his head. "No. If you want my weapons, you will have to take them from me."

Sun ramped up the power in his *Strahlgewehr* and pressed the button. There was a fizzling sound and the device went dead.

Quickly, Saint-Germain reached out with telekinetic power and the plasma tube leaped from the ground into his hands. It was aimed right at Sun Koh. From the shadows, three shots rang out from Sturmvögel's automatic rifle. They struck the golden figure in his center of mass with no effect.

Saint-Germain laughed. "I will now end this and free the resonator to do its job." The backpack started humming more loudly. Suddenly, Saint-Germain became aware of a red blur moving towards him from his left at high speed. Instinctively, he turned to face it just as it collided with him. Sun Koh took the opportunity to leap forward and grab the tube. He pulled it out of Saint-Germain's grasp and twisted. There was a grinding sound followed by a snap as the cable from the tube snapped off of the backpack. The humming from the backpack got louder with intermittent harsh growling noises. It did not sound good.

The red blur was a tall figure dressed in a Crusader's armor. He tumbled with Saint-Germain to the pavement. The two figures rolled to their feet and faced each other. Rapier X with his Crusader's shield and his rapier in hand called out in English.

"If you want a fight, I'll give it to you." Saint-Germain drew out his huge naval saber. It was heavy enough to use as a club but sharp enough to transect a man's body with one blow. He lunged at Rapier hacking and slashing.

Rapier defended himself with the shield and counterattacked with the tip of his rapier. While the golden armor could stop bullets and even attenuate some blunt trauma, the weave of its mail was not tight enough to keep out the rapier's tip. Rapier moved with blurring speed faster than the eye could see. He blocked the huge saber with his shield and poked his rapier expertly through Saint-Germain's defenses stabbing him several times through the golden mail. The punctures were not deep but they drew blood. Meanwhile the growling of the back pack increased.

Saint-Germain tried to push the fight towards the trailer with the jamming equipment, but Rapier effectively backed him away from it. The tall black man fought tenaciously. Saint-Germain could not get past him, and every time that damned rapier tip slipped between the mail weave, it felt like a hot poker.

Meanwhile the saber was demolishing the steel shield bit by bit. Saint-Germain was no slouch with a sword and his armor increased his speed, strength and endurance. He struck Rapier in the torso a few times and once hit his sword arm. Rapier nearly dropped his weapon. He rolled with the blow. Saint-Germain took that as an opening and struck Rapier hard on the helmet. This caused him to stumble. The golden man seized the opportunity and leaped towards the truck. His intention was to sever the power cable leading to it to disable the jamming.

But Rapier came up behind him and put the tip of his sword into Saint-Germain's back stabbing deep enough to hit the right kidney. Saint-Germain crumpled with agony but he slashed back hitting Rapier's side with the flat of his saber. The blow lifted Rapier off his feet and made him drop his sword. If he had not had his upper arm pinned against his chest at the time of that blow, it would have been broken. He hit the ground and his head struck resoundingly on the curb. Saint-Germain turned and moved in to finish him. Dazed, Rapier kicked out with his feet pushing his shield at his opponent. Saint-Germain knocked it aside. Then with a blurring movement faster than any human could possibly have accomplished, Rapier came up with the stiletto in his left hand and plunged it into Saint-Germain's chest to the hilt. The thin triangular blade slipped under the rib cage and into the golden figure's heart. Saint-Germain dropped his saber and stumbled back. His back pack was vibrating violently with an angry growl.

Rapier collapsed to the ground. Sun Koh had been circling the fight trying to get in to help, but they had moved so fast he did not get a chance. With the two combatants down Sun moved in. The backpack sounded like it would blow any second. Sun knew that if it did, the electromagnetic pulse would disrupt the Lethe device and the resonator field would connect. To prevent this he needed to get the backpack underground and fast! He grabbed the golden figure and dragged him to a nearby manhole cover. Sun lifted the cover off and dumped the figure into it. He then slammed the cover back in place and collapsed on top of it. A few moments later there was a loud explosion and several manhole covers for blocks around were blown off. The Lethe device continued its jamming undeterred.

•••

Rapier X woke up to find himself lying in his bed back in *Schloß Valhalla*. His entire body felt immobile, but especially his right upper arm and shoulder. His right arm was in a sling. He had bandages on his face and felt more than a little woozy.

Shani was on a chair next to his bed. There was a nurse in the room as well. As soon as Rapier regained consciousness, Shani sent the nurse to get Sun Koh. The Atlantean prince came into the room and sat next to Rapier.

"How do you feel?" he asked.

Rapier grunted, "Okay, I guess. The last thing I remember, I had just stabbed that golden suited figure in the heart. I must have really hit my head hard."

Sun Koh nodded. "You certainly did. You had a concussion and have been semiconscious for ten days. Your brain has been through a lot in the last month and I wasn't sure you were going to make it. You looked pretty bad at first, but your neurological exam began to normalize after two days and I realized that your brain was continuing to heal. You started babbling a week ago and could answer some questions but I doubt you remember any of that."

Rapier shook his head and winced. "Why do I have bandages on my face?"

Sun smiled. "When I was sure you would recover, I decided to do a little repair work on the scar on your face. I excised the keloid and used a special gel to seal the wound. It enhances wound healing and suppresses scarring. It also holds the wound together so that stitches are not necessary. Let me show you."

Sun Koh cut the bandages and removed them from Rapier's face. He then gave him a hand mirror. "What do you think?"

The ugly scar that ran across his face was gone. There was a thin line in its place which was shorter than the scar had been. "The incision is healing from the ends inward. Once healing is complete, you won't be able to see where it was."

Rapier then asked. "What happened after I passed out?"

"I threw Saint-Germain's body into a flowing sewer and it got washed away. The back pack exploded in a cistern just down the road from that manhole. It did little damage except for blowing off a few manhole covers. We never did find the body.

"The rest of the Rally went off without a hitch. The Tesla coil at the Hangman's Bridge overheated and the whole device melted to slag as it was designed to do. No harm was done." Sun did not mention it, but when they went to examine the Telefunken transformers on the rail car, they had similarly melted down internally. It would be impossible to reconstruct those devices.

"We all owe you a debt of gratitude, Rapier. You saved my life and the lives of thousands of people in Nuremberg. If you had not overcome Minx's command to stay in the hotel, we would likely all be dead now."

Rapier sighed, "I know you did not want me out of the hotel for my own good, but it was my decision, not yours. I refused to let him kill you. After all, you had saved my life and I owed you. I made my choice and I acted on it. I am a man, not a pet or a machine. I can think for myself."

Sun reached into his pocket and took out a bank book that he tossed to Rapier. "This is a sign of our gratitude."

It was a Swiss bankbook for an account in the name of Mordechai Jonathan. Rapier looked at the balance and whistled softly.

"That's not dollars, is it?"

"No. Swiss francs."

Rapier huffed. "Francs, eh? That's still no small piece of change."

"Well you earned it. I also have a new passport for you from the American embassy. I have a few friends there."

Then Sun looked embarrassed. "Rapier, there is no place in Germany for a *man* like you." Sun Koh emphasized the word "man" as a sign of respect. "You can't stay here. They won't understand. Even though you saved them, they will never accept you."

"It's the 'Black Man's Burden' I guess", Rapier replied dryly.

Sun continued, "But, you know, there is always a place for a man of color in Paris. There are many Negro American expatriates there. And you have enough money now to live like a gentleman. How about it?"

"The best days of my life were in Paris after the Armistice," said Rapier. "I hated to leave. I always wanted to go back."

Rapier turned to Sun Koh and smiled, "I guess we're even now."

Sun stood up straight and extended his hand to the black man. "One never needs to be even with a friend." They shook hands.

Later Sun Koh mused about the whole affair. He had seen Leni Riefenstahl in Berlin that week at her offices. She was with a tall handsome young actor who had his arm around her. Sun knew that they had been romantically connected in the newspapers for some time now. He could see in Leni's eyes the same regret and guilt that he felt. Theirs had been a onetime fling and they both had serious relationships with other people. Sun had been worried about how to break up with Leni, but that was already taken care of.

Meanwhile, Sun had sent Gretchen a token of thanks for her excellent work. It was a small diamond pendant, but the gem was flawless, and the setting made it sparkle like the sun. Gretchen's eyes lit up and she gave him a grateful peck on the cheek. There would also be a little bonus for her this month as well.

Sturmvögel had really enjoyed visiting his mother. As usual, she had stuffed him with home cooking and tried to have some of the daughters and granddaughters of her friends "just come by" to meet him. Sturm did not mind. They usually brought some food or baked goods when they came, and every now and then one of them would be worth meeting. Now that he was back in Berlin, he missed his mom. He also missed that cute little Lisle from down the block. She was more than ten years younger than he was but she was a spirited girl and full of fun. He smiled. What his mother did not know wouldn't hurt her. He hoped Sun Koh and his team would attend the 7th Party Rally next year. It gave him something to look forward to.

THE END

EPILOGUE:

Rapier X became the toast of Paris. He opened up a nightclub *Au Coeur Des Ténèbres* that catered to black patrons.

The failure of Nikola Tesla's demonstration was a great blow to the man. He blamed "Pyrrhon Quick" for the failure. Pyrrhon on the other hand was furious that the Nazis had gotten wind of the mission through Tesla's carelessness and had come within days of capturing him. They had a falling out and did not speak for several months. Meanwhile, all of Tesla's weapons projects went unfunded. No nation was interested in pursuing them. When Tesla died in 1943, the US Government seized his papers and labeled them "Top Secret." They are still being held under that classification as of 2018.

During the time "Pyrrhon Quick" was in Nuremberg, his wife and business partners told everyone that he was "in Europe collaborating in experiments with another electrical expert" on an apparatus that "could be used to kill insects with electric waves." He continued to have further adventures by himself and with his adventurer comrades. Eventually, his company became a major US Defense contractor. His son would inherit his father's inventive genius and carry on the family name with his own adventures.

Helene "Leni" Riefenstahl completed the editing of her film of the 6th NSDAP Rally and gave it the title *The Triumph of the Will*. It opened to wide international acclaim in 1935 and is still considered the greatest political documentary in history. Political propagandists in the 21st Century still study it and use her filming techniques. She had many lovers over the years and only married her long-term lover on her death bed. Leni died in 2003 at the age of 101.

SUPER MAN VS. ÜBERMENSCH: DOC SAVAGE AND SUN KOH

BY ARTHUR SIPPO MD, MPH

In 1933, the Street and Smith Company decided to publish a series of stories about a man trained from birth to reach the peak of human perfection. The character was to be called "Doc Savage," a name intended to reflect both his intellectual prowess and his raw physical abilities. He would be both a mental and physical marvel. He had bronzed skin and swirling flake-gold colored eyes. But he would not come by his abilities through magic or some strange scientific accident, Doc Savage would have been made a super-hero by his own efforts. He would obtain his knowledge and powers through study and hard work.

The first story in the series *The Man of Bronze* introduced Doc and his five aides—all educated experts in different fields. These characters were intended to emphasize the American work ethic and to represent the goal towards which American culture had always aimed: the independent, self-made entrepreneur. Doc and his aides were all cut from the same mold.

Doc was the centerpiece of the stories and he did not owe his success to family ties (of which he allegedly had none at the time of his initial creation) nor to any inherent superiority over his fellow men. Doc Savage was to be the product of his own hard work and training. In fact, in the early novels, the point was made more than once that anyone could be like Doc if they worked at it. Over the years, issues of Doc Savage Magazine included a special section of exercises that were designed to make the readers more like Doc himself. This reflected the prevailing theory of the Ethical Culture movement that was very popular in early 20th Century America.

Doc was a morally upright man who fought evil as a matter of principle. As the character developed he became more humane and eschewed taking human life unless it was absolutely necessary. He was a model of fair play and conventional morality. He did not lust after women nor seek to enrich himself or dominate other people. The writer chosen to do the series, Lester Dent, mentioned in correspondence that he wanted Doc to possess Lincolnesque traits and Christliness. Doc Savage was intended to be a paragon: a hero who was perfect in almost every way. This formula began to unravel towards the end of the run of 181 published novels in 1949, but by that time Doc Savage had inspired several other paragon characters such as Jim Anthony, Thunder Jim Wade, Captain Hazzard, and the ultimate American icon, Superman.

The Doc Savage pulp series had no recurring villains (except John Sunlight who figured in two stories) and had no over-arching theme. The very last story in the series was *Up From Earth's Centre* which was a Dantesque tour of what appeared to be the infernal regions of Hell located beneath New England. This was not intended to be the last story in the series, but it was a fitting apocalyptic terminus in which the mystery of what really happened underground was never solved.

It had not dawned on me until recently how terribly "American" the whole premise of Doc Savage was. He was an Everyman hero. He was not a member of the cultural elite. As the ideal American hero, Doc would not come from any one ethnic, religious, or political background. He was a man of mystery because he was precisely a product of the melting-pot. Doc Savage showed what free men could do if they cast off the encumbrances of the Old World and its social, political, economic, and religious hierarchy. As an American, I didn't realize there was any other way to create a paragon character.

Then I discovered a copy-cat character from the German pulps called Sun Koh. By all indications, Sun Koh was conceptualized and published in imitation of Doc Savage, making Sun Koh the very first fictional character to be created as an homage to Doc. But Sun Koh was created in a very different cultural matrix: emerging Nazi Germany. The values that he would espouse—and in fact the very basis of his appeal in Germany—would come from a very different vision of what represented the pinnacle of human perfection.

Unlike Doc Savage who had been educated by scientists to reach perfection, Sun Koh was a prince from Atlantis who had been sent forward from the past to claim his right as the sovereign of Atlantis when it emerged again from the Atlantic Ocean at the start of the next Ice Age. Sun Koh was an ethnic "Aryan" and it was his innate genetic endowment that made him superior to other men.

From 1933 to 1938, German writer Paul Müller (under the house name Lok Myler) wrote 150 Sun Koh adventures. This was an average of one story every two weeks. The only single character American pulp output even close to this was that of Walter Gibson's character The Shadow. For several years Gibson cranked out two Shadow stories a month, but overall, there were only 325 published Shadow stories published over 25 years. Meanwhile Müller wrote several other series simultaneously with Sun Koh including stores about Jan Mayen, Rah Norten, and Mark Powers.

"In the first Sun Koh Story *Ein Mann fällt vom Himmel* ("A Man Falls from Heaven") Sun Koh floats down from the sky during a rain storm and lands in London. He was a blue-eyed blonde giant of a man who had no memory of who he was. All he knew was that he had to get to a particular hotel in that city. There he meets up with the bellboy, Hal Mervin, and an Afro-American boxer named Jack Holigan both of whom become his servants.

As the series progressed he eventually finds his way to Germany and becomes associated with several already established pulp characters such as Alaska Jim Hoover, the adventurer Sturmvögel, and scientist-inventor-detective Jan Mayen. There also is a recurring love interest, Joan Martini and a recurring villain Juan Garcia. All of Sun Koh's aides (with the exception of Dr. Peters who was a bench-work scientist) were men of action, not men of intellect or education. Even Jan Mayen was more of an action hero than a seeker of knowledge. This was in stark contrast to Doc Savage's aides who were often described as the five greatest minds ever collected in one group.

It is interesting that Holigan was depicted as being Prince in his ancestral African tribe and is known throughout the series as Nimba. As a black character, he is treated much better in the Sun Koh series than the character "Eradicate" Sampson was in the original Tom Swift stories. Nevertheless, he was still made subservient to his Aryan master both physically and mentally. Holigan was eventually killed in adventure 139, *Nimba Todt*. One may speculate if the strong Nazi racial sentiments put pressure on Müller to eliminate a racially "inferior" major character.

The Doc Savage stories had very little to say about blacks. There was one intriguing scene in the story *Land of Long Juju* (ghost written by Lawrence Donovan but edited by Dent) where a farmer has been having black men trespassing on his property. He sees Doc Savage for the first time and the following dialog transpires:

"I don't know who you are," said the older farmer suspiciously. "You ain't much whiter'n them dang skunks!" The farmer's flashlight had picked out Doc's bronze face. Doc smiled slightly."

It makes me wonder if Doc's skin color had been intended to blur the color distinction between Americans.

The recurring theme in the Sun Koh stories is that a second Ice Age is imminent, and that Atlantis will rise again from the sea. Sun Koh has come forward in time to claim his rights as the Heir to Atlantis and to assist the Aryan people in their struggle to obtain their rightful place as masters of the world. The "inferior races" of the world are expendable, and their sole function is to facilitate the triumph of the Aryan Master Race.

Sun Koh was depicted as a man of destiny, very much like Adolph Hitler described himself in Mein Kampf. He had unerring luck and a "Danger Sense" that warned of any imminent danger to his person. Sun Koh was also a genius and a physical marvel just like Doc Savage. He rarely made a mistake and always outsmarted and outfought the villain in the end. He faced a number of dastardly plots often involving some scientific menace or some threat to Aryan supremacy in some exotic locale of the world. Sun Koh had no scruples about killing, especially if those opposing him were of some "degenerate" racial group. The main driving force for this character was his willpower and his sense of purpose. He had a destiny to fulfill and nothing would stand in his way. This Nietzschean amoralism was the ideal espoused by the Nazis and Sun Koh became a standard bearer for Nazism and its social and political programs.

The series came to a premature end in 1938 when the Nazi authorities decided that it was a waste of resources to publish such frivolous entertainments. The pulp magazines were therefore shut down by government order. But Paul Müller, knowing the end of the series was near, had Sun Koh discover the resurrected continent of Atlantis inside the Hollow Earth. With the aid of Jan Mayen's atomic aircraft, Sun Koh flew through the secret entrance to that world hidden in Greenland and conquered it. At the series end, there was plenty of *lebensraum* for the Aryan races to migrate to so that they would escape the New Ice Age as the lesser races perished.

The differences between the two characters are indicative of the social matrix in which their stories were published. Doc and his men had an open attitude towards life and enjoyed the thrill of righting wrongs and having adventures. They "did not go out for personal gain, but to use their talents to help those in need." Sun Koh and his men were ideologues who shared racial and political prejudices. They were not entrepreneurs open to new adventures, but men who thought they were destined to rule the world and to be the instruments by which destiny would achieve an intended goal.

The contrast is between a self-made Super-Man who makes his own way in the world and a genetically superior Nietzschean *Übermensch* who seeks a predetermined destiny. The American vision is open-ended and flexible while the Nazi vision is constrained and rigidly determined by the goal it seeks. Yet it is the American who is bound to a moral code while the Nazi is free to do whatever he wills to bring about his desired end.

Paradoxical as it may seem, the freedom to make choices actually places greater moral responsibility on the individual while the one who seeks an inevitable destiny believes that his end justifies his means.

These two characters were standard bearers for competing ideologies at a critical point in human history where the world tottered on the brink of totalitarian domination and genocidal racialism on the one hand or egalitarian freedom on the other.

As it turned out, the Nazis themselves suppressed their own iconic standard bearer. The very totalitarian restraints that Sun Koh espoused forced him into irrelevance even among those who should have appreciated what he stood for. After the war, his stories were reprinted but in bowdlerized form eliminating their racist and anti-Semitic content.

Meanwhile, Doc Savage continued to be an American hero during the war that defeated the Nazis and beyond. His stories were reprinted a generation later with no need for censorship. What he stood for inspired several generations of young people and he is still a beloved icon and an inspiration to writers of the hero genre.

Everyone knows who Doc Savage was and many writers world-wide pay homage to the character and his creators. Contrarily, Sun Koh is a footnote in pulp history which is little known outside of Germany. In many ways he is an embarrassment and his legacy is mixed.

I think there is a lesson to be learned from this. The Super-Man or the *Übermensch* : which represents the true pinnacle of human perfection?

SUN KOH'S CREW

BY ART SIPPO

Ashanti Garuda: (aka "The Daughter of Kali") Ashanti is the mistress and chief assassin of Sun Koh. Her nickname is Shani. She is a true Aryan from India who has mastered all forms of Yoga, Ayurvedic/ Unani/Siddha medicine, Indian Mysticism, Sorcery, Alchemy, Kalaripayit, Marma Adi, Silambam, Varma Kalari, and other Indian martial arts. Her true age is unknown, but she appears to be in her twenties thanks to her Ayurvedic *Elixir of Life.* She is a devotee of Kali and of the Left-Hand Path of Tantra who has vowed eternal hatred on the British for oppressing her people. The six powers granted to her by Kali are pacifying (glamour, seduction), subjugating (hypnosis, sexual obsession), paralyzing (pressure points), obstructing (grappling and throws), driving away (breaking kicks and punches), and death-dealing (strangulation, death blows, death points). Ashanti has a berserker attack that uses all four extremities and her head which is utterly devastating. She wears different colored Spider-web silk Saris that are light and airy and do not impede her leg movements, but which can stop a pistol bullet or a knife. She has a blood red oval tikala mark on her forehead with a golden Swastika in the middle to honor Kali. She also has 12 swastikas tattooed on her body to protect her from harm (i.e., on the soles of her feet, the palms of her hands, inside of her thighs, the inner side of her arms, the outsides of her buttocks, and the lateral sides of her breasts). She has a pet miniature Golden Spitting Cobra with green eyes named Shakti that she wears as a bracelet entwined around her right upper arm or forearm. The snake remains still and appears to be just a bracelet until Shani awakens it. The snake can spit venom precisely from a dozen feet away on Ashanti's command to temporarily blind an opponent. It's

bite though is quite deadly. Sun Koh had given her a Tiger's Eye ruby which she sometimes wears in place of the tikala mark. It adheres to whatever part of her body to which she attaches. This ruby enhances her senses, her strength, and her agility, and enhances her psychic powers. She can also make it glow at will. She is tall for a woman (5' 9") with solid muscular body and a full female figure. She exudes sex appeal and is used to men doing as she asks. Her preferred mode of dress is a Sari with Sandals. Her fingernails and toenails are painted red with an occasional golden Indian-style swastika imbedded in her great toenails. She is always armed in some way and favors the subtle use of various poisons.

Alaska-Jim (real name Jacob Hoover) was a hunter and trapper in the Old West who also worked for the Canadian mounted police. He was an associate of Sun Koh and was known for his riding, roping, and shooting skills. Jim was a giant mountain man with the ferocity and fighting prowess of the legendary Jeremiah Johnson. He was a Canadian Citizen of German descent who lived in the Yukon. Alaska Jim came to the United States as a Hessian mercenary during the Revolutionary War. He was romantically involved with a woman who was coveted by the local nobleman of his home city in  Germany and was sent to the United States in the hopes that he would be killed in battle. When he arrived in America, he deserted on the promise made by the American Colonists that he would be granted citizenship and a monetary stake. Jim took the money and went out west away from the battles. He wandered around for a few years living with various Indian tribes and basically "went native." His travels brought him to the southwest of north America and he was captured by the underground nation of Ch'iny'n which lay below the Rocky Mountains. Because of his size and fighting prowess, his captors surgically altered him to be a gladiator in their arena. He was toughened physically and mentally to be very hard to injure or kill. He became the recipient of numerous xenografts that changed his histology and biochemistry. It also extended his lifespan indefinitely. Eventually, he was able to escape and returned to the surface world. He then went to South America and wandered there for several decades before daring to return to the US. Even so, he found it safer to eventually settle in Canada and he joined the Mounties as a scout. Alaska Jim also took over an abandoned Russian Orthodox Monastery in the mountains of Alaska which he made his personal retreat and where he stored mementos of his adventures. He married an Indian woman who at the time of the Sun Koh stories had been dead for many years.

Jim always dressed in furs or Buckskins and wore a coonskin cap with a striped tail. He stood just over 6' tall and was very bulky and muscular. His skin had been so toughened by the Ch'iny'n that he could not wear normal clothing without destroying it rather quickly. He also found that his body could not hold tattoos. They would eventually slough off. He also gained some willful control over the growth of his body hair and even the coloration of his skin and eyes. Insects avoided him because he did not taste right to them. Complex poisons like snake or frog venoms had no effect on him. Only simple poisons like sulfuric acid or sodium hydroxide had any effect on him. Even so, he could regenerate whole limbs and healed without scarring. His skin was so tough that small caliber bullets would not penetrate it and small sharp pointed objects like knives or spears were likewise deflected. He generally suppressed his beard growth to be more like his Indian friends but on occasion, he would let his face and body hair grow if need be to keep warm. In the 1930s he was over 180 years old.

Jan Mayen was an Austrian detective inventor-adventurer-industrialist who flew around the world in an atomic powered aircraft/submarine called *Schimäre* under the secret identity of **Der Kapitän**. (aka, The Captain). Jan was a light featured with reddish-brown hair and intelligent blue eyes that missed nothing. In his guise of Der Kapitän he was the terror of smugglers and human traffickers. He is the grandson of Robur the Conqueror and heir to the Technocrat movement started by Captain Nemo. The movement controls an island in the poorly charted areas

of the Indian Ocean which had been used by Captain Nemo and the crew of his submarine, the Nautilus. Jan Mayen had adventures on every continent. He was like Captain Nemo in having advanced technology at his finger-tips derived from savants in the Himalayas who had preserved some Atlantean and Muvian technology after the Great Cataclysm 11,000 years ago. As Der Kapitän, he dressed in the paramilitary uniform of an airplane captain with a round service cap and a black domino mask to shield his identity. Four lines of golden pipng on each cuff identified him as the captain of his ship

His Co-pilot is Tyrann (German for Bully) who was a mid-sized wide shouldered man. He has been likened to a human fireplug. He dressed similarly to his boss and had 3 lines of piping on his sleeves. Tyrann had been a German Air Ace during the Great War.

Sturmvögel : (Storm Bird) Rudolf Rauhaar, aka Rolf Kraft, aka  Sturmvögel was an associate of Alaska-Jim. Sturmvögel was over seven feet tall and a well-trained paratrooper, commando, and soldier in the manner of Oskar Skorzeny or Rambo. He has a dueling scar on his left cheek. While he had many adventures in the American and Canadian west, he also could handle himself in Jungle and desert terrain. He combined stealth with strength, speed, and lethality. He usually wore black fatigues and combat boots with either a German infantry helmet or an alpine military hat. He was the quintessential Storm Trooper. He was blond haired and blue eyed and had a very rangy build. He was light on his feet and practiced gymnastics to stay fit. Looking at him, it was hard to believe that he weighed over 300 pounds. He had served with the German Irregulars (i.e., Special Forces) in the Great War. Afterward after the armistice, he eventually gravitated into the SA. He had moral qualms about a particular "mission" on which the SA sent him which led him to kill his immediate superior. He fled Germany and took up residence in Canada under an assumed name. he has a peculiar mutation that prevents his body from building up lactic acid during heavy exertion. He does not get physically tired and can function at high physical stress almost indefinitely.

Rolf Karsten : Rolf Karsten was a consulting detective and was known as der Schrecken der Berliner Unterwelt (The Terror of the Berlin Underworld) or Schreck for short.. He was a private detective with edge who could match wits with urban criminals and who had no limits to what he would do to solve a case. Good with his fists and fast with a gun or a knife. Also, he was an astute judge of human nature and human vices. He wore cheap suits with a small brimmed hat and was constantly smoking a cigarette. Sun Koh eventually used hypnosis on him to get him to quit smoking.

During the Great War, Schreck ran an intelligence network in London for the German government. He has a very plain face that is almost impossible to describe and this helps protect his anonymity. He is an average sized man, of non-descript manners, whom no one remembers seeing. He was the perfect spy.

Gretchen Schulman is Rolf 'Schreck' Karsten's 'Gal Friday. ' She is the best documentary researcher in Germany and probably in western Europe. She is an incredible linguist who can speak at least 5 modern languages fluently and several others passibly. She is of course able to read Latin, Greek, Old Church Slavonic, Coptic Demotic, and even Egyptian Hieroglyphics! Gretchen is a petite blond with a smashing figure who dresses in a way that shows off her womanly curves without appearing cheap. She keeps her blond hair in a large puffy hair-do that floats around her head like a cloud. She has a musical voice and is very conscious of the way people (especially men) perceive her. She can get the crustiest document guardian to let her "just take a peek." She exudes sexuality but is morally very conventional. She has been married and divorced twice and is Schreck's on-again/off-again lover. Even Sun Koh finds her very attractive, but out of respect for Schreck, he restrains himself.

Minx : Ludwig Minx was a man of mystery: a ghost hunter, ghost breaker, and professional magician who usually wore a Top Hat, white gloves, a tuxedo, a collared cape, a large wand/cane, and a goatee. He not only dealt with fantastic mysteries but more mundane ones as well. He possessed a wide range of mental powers, including hypnosis, telepathy, psychometry, and levitation. He was an expert in all forms of prestidigitation, and there was no phenomenon of somnambulism, of telepathy, of "telepsychics," of levitation hypnotism, magnetism, mentalism suggestion, and autosuggestion that was beyond him. He was trained by the adepts of the Agartha, the lost Aryan civilization allegedly residing inside the Hollow Earth. He is a member of the Thule Society. Minx was very much like the Shadow, Mandrake the Magician, and the Spider all rolled into one. He usually wore evening dress all day long which contained several trick devices. Minx is the "real deal" and one of the most

powerful true adepts in the world. He has mastered various white and dark arts. When he performs on stage, he is known as Dr. Baphomet. He has a crush on Shani which is not requited.

Gertrude Reinhardt née Shumann is the middle-aged secretary who

is the office manager for Sun Koh's offices on *Friedrichstraß* in Berlin. She is the daughter of an Admiral and the widow of a battleship captain. She had worked as a government secretary for 20 years when she started working for Sun Koh. She had four sons and two daughters. Her sons each went into a different military service: the Army, the Navy, the Air Force, and Military Intelligence. Her two daughters married military officers as well. Gertrude had the highest possible security clearance for a civilian civil servant. She also had no sense of humor and a frown that could turn

a basilisk to stone. She ran a tight ship and could be trusted to hold down the fort in a crisis. On her desk she kept pencils in a pewter stein that her husband always took with him on his ships in the Great War. She also had a human skull with the top of the cramium removed in which she kept black-and-red wax wrapped sweets. These sweets had a smoked caramel center surrounded by dark bitter chocolate. To say the least, they were an acquired taste. In her desk drawer she kept her father's old Mauser C96 "Broomhandle" pistol. It was one of the 9x25mm Mauser versions of this classic pistol from World War I configured for full automatic operation and designed to use ammunition magazines of different capacities. Gertrude prided herself on her ability to fire the weapon accurately even on full automatic. She carried it with her going back and forth to work every day. In 1930s Berlin, a girl could not be too careful!

Mordechai Absalom Jonathan aka Jack Holigan aka Rapier X aka Nimba was an Afro-American who had served in the US Army during the Great War and had been awarded the Croix de Guerre. His African ancestry was in direct descent from tribal kings, and Nimba looks and plays the part. His father had been a professor at Tuskegee Institute. Mordechai was the 'black sheep' of the family and ran away to New York to earn a living as a boxer under the alias Jack Holigan. He ran afoul of the mob when he refused to take a dive. To escape them he volunteered for the US Army to fight in World War I. He was attached to a French Army unit and fought with distinction. Despite his decoration, he could not find a decent job after the war and the mob was still looking for him, so he went out west as a cowboy. He carried a stiletto which he had obtained in France and used it in knife fights to kill his opponents. He was forced to flee the US and went to work in Canada under the alias Rapier X. He was rescued from captivity there by Sun Koh and brought back to Europe. Mordechai was a heavy weight boxer and remained undefeated, winning every professional bout with a knock out. He was also an expert swordsman whose preferred weapons were the rapier and the stiletto. In gratitude for services rendered, Sun Koh gave him a small fortune with which Mordechai purchased a club in Paris which he named *Au Coeur des Ténèbres* (The Heart of Darkness). In the War between Italy and Ethiopia, Mordechai fought for the Ethiopian side under the pseudonym "Nimba" and wore bullet-proof body armor. He is the only man who ever fought Sun Koh to a standstill in fencing.

ingramcontent.com/pod-product-compliance
ing Source LLC
ersburg PA
051121260626
CB00005B/1606

8 1 9 4 6 1 8 3 5 0 7 *